THERE WAS LIFE ON MARS

—and out among the stars, and even in the fiery hearts of the suns themselves. So just where did that leave Man and his one small, blue planet and his grand, anthropocentric dreams? Frankly, most people didn't care; their lives never led them to look up so far, and they could ignore the vast issues above their heads as mice ignored the clouds.

But to Bradley Reynolds it was the most important question there could ever be, and his search for an answer—*the* answer—was to take him deep into his own mind and out to the farthest edges of space. . . .

IF THE
STARS ARE
GODS

GREGORY BENFORD
GORDON EKLUND

ACE BOOKS, NEW YORK

This book is an Ace original edition,
and has never been previously published

IF THE STARS ARE GODS

An Ace Book / published by arrangement with
the authors

PRINTING HISTORY
Ace edition / November 1981

All rights reserved.
Copyright © 1977 by Gregory Benford and Gordon Eklund.
This book may not be reproduced in whole or in part,
by mimeograph or any other means, without permission.
For information address:
The Berkley Publishing Group, a member of Penguin Putnam Inc.,
200 Madison Avenue, New York, New York 10016.

The Putnam Berkley World Wide Web site address is
http://www.berkley.com

Make sure to check out *PB Plug,*
the science fiction/fantasy newsletter, at
http://www.pbplug.com

ISBN: 0-441-37066-7

ACE®
Ace Books are published by
The Berkley Publishing Group, a member of Penguin Putnam Inc.,
200 Madison Avenue, New York, New York 10016.
ACE and the "A" design are trademarks belonging to
Charter Communications, Inc.

PRINTED IN THE UNITED STATES OF AMERICA

10 9 8 7 6 5 4 3 2

IF THE STARS ARE GODS

ONE
1992
MARS

I

It was a fact, Major Paul Smith reasoned as he gazed at the cratered terrain now sweeping past, that life existed on the planet Mars.

No, not just the present landing party–Kastor, McIntyre, Reynolds, and Morgan–who were surveying the northern reaches of the basin of Hellas, but native Martian life. Up to and most definitely including a number of related varieties of complex spores. The proof was there. For two decades a succession of robot probes, both American and Russian in origin, had relayed the evidence to a supposedly stunned populace of Earth.

It resembled the assassination of a famed political or religious leader: one never forgot his own first experience. For Smith, the moment chanced upon his final year at the Academy, during a physics course. The instructor, a former NASA technician, halted the class in mid-session while he scurried to huddle with three beaming colleagues. "Gentlemen, gentlemen," he announced at last, spinning free to face the class. (His hands actually shook; Smith now envisaged them trembling.) "I have just been informed that apparent evidence has been received at Pasadena which tends to indicate the possible presence of life on Mars."

Fear. He recollected the sweep of emotion like a bitter taste on his tongue. Fear crawled up his spine, held taut and secure in the stiff-backed chair.

We are not alone. Green men. Flying saucers. Slitherly lizardly fiends . . . Are they watching us? Smith grinned now, almost as if in embrassassment, remembering the automatic assault of old clichés. In spite of the instructor's carefully placed qualifiers, his soul had quivered fearfully.

The evening headline, with no place for *apparents, tends,* or *possibles,* had screamed bluntly:
And even though Smith knew, by then, that this "life" indicated nothing more frightening than the presence of organic matter in the Martian soil, the icy fingers clutched his spine again.

Life on Mars. For the hell of it, Smith uttered the phrase aloud into the tomblike silence of the orbiting command chamber: three such simple little words. Substitute most any other word for that final noun and the result ranged between banality and silliness. Smith experimented with some examples. "Life on Earth. . . Life on Tibet. . . Life on the barroom floor. . . "

"Life on Mars," Paul Smith said. A big crater drifted past the window, the circling slopes standing like the spiney ridges on a horned toad's back. Sure there was life down there, but the old fear had long ago been eroded. Even the continuing reports from the landing party in Hellas of new and remarkable strains of life failed to stir Smith deeply. The human mind, he realized, possessed an awe-inspiring talent for converting in remarkable time the most fantastic truths into the most banal facts.

Speaking of time, he guessed he ought to prepare.

Smith hung curled in the command chamber nook nearest the window that presently overlooked the passing Martian surface. This vehicle, the *Fresno,* named by Colonel Kastor in honour of the U.S. President's birthplace, orbited at a mean distance of some two hundred kilometres above Mars. Each successive orbit occupied slightly more than one hour. Except in cases of dire emergency, the landing party below (Nixon Base, Kastor had named them, supposedly in honour of the politician who had served as President during the first manned lunar expeditions, but more likely as another stroking device aimed at soothing the present administration) transmitted every fourth pass. This, as Smith well knew, was number four.

The transmissions, dull and impersonal as Kastor normally made them, served to snap the monotony, but they also forced Smith to move. God, he hated Mars!–an incredible truth, and not yet banal. Paul Smith had given up five years of his life and journeyed through some sixty million kilometres of space, only to discover that he passionately loathed the objective of all these efforts.

Mars seemed to mock his own world. The mountains climbed higher; he passed the dome of Olympus Mons each orbit and now refused even to glance that way. The canyons ploughed deeper, the plains swept wider. And the life–life on Mars!–was a mocking life. Life that may have once been spawned amid relative beauty (or so some scientists theorized), but which now certainly existed in infernal ugliness. That's why he hated the damn planet: it was ugly–and through no lack of his own imagination, either. Ugly, ugly, ugly!

Smith remembered the view of Earth seen from space, a sight familiar to him, but never monotonous, after nearly a full year of preparatory experiments and manoeuvres in the orbital lab. The Earth shook the breath right out of your chest. Green and azure blue, brown and puffy white . . . Not this–not *red.*

He studied the cratered terrain. This was part of the Southern Hemisphere; the Northern, more volcanically active, was less tedious. Still, he sometimes guessed that Kastor understood his real attitude–which helped explain why, in an unanticipated, unexplained change of plans, Kastor had elected to take young Reynolds down to the surface instead of the more experienced Smith, who had not disputed the decision at the time. Kastor had insisted that it was because they needed experience in orbit, while there was already plenty of that below in Morgan and McIntyre. Smith had said nothing. Kastor had pointed out that Reynolds, an astronomer, already knew more about Martian life forms than Smith, a military officer. Smith had not argued. Much later, while others slept, Smith had asked young Reynolds if he'd ever read *A Princess of Mars* by Edgar Rice Burroughs. When Reynolds looked blank, Smith had laughed and said, "Then I guess you don't know so damn much about Martian life as Kastor thinks."

Paul Smith forced himself to move. Releasing the straps that bound him, he floated gently up, then kicked out. He drifted across the length of the command chamber, struck a wall softly, then slipped straight on the ricochet into the chair fronting the radio. He checked his altitude and confirmed his location in terms of the Martian surface. Though Hellas itself would not come into view for another ten minutes, he decided to call now. He spoke softly, but his voice boomed. "Nixon Base, this is *Fresno.* Nixon Base, this is *Fresno.'*

Silence. Apparently Kastor wasn't quite so eager.

A sudden, angry impatience gripped him. Smith wanted this finished so he could go back to his window. Even in the time so far, he had grown inordinately fond of isolation. During the second week, he had discovered the fragile, spiderlike webs woven by the taut blue veins on the backs of his hands. "Nixon Base, this is *Fresno*."

Kastor stirred. "Hello, *Fresno*, this is Nixon Base. Paul, is that you?"

No, sir, it's Edgar Rice goddam Burroughs. "Yes, Jack."

"How about it? Anything especially interesting up there?"

"Nope. Quiet as a little mouse." Smith tried to envisage them down there. The plain of Hellas flat as a child's chest. The red dust heaped and piled. The howling, oddly forceless wind. The horizon near enough to touch. Four figures in matching bulky suits. The mantislike crawlers. . .

Kastor controlled the radio. Once he had permitted McIntyre to speak, but the subject had been a geological matter. After Smith received the party's transmissions, he relayed them to Houston, where the highlights were played–against old images of Mars–on the evening news shows.

"There's a light storm brewing at one hundred twenty degrees longitude, thirty degrees latitude south, but that shouldn't affect you."

"It doesn't seem likely–half a planet away."

"I guess not." *You bastard, I'm only trying to do my job up here:* to scan the Martian surface for duststorms. So far–more mockery–Mars had remained uncharacteristically quiescent. The annual Great Dust Storm was not due to hit till well after their departure, a cautiously predetermined fact: the Storm originated in the Noachis region near the edge of Hellas. Still, there was usually some lesser activity.

"We've made some atmospheric samplings and I want to transmit the preliminary results," Kastor said.

"Sure, go ahead."

While Kastor spoke (repeating, no doubt word for word, only what Morgan had told him), Smith listened with no more than half an ear. He remained vaguely curious, but not obsessed. Spores. Organic compounds. Microbiotic life. He'd heard this all before. Why not, he wondered idly, a silicon giraffe? How about a two-hundred-foot, green-skinned, horn-rimmed Martian worm with a funny nose?

And he missed Lorna. Horny for his own wife. How little the average citizen knew of an astronaut's agony. With Morgan in the crew, maybe they got the wrong idea. Prolonged nightly orgies. A pornography of the spaceways. They didn't know Loretta Morgan. He grinned at the thought of the old bag stricken with mad lust.

Kastor screamed: *"Oh, my God, hold on! Jesus, we're shaking like—!"*

Silence.

Paul Smith felt icy fingers of fear creeping along his spine. "Jack!" He spoke softly this time. "Nixon Base!"

And in this emergent moment of crisis his eyes unfilmed, the padding illusions of the mind fell away, and Paul Smith saw suddenly that this world had now turned on them in some unimaginable way. And that they were unprepared. So many months of stress, boredom . . . Each of them was now tipped at some angle to reality; each had made his own private pact with the world . . . and had been twisted by it. He, Smith, was now clutched in his Mars-hating neurosis. Below, each member of the ground team was no longer the well-balanced crewman he'd been Earthside. No, the one thing they'd never been able to check–the effects of prolonged isolation and work in deep space –had slowly wrought some new change in each of them, gnawing away at their personal defences. And now they were exposed . . .

Smith grimaced. He needed the others to navigate the return module to Earth. Alone, he would die. Starve or strangle or suck vacuum above the bloated

crusted carcass of red, blotchy Marscape, the leering
land crushing him to it . . . "Nixon Base, this is
Fresno. Nixon Base, this is *Fresno*."

Smith had to tilt his head to see the ten-inch video
screen set at an angle in the hull to his left. The flat
pink basin of Hellas crept into view past jagged, towering mountaintops. There was life down there on
Mars.

II

Colonel Samuel J. Kastor squirmed in the
aluminium frame of his crawler seat and struggled to
be content with the worm's-crawl pace Loretta
Morgan maintained as she drove across the basin.
After all, he reasoned, there was no reason to hurry.
Smith wouldn't fly away, the landing module lay safe-
ly secured, and the orbits of Earth and Mars remained steady. *Hell,* he thought, *we've already uncovered more firm data in a few weeks down here than
fifteen robot flights over a twenty-year period*. That
twenty-billion-dollar cost figure for the entire expedition irritated him. Kastor didn't want to have to pay
it back out of his own sixty-five-thousand-dollar
salary. *We're giving them more than they have any
right to ask for,* he decided.

Hellas, which from above resembled an elongated
pancake, stretched its features around the two
crawlers. He saw rocky ridges, smooth bumps, a few
boulders, but mostly dust. The wind was a constant
factor but when one was buried inside the hulk of a
suit, it was easily discarded. Kastor regretted the necessity of landing here. McIntyre, the geologist, had
fought hard against the decision. His reasons were
professional; Kastor's were artistic. McIntyre had
loudly asserted that it was ridiculous to send a
manned expedition to Mars and ignore the volcanic
constructs and plains; he favoured a landing site

somewhere on the volcanic plain between Tharsis Ridge and Olympus Mons. NASA had rejected the suggestion. Life forms, not rocks, had motivated the twenty-billion-dollar investment, and life forms happened to be most plentiful in the southern Hellas region. All Kastor had desired were the best, most dramatic videotapes possible. The sight of a volcano twenty-five kilometres high or a canyon seventy-five kilometres wide could have pried open a lot of weary eyes back on Earth. Still, Kastor damn well realized, if the expedition succeeded in solving some of the puzzles of Martian life, then the wildest pictures under creation would mean nothing beside that accomplishment. Maybe that was why he was in such a hurry now. Surrounded by these bleak wastes, he knew that it was life or nothing. He had expended five years of his own life on a cosmic gamble. Would it pay off?

McIntyre was driving the second crawler, with Bradley Reynolds strapped to the seat beside him. The two vehicles rode nearly side by side. Reynolds, his form concealed by the heavy suit, waved an arm high in the air. Understanding the signal, Kastor glanced at his chronometer and then, involuntarily, at the clear, powder-blue sky. No, Smith wasn't up there yet. At dawn and dusk the *Fresno* would streak through the sky, a bright yellow star on a frantic course. Except for Morgan, none of them bothered to look anymore.

Reaching lightly across, Kastor waved a hand in front of Morgan's bubble helmet. When she glanced his way, he pointed toward the ground. By common consent the four of them avoided radio contact whenever possible. Kastor wasn't sure he understood why. Perhaps the reason had to do with their constant mutual proximity these last years. In other words, they were sick to their stomachs of one another.

As soon as Morgan brought the crawler to a

smooth halt, Kastor bounded off the side into the piled dust. When the other crawler stopped, he motioned Reynolds to join him. He waited until the other man had approached near enough so that his narrow, angular, bearded face showed distinctly through his helmet, then said, "Brad, would you mind going over with me the data you collected from the last atmospheric sampling?"

"No, sir, not at all." Reynolds began to repeat what he had already told Kastor an hour before. Kastor listened intently, refreshing his own memory. Over the radio he heard Morgan's sour sigh. *Screw her.* Sure, it would have been easier to permit Reynolds to do his own talking, but Kastor knew full well the value of public exposure. This was his expedition –he was the commander. He didn't intend to allow some bright kid to sneak up and erode that bitterly achieved position.

"Then there's another quantitative increase?" Kastor asked.

Reynolds said, "Yes, sir, that's true."

"Which fits your previous findings?"

"Perfectly. Would you like to see?"

Kastor said, "Yes, show me."

Reynolds trudged back to his crawler and returned shortly with a crude map he and Morgan had drawn of Hellas basin. Various scribblings–lines, circles, dots, and figures–littered the face of the chart. Kastor began to shake his head inside his helmet, then realized the danger of letting Reynolds guess his confusions. "Where's the focus again?"

Reynolds laid a thick finger on the northeastern corner of the map. "Everything seems to be pointing this way, sir."

"The closer we approach, the greater the quantity of life."

"And the variety and complexity, too."

"I remember that."

"But you still don't think we should tell Houston."

"We've given them all the data."

"But not our own conclusions."

Kastor sighed inwardly. Morgan also hounded him constantly on this. "We don't want to look like fools, Brad. We have no explanations for this."

"Maybe if we told them, they could find one." This argument was also Morgan's favourite.

"There's plenty of time for that later."

"But, sir, don't you—?"

Kastor backed off. "I've got to talk to Smith. We can discuss this later."

"But, sir—"

"Later, Reynolds," Kastor said rudely. The communication equipment occupied an aluminium crate in the back of his crawler. Kastor believed he had made a wise choice, selecting Reynolds over Smith for the landing party. Reynolds was damn bright–even Morgan failed to detect the peculiar patterning of Martian life. But brightness wasn't the reason Kastor had chosen Reynolds. Kastor prided himself on his own ability to see past people's surface manoeuvrings to their core motivations. For himself, he wanted one thing from life, and that was power. Kastor believed that ninety-five per cent of the human race acted for similar aims, but most, ashamed, concealed this fact behind meaningless phrases like "the good of humanity", "the future of the planet", and "the joy in helping others." Kastor didn't give a hoot about humanity, the planet, or any others. Unlike most people, he didn't try to hide his feelings from himself. Twenty-five years ago he had sought an Air Force commission because he had believed that was where the power lay. A mistake. War, once the primary pursuit of mankind, had dwindled to a vestigial state. He now knew fame was the answer, and that was why he was here. Bradley Reynolds–there was a weird one. Kastor believed Reynolds was part of the five per cent; power failed to interest him. But what did? Paul Smith–tough, young, ambitious–an obvious rival. But Reynolds was unreadable.

Kastor hauled the communication gear out of the crawler and set up the radio on the Martian sand. Morgan and Reynolds crowded around him, while McIntyre remained seated in his crawler.

Kastor twisted the antenna and twirled a dial. He suddenly heard a hollow disembodied voice: "—this is *Fresno*. Nixon Base, this is *Fresno*."

Adjusting his suit radio so that his voice would transmit above, Kastor spoke evenly: "Hello, *Fresno*, this is Nixon Base. Paul, is that you?"

"Yes, Jack."

"How about it? Anything especially interesting up there?"

"Nope. Quiet as a little mouse. There's a light storm brewing at one hundred twenty degrees longitude, thirty degrees latitude south, but that shouldn't affect you."

Kastor spied the opportunity for a lightly sarcastic jeer. "It doesn't seem likely–half a planet away."

"I guess not."

Kastor grinned. Poor Smith, getting bored up there. It took a damn strong man to withstand total isolation; you had to be able to bear your own company. Kastor said, "We've made some atmospheric samplings and I want to transmit the preliminary results."

"Sure, go ahead," said Smith.

Kastor spoke slowly, repeating as nearly word for word as his memory allowed what Reynolds had told him. He tried to envisage Smith up there listening, but it was the bigger audience that interested him. The people of the planet Earth. The late evening news. He tried to add some drama to his voice, but the dry words refused to be manipulated. This was heady stuff, he knew. It was life. The Martian Garden of Eden. Reduced to facts, the truth sounded not only dull but obvious.

The quake struck without warning, as suddenly as a bolt of pitchfork lightning. The ground trembled and Kastor tottered. He fell flat on his rump and got tossed into the air. Reaching out to grab a secure hold, he realized that the whole world was insecure. He screamed, *"Oh, my God, hold on! Jesus, we're shaking like—!"*

He saw Morgan fall. Reynolds sprawled on top of her. The radio bounced like an energized ball. Kastor threw out his arms and covered it. He hugged the radio. If the world collapsed around him, he wouldn't be alone.

A barrage of voices pounded in his ears. Reynolds shouted. Morgan cried. McIntyre screamed. "It's a goddamn quake!" yelled Kastor. "Shut up and hold on." Incredibly, he saw one of the crawlers flop on its back. A burst of dust and sand covered his helmet. He was blinded, buried. He clawed for the sky and realized he still had hold of the radio.

Silence.

The land had stopped shaking.

Kastor shoved away the blanket of debris covering him and stood up. Tentatively he tested his limbs. Crouching, he unburied the radio. "Men," he said softly, adjusting his suit to receive.

A woman's voice answered, "Jack."

"Morgan, where are you.?"

"Here, behind you."

"Oh." He realized he could see. Turning, he saw Morgan crouched upon the sand. A body—Reynolds—lay sprawled beneath her heavy arms. Deserting the radio, Kastor hurried over. "He's dead."

"I don't think so," said Morgan. "He may have banged his head on his own helmet. Turn up your radio. I think I can hear his breath."

Kastor didn't care about that. His gaze caught

hold of the upturned crawler. Much of their gear–
food, testing equipment, bundles of paper–covered the
ground. A trickle of water from a ruptured vat seeped
into the Martian soil. The second crawler remained
upright and undamaged.

Morgan's voice spoke into his radio. "Brad, can
you stand?"

Reynolds (weakly): "Yeah, but I'm bleeding."

Kastor saw McIntyre and groaned. The poor
bastard had been sitting in the crawler. When it
turned over, he had flipped out. A sharp, heavy strut
had cracked his helmet. Kastor looked down at the
mangled skull and felt ill. "Jesus Christ," he cried,
"he's dead."

III

Loretta Morgan believed they had underestimated
the terrible hostility of this planet. Left undisturbed
for aeons since creation, Mars lay passive. *We're like
fleas crawling through the fur of a dog,* she thought.
And Mars may give a twitch and shake us off.

She remembered how they'd buried poor McIntyre
–the body sealed up like a sack of their own garbage to
avoid any possibility of contamination. Kastor had
called her a cold bitch because of her refusal to
mourn. She could have laughed in his face. To her,
life was a gift, and weeping because it was gone was
like a brat whining because Santa had brought only
four presents and not the anticipated five. *We've
come to Mars where we don't belong,* she thought, *and
so we're all going to die. We've no right to expect a
damn thing from this cold universe, and that includes
the gift of precious life itself.*

Thinking of life made her think also of death. And
thinking of death made her think of poor McIntyre.
And McIntyre brought her right back to Colonel
Kastor again.

The silly simple son of a bitch, she thought. He'd

wanted her to mourn before and now, when it really ought to matter deeply to him, there was absolutely nothing he could do one way or the other.

Colonel Kastor had died today. He'd driven a crawler into a twenty-metre chasm and perished. An accident. A damned stupid, senseless, careless, pointless accident.

Bullshit, she thought. *That was no accident.*

Mars had risen up–a sleeping dog disturbed–and scratched a second life.

First McIntyre and now Kastor.

Two remained: she and Reynolds.

Soon that number would be just one.

The hard, tight surfaces of the life-support tent encircled them both. It was cold Martian night outside, but she'd already completed her evening walk. After sunset, as soon as the cocoonlike webbing of the tent stood upon the sand, she went strolling alone. Kastor, when he was alive, had called these private walks a sure sign of feminine sentimentality. She didn't know about that. She did know that she stood poised upon the tip of a dune and peered through her bubble helmet at the steady green orb of the shining Earth. For five minutes she did this, looking away only to blink, saying a final passive goodbye. Humankind had invaded space, she thought, to learn once and for all how damn inconsequential it really was. That's what the green star told her. So did this: life on Mars. So did McIntyre and now Kastor, both dead and unmourned seventy million kilometres from what each called home. So would she, when her turn came, when she was just as dead as either of them. Who (or what), she asked, gave one tiny damn for any individual human being, dead or alive or indifferent?

No, she didn't think she was crazy. Smith was crazy and Kastor, too, probably, but not her. This was Mars, and she had known all along that this was where she would die. It wasn't a premonition—a furtive glance at a possible future. No, it was knowledge—it was necessity. They had come here to understand the conditions of life on Mars, but each had brought, willingly or not, the conditions of death on Earth. She didn't want to die. The end frightened her as much as anyone. But she would go. She was ready now. It could be tonight or tomorrow or the day right after. The exact instant did not matter. Life was gone, finished, complete. Loretta Morgan, such as she once had been, was dead.

She sat naked beside young Reynolds. Kastor's death had at last freed her at night of the burden of her own clothes. Not that he would ever have noticed; sex, Kastor had likely believed, was a sign of feminine sentimentality. She would have noticed, though.

"Well, what do you think?" asked Reynolds, who was straining hard to act as though he had seen a naked woman before. In fact, she believed that he had. Despite the boyish smiles and mere twenty-seven years, Bradley Reynolds was a man whose natural impulses sprang too suddenly to the surface for him ever to know true naiveté; Reynolds might occasionally be artless, but he was never just simple.

Letting her heavy breasts fall naturally, she leaned over and touched the map with a finger. "I think we're getting damned close. The source of life ought to be here."

"The Garden of Eden," he said, peering at the heavily notated northeastern corner of the map.

She drew back. "Don't call it that. That was Kastor's need for dramatics. Life on Mars is drama enough. We don't need PR slogans."

"Maybe we don't, but NASA may." There he was again. Artless, but not simple.

"Then call it what you like."

"How about Agnew Point?"

"Who?"

"The base. Agnew was one of Nixon's vice-presidents. He was chased from office for accepting bribes."

"You're not interested in the Senate too, are you?"

His lips formed a boyish smile. "I'm not old enough." Reynolds sat with the radio between his clothed legs. Smith would soon be passing. "How long do you estimate it will take for us to reach this source?"

She thought, chasing briefly away all intimations of certain death. "With only one crawler and three quarters of our supplies expended, I'd guess three weeks."

"We may get hungry on the way back."

"We'll live," she said, battling not to smile.

"I suppose so." He shrugged. "But the only solution I can devise that explains the source is that Martian life has evolved so recently that it's still centred in this one place."

She shook her head. "It's evolved too far for that."

"Not necessarily. Look, how do we know? Without an ozone layer, in a carbon dioxide atmosphere, the rate of mutation may be fantastic."

Her thoughts came with a clarity that amazed her. "The first probes found evidences of life as far from Hellas as Elysium. Maybe the apparent centralization is merely a matter of environmental convenience. On Earth, there's more life in Florida than Greenland. Hellas might be the Florida of Mars." She studied the chronometer strapped to her wrist. "It's almost time."

He acted surprised. "Smith already?"

"Look," she said quickly, "you *are* going to tell them, aren't you?"

"Because Kastor's dead?" He shook his head. "That doesn't really seem fair. It would make him look like a fool for keeping it secret—a fool or worse."

"But he was a fool—and worse."

"No. I've thought about this. I'll tell them later, but not right away, not the same day. I don't want to ruin a man's reputation."

"But the man's *dead,* damn it!"

"I'm sorry, Morgan."

"But you do intend to tell them later? You aren't going to play silly dramatic games like Kastor?"

"No, I'll tell them."

"Then promise."

He seemed puzzled but nodded. "All right, I promise."

All of this was forcing her to realize how awfully alone she was. Wasn't there anyone–man or woman or beast–who truly understood how utterly minute a human being was? This was *Mars*, damn it; native life existed here. Who could worry about the reputation of a dead man at a time and place like this?

Smith's high, shrill voice came over the radio: "—this is *Fresno*. Nixon Base, this is *Fresno*."

Reynolds said, *"Fresno,* this is Hellas Base. Paul, I've got some terrible news. Colonel Kastor died today in an accident."

"Oh, no," said Smith.

Loretta Morgan smiled tightly. *You damned hypocrites,* she thought. When the time came, would they be mourning for her, too?

IV

Bradley Reynolds held his arms around Loretta Morgan as she lay stiffly beside him. Outside the life-support unit, the winds raged, tossing dust and sand in great, huge puffs that obscured the light of day. Reynolds knew that the annual Great Martian Dust Storm normally originated in the northeastern Noachis region where it bordered upon the Hellas basin. That storm, though slow to develop, eventually expanded to the point where it circled the Martian globe. Occasionally the storm reached clear into the Northern Hemisphere and covered the entire planetary surface. According to Smith, this particular storm had similarly originated in Noachis as a white cloud perhaps two hundred kilometres in length. The storm was much larger than that now, but it still wasn't the Great Storm. That wasn't due until spring. Morgan said she thought this storm was just Mars scratching her fleas. Her odd wit aside, the storm had kept them pinned down in the tent, unable to move, for two weeks now. Smith reported that the storm seemed to be dwindling. By crawler, the source point of Martian life (if such a point even existed, Reynolds reminded himself) remained a full week distant.

"I love you," Reynolds told Morgan, but both knew that was not true.

They lay in darkness. An equalizer. Not only were all men and all women no different in the dark; all worlds seemed the same. Except for the howling, raging wind, the noise far in excess of the actual force, this could have been the Earth. A camp high in the Sierras. A man and woman in love. Not extraordinary. "Bradley, let me go. I have to pee."

But this was Mars.

"Sure," Reynolds said, removing his arms.

He couldn't hear her moving across the tent. The wind obscured that, too. Life was precious here, and precarious, too easily ended. McIntyre and Kastor, Morgan's tiny pattering feet. *I am alive,* Reynolds reminded himself. *So are they.* He meant the Martians. The others refused to use such terminology, but the Martians (spores, microbes, bacteria) were alive. Reynolds felt his relative youth caused the difference. By the time he became aware of a physical universe extending beyond the barriers of his own home, the fact of life on Mars had been known. Alien life was thus an integral factor in the fabric of his consciousness—a given quantity. Even Morgan sometimes revealed a careless fear and bitter anger that life, which had seemed one of the few remaining characteristics separating man from the universe, was no longer unique to Earth. Morgan would deny this. She would say that most intelligent people (and many who were not) had accepted for decades the knowledge that life could not be limited to one world. But Reynolds knew that theory and fact were never the same. The majority of Earth's population believed that a God existed, but if one appeared tomorrow in the flesh, this belief would in no way lessen the shock of the physical fact. It was the same with alien, Martian life.

But Reynolds, born at a time when God was known, not only accepted but actually expected alien life. These puzzling Martian spores, existing and thriving where they should not, could only be a beginning. There were worlds beyond–Jupiter, Saturn, Titan–and then the stars. When he talked this way, Morgan accused him of idealism, but life was no longer an ideal; life was real.

He pushed aside the blankets that covered him and stood up. He called, "Loretta?" screaming to be heard above the wind. She didn't answer. He was cold. Even in the ultimate privacy of the life-support tent, his own nudity disturbed him. He padded forward and banged his knee against a water vat.

"Ouch!"

He searched the floor for a torchlight. "Loretta? Hey, where are you?" A sudden anxious chill touched his heart. She must be eating. His fingers closed around the slick handle of the torch. He flicked a finger, ignited the beam, swung the light.

He saw nothing against the far wall.

She couldn't have gone out.

Reynolds turned the light. He recalled now, before the storm, Morgan had gone out alone every night to gaze ritualistically at the green beacon of the Earth; but both remaining suits and their helmets lay neatly packed in crates on the floor of the tent.

Reynolds completed a full three-hundred-sixty-degree

turn. "Loretta!" he screamed, continuing to spin.

She was nowhere present in the tent.

As he struggled into the suit–realizing too late that it was her suit and contained the rank residue of her scent –he remembered how she had been: forty years old but still lovely. Her body–squat and too stout, tiny stubby fingers and small delicate feet, wide hips, lines of three children on her belly, loose breasts.

He carefully fitted the bubble helmet over his head.

Sealing the inner airlock door, he waited impatiently for the outer door to cycle open. The shrieking wind would cover the sound of its closing; she could have left unheard.

Inside the suit he could not hear the terrible wind. Dust and sand scoured the surface of his helmet. He used his hands as claws to see. Her body lay half buried no more than a metre from the airlock. Lifting her dead weight easily in his arms, he hurried back inside.

Reynolds hoped that the brief exposure of the body to the open Martian atmosphere had not been sufficient to contaminate the land.

Before leaving the area, he would have to run a careful check to be sure.

V

The last man on Mars, Bradley Reynolds, cautiously steered the battered crawler across the dunes to northeastern Hellas. He carried with him only sufficient equipment for one man: the radio; a shovel; two picks; concentrated food, primarily cereals; five water vats; emergency oxygen; a portable life-support bag; and, most important, the atmospheric and soil-detection devices. Everything else–including his samples and records –remained behind in the big tent. On his way back he would stop and retrieve what he needed.

The dust storm had greatly altered the shape and texture of the land. Piles of loose dust and sand lay scattered in great peaks, waves, and swirls. In some places, slabs of hard rock stood exposed to view. The sun directly above shifted subtly in colour from powder-blue to sable. The horizon loomed so close he thought of touching it. The source–the focus–the Garden–lay nearby. As often as every hour, Reynolds stopped the crawler and collected new samples. He uncovered many new and complex strains of microbiotic life. When he went on, he left the samples behind. There were too many to carry now, and it was the source of life, not merely life itself, that interested him.

With Morgan dead, Reynolds had not hesitated telling Earth of his own theories. The manned space programme had been allowed to atrophy for nearly three decades. Only the presence of life on Mars had sparked this revival. For that reason, because Reynolds believed in the necessity of man in space, he knew he must find something now. A failure–and three deaths would not likely be viewed otherwise–and the programme might again shrink or even vanish forever. And they had barely started yet. Mars, he fervently believed, was no more than a wart on the snout of a giant elephant. The physical universe did exist–in that regard, he accepted the testimony of his senses–and humankind had a right and duty to experience it all.

It was these beliefs that had allowed him to gain a place among the crew of this expedition, but it was also those beliefs that had forced him, at least until now, to keep quietly in the background. He had allowed poor Kastor to lead–Kastor and his pretty ambitions of power and fame–and then, during the brief period while she was living, Loretta Morgan. But now Bradley Reynolds was alone on Mars. The planet was his to control. What the Earth learned would be filtered first through his senses and his mind. He could easily imagine his colleagues on Earth frantic over the possibility. But there was nothing they could do. He was on Mars, they were on Earth, and he never intended to forget that fact for one moment.

He was an astronomer. *A brilliant astronomer* was the phrase most often used, but that was not true. As long as five years ago a youthful interest in the possibility of life on other planets had become an obsession. Reynolds was young, handsome, articulate, and intelligent. He had become a sort of one-man proselytizing force for the long-neglected religion of Man. In Space. He appeared on television. He wrote books. He made frequent public appearances, usually on college campuses, where the audiences were young, intelligent, and impressionable. He had met with the president and testified before several Congressional committees. His message was always the same. Life existed out there. It was the proper duty of mankind to find and know that life. Mars was the perfect place to begin, but after that, inevitably, would come Jupiter, Saturn, and then the stars themselves. He had spoken well. He had agitated intelligently. The end result had been the fact of this expedition. But the end result of that, he now fervently believed, had to be success. Failure would destroy everything, and he knew he would do almost anything to guarantee success. The future of humankind dangled in the balance. What happened on Mars would determine what would happen later, if anything, on all those other planets and stars.

Kastor, McIntyre, and Morgan were dead. He missed none of them, had liked one of them, but mourned them all equally. It was better this way–better alone. None of them, not even Morgan, had glimpsed the full truth. But he knew it. He knew it all.

And so now it was up to him to expose the truth to the waiting eyes and ears of the Earth.

Smith, after relaying the data concerning the source, returned in less than a day with a reply. "Mission Control said tell you this idea about a source for Martian life is nonsense."

Reynolds controlled himself. The storm outside groaned angrily. "But they can't dispute my findings."

"They said it was probably a coincidence."

"That's absurd. Coincidence can't—"

Even over the radio, Smith's voice rose shrilly. "I'm telling you what they said, Brad."

Reynolds remained calm. It was happening again: human frailty disrupting the truth of the universe. But he had beaten them before. "What do they want from me, then?"

"They say you'd better return. Three out of four dead is a terrible price to pay. I can't pilot the *Fresno* to Earth alone. They say you'd better return at once to the module."

"I'd like to do that," Reynolds said. "But we came here to study life. Even three deaths can't alter that, Paul."

"It was an order, Reynolds."

He decided not to disguise his suspicions any longer. "Whose?"

"What?" said Smith.

"I'm asking if you even told them. About the source. Did you keep quiet to get me to come back this way?"

"That would be a stupid thing to do, wouldn't it?"

"Maybe. I don't know. Just don't lie to me, Paul."

"For Christ's sake, believe me, I'm not. Houston gave an order."

"Then I'm afraid I'm going to have to disobey it."

"Reynolds, you can't."

"Paul, I am."

And he did. Reynolds went on. Every fourth pass, he spoke with Smith. He found that isolation was a thing he could easily bear. Smith told him, "Brad, what you're doing is crazy. The others are dead. Do you want to die, too?"

It wasn't a question he had ever allowed himself to consider. "I won't die."

"But there's no reason. We know life exists down there. What else is there?"

"We don't know why."

"Who cares?" Smith cried.

"I guess I do," Reynolds said softly.

VI

The butt of the tiny probe rose out of the sand, a dull gleam that caught his eye and burned his soul.

Reynolds did not have to take a sample to know. Using his hands like the paws of an animal, he uncovered the probe. It was shaped like a crazy wheel on a pole, all struts and nuts and bolts. The message inscribed on one wing, though warped and weathered by the erosion of wind and sand, could be read. There was even a date.

Reynolds read, 1966.

The message itself was written in Russian.

Here lay the source of Martian life. The Garden of Eden shone in the dust.

Tottering on his haunches, Reynolds stared at the distant sky, flecked by a single wispy strand of cloud. My God, why didn't they tell us? It was a product of the secrecy of that distant age–the Cold War. And now: contamination. A Russian probe, reeking with Earth bacteria, placed down here in the basin of Hellas.

Reynolds lowered his gaze and peered at the landscape cloistered around him. Life on Mars–yes, but whose? Ours, brought with this probe? Or theirs?

He knew this question was one that would never be answered.

His sorrow turned immediately to bitterness and then rage. He leaped to his feet and began kicking at the probe. His boots clanged against it. The Cyrillic script dented. The paint chipped off and then the metal split.

Reynolds made himself relax. He sat down heavily in the powdery dust. He blinked back tears. So much, so goddamned much, and now this insane, comic, fool's finish.

Smith would arc overhead any moment. He would have to be told.

Reynolds rummaged through the facts. Was *all* the Martian life a contaminant? Or only part? If merely a part, how to explain the Garden of Eden effect?

If if . . .

Suppose the probe had added a new element to the genetic menu of Mars. New biological information, new survival mechanisms. Something basic, like sexual reproduction itself, on the cellular level. Like adding rabbits to Australia, only symbiotic: the children of the breeding survived better than either the natives *or* the contaminants. A new breed of Martians, spreading out from the Garden of Eden. Injection of a new trick into the genetic heritage would or *could* cause such a runaway effect.

Two hypotheses: (*a*) All Martians were contaminants. (*b*) This was merely a new breed.

Which was right?

There was no way to tell. None.

Until the next expedition, which could make a careful study of the Garden and its blossoming life.

But this wasn't a simple scientific issue.

Once they heard about this absurd Soviet gadget, they'd leap to the same immediate assumption that he had: hypothesis *a*. Only on Earth they wouldn't be able to kick and claw at the probe. They would strike out at whatever seemed handy. And the space programme was temptingly handy.

Given two hypotheses, each equally likely in the face of the first facts . . . which do you choose?

The one which leads to more research, a second manned expedition?

Or the idea that closes off discussion? That slits the throat of the inquiry itself?

Reynolds sat in the powder and thought. Silence enclosed him.

Then he went to the battered crawler, fetched the radio, and set it up on the sand.

"*Fresno,*" he said, "this is Morgan Base."

"Roger. Reading you."

"Nothing special to report. Nice landscapes, rusty sand. Microbes everywhere. It's just a good place to live, I guess. Back on Earth, you can tell them . . . tell them Hellas is Florida."

TWO

2017

THE MOON

A dog cannot be a hypocrite, but
neither can he be sincere.
          —*Ludwig Wittgenstein*

I

It was deceptively huge and massive, this alien starship,
and somehow seemed as if it belonged almost anywhere
else in the universe but here.

Reynolds stepped carefully down the narrow corridor
of the ship, still replaying in his mind's eye the approach
of the air lock, the act of being swallowed. The ceilings
were high, the light poor, the walls made of some dull
burnished metal.

These aspects and others flitted through his mind as
he walked. Reynolds was a man who appreciated the
fine interlacing pleasures of careful thought; but more
than that, thinking so closely of these things kept his
mind occupied and drove away the smell. It was an odd
thick odour, and something about it upset his careful
equilibrium. It clung to him like Pacific fog. Vintage ma-
nure, Reynolds had decided the moment he passed
through the air lock. Turning, he had glared at Kelly
firmly encased inside her suit. He told her about the
smell. "Everybody stinks," she said, evenly, perhaps
joking, perhaps not, and pushed him away in the light
centrifugal gravity. Away, into a maze of tight passages

that would lead him eventually to look the first certified intelligent alien beings straight in the eye. If they happened to have eyes, that is.

It amused him that this privilege should be his. More rightly, the honour should have gone to another, someone younger whose tiny paragraph in the future histories of the human race had not already been enacted. At fifty-two, Reynolds had long since lived a full and intricate lifetime. Too full, he sometimes thought, for any one man. So then, what about this day now? What about today? It did nothing really, only succeeded in forcing the fullness of his lifetime past the point of all reasonableness into a realm of positive absurdity.

The corridor branched again. He wondered precisely where he was inside the sculpted and twisted skin of the ship. He had tried to memorize everything he saw but there was nothing, absolutely nothing but metal with thin seams, places where he had to stoop to crawl and the same awful smell. He realized now what it was about the ship that had bothered him the first time he had seen it, through telescope from the moon. It reminded him, both in size and shape, of a building where he had once lived not so many years ago, during the brief term of his most recent retirement, 2008 and '09 in São Paulo, Brazil: a huge ultramodern apartment complex of a distinctly radical design. There was nothing like it on Earth, the advertising posters had proclaimed; and seeing it, hating it instantly, he had agreed. Now here was something else truly like it—but not on Earth.

The building had certainly not resembled a starship, but then, neither did this thing. At one end was an intricately designed portion, a cylinder with interesting modifications. Then came a long, plain tube and at the end of that something truly absurd: a cone, opening outward away from the rest of the ship and absolutely empty. Absurd—until you realized what it was.

The starship's propulsion source was, literally, hydrogen bombs. The central tube evidently held a vast

number of fusion devices. One by one the bombs were
released, drifted to the mouth of the cone and were deto-
nated. The cone was a huge shock absorber; the kick
from the bomb pushed the ship forward. A Rube
Goldberg star drive. . .

Directly ahead of him, the corridor neatly stopped
and split, like the twin prongs of a roasting fork. It
jogged his memory: roasting fork, yes, from the days
when he still ate meat. Turning left, he followed the
proper prong. His directions had been quite clear.

He still felt very ill at ease. Maybe it was the way he
was dressed that made everything seem so totally wrong.
It didn't seem quite right, walking through an alien
maze in his shirtsleeves and plain trousers. Pedestrian.

But the air was breathable, as promised. Did they
breathe this particular oxygen-nitrogen balance, too?
And like the smell?

Ahead, the corridor parted, branching once more.
The odour was horribly powerful at this spot, and he
ducked his head low, almost choking, and dashed
through a round opening.

This was a big room. Like the corridor, the ceiling was
a good seven metres above the floor, but the walls were
subdued pastel shades of red, orange, and yellow. The
colours were mixed on all the walls in random, pattern-
less designs. It was very pretty, Reynolds thought, not at
all strange. Also, standing neatly balanced near the back
wall, there were two aliens.

When he saw the creatures, Reynolds stopped and
stood tall. Raising his eyes, he stretched to reach the
level of their eyes. While he did this, he also reacted. His
first reaction was shock. This gave way to the tickling
sensation of surprise. Then pleasure and relief. He liked
the looks of these two creatures. They were certainly far
kinder toward the eyes than what he had expected to
find.

Stepping forward, Reynolds stood there before both
aliens, shifting his gaze from one to the other. Which

was the leader? Or were both leaders? Or neither? He decided to wait. But neither alien made a sound or a move. So Reynolds kept waiting.

What had he expected to find? Something like a man, that is, with two arms and two legs and a properly positioned head, with a nose, two eyes, and a pair of floppy ears? This was what Kelly had expected him to find–she would be disappointed now–but Reynolds had never believed it for a moment. Kelly thought anything that spoke English had to be a man, but Reynolds was more imaginative. He knew better; he had not expected to find a man, not even a man with four arms and three legs and fourteen fingers or five ears. What he had expected to find was something truly alien. A blob, if worst came to worst, but at best something more like a shark or a snake or a wolf than a man. As soon as Kelly had told him that the aliens wanted to meet him–"Your man who best knows your star"–he had known this.

Now he said, "I am the man you wished to see. The one who knows the stars."

As he spoke, he carefully shared his gaze with both aliens, still searching for a leader, favouring neither over the other. One–the smaller one–twitched a nostril when Reynolds said, "the stars"; the other remained motionless.

There was one Earth animal that did resemble these creatures, and this was why Reynolds felt happy and relieved. The aliens were sufficiently alien, yes. And they were surely not men. But neither did they resemble blobs or wolves or sharks or snakes. They were giraffes. Nice, kind, friendly, pleasant, smiling, silent giraffes. There were some differences, of course. The aliens' skin was a rainbow collage of pastel purples, greens, reds, and yellows, similar in its random design to the colourfully painted walls. Their trunks stood higher off the ground, their necks were stouter than a normal giraffe. They did not have tails. Nor hooves. Instead, at the bottom of each of their four legs, they had five blunt short fingers and a single wide thick offsetting thumb.

"My name is Bradley Reynolds," he said. "I know the stars." Despite himself, their continued silence made him nervous. "Is something wrong?" he asked.

The shorter alien bowed its neck toward him. Then, in a shrill high-pitched voice that reminded him of a child, it said, "No." An excited nervous child. "That is no," it said.

"This?" Reynolds lifted his hand, having almost forgotten what was in it. Kelly ordered him to carry the tape recorder, but now he could truthfully say, "I haven't activated it yet."

"Break it, please," the alien said.

Reynolds did not protest or argue. He let the machine fall to the floor. Then he jumped, landing on the tape recorder with both feet. The light aluminium case split wide open like the hide of a squashed apple. Once more, Reynolds jumped. Then, standing calmly, he kicked the broken bits of glass and metal toward an unoccupied corner of the room. "All right?" he asked.

Now for the first time the second alien moved. Its nostrils twitched daintily, then its legs shifted, lifting and falling.

"Welcome," it said, abruptly, stopping all motion. "My name is Jonathon."

"Your name?" asked Reynolds.

"And this is Richard."

"Oh," said Reynolds, not contradicting. He understood now. Having learned the language of man, these creatures had learned his names as well.

"We wish to know your star," Jonathon said, respectfully. His voice was a duplicate of the other's. Did the fact that he had not spoken until after the destruction of the tape recorder indicate that he was the leader of the two? Reynolds almost laughed, listening to the words of his own thoughts. Not *he*, he reminded himself: *it*.

"I am willing to tell you whatever you wish to know," Reynolds said.

"You are a . . . priest . . . a reverend of the sun?"

"An astronomer," Reynolds corrected.

"We would like to know everything you know. And then we would like to visit and converse with your star."

"Of course. I will gladly help you in any way I can." Kelly had cautioned him in advance that the aliens were interested in the sun, so none of this came as any surprise to him. But nobody knew what it was in particular that they wanted to know, or why, and Kelly hoped that he might be able to find out. At the moment he could think of only two possible conversational avenues to take; both were questions. He tried the first: "What is it you wish to know? Is our star greatly different from others of its type? If it is, we are unaware of this fact."

"No two stars are the same," the alien said. This was Jonathon again. His voice began to rise in excitement: "What is it? Do you wish to speak here? Is our craft an unsatisfactory place?"

"No, this is fine," Reynolds said, wondering if it was wise to continue concealing his puzzlement. "I will tell you what I know. Later, I can bring books."

"No!" The alien did not shout, but from the way its legs quivered and nostrils trembled, Reynolds gathered he had said something very improper indeed.

"I will tell you," he said. "In my own words."

Jonathon stood quietly rigid. "Fine."

Now it was time for Reynolds to ask his second question. He let it fall within the long silence which had followed Jonathon's last statement. "Why do you wish to know about our star?"

"It is the reason why we have come here. On our travels, we have visited many stars. But it is yours we have sought the longest. It is so powerful. And benevolent. A rare combination, as you must know."

"Very rare," Reynolds said, thinking that this wasn't making any sense. But then, why should it? At least he had learned something of the nature of the aliens' mission, and that alone was more than anyone else had managed to learn during the months the aliens had slowly approached the moon, exploding their hydrogen bombs to decelerate.

A sudden burst of confidence surprised Reynolds. He had not felt this sure of himself in years, and just like before, there was no logical reason for his certainty. "Would you be willing to answer some questions for me? About *your* star?"

"Certainly, Bradley Reynolds."

"Can you tell me our name for your star? Its coordinates?"

"No," Jonathon said, dipping his neck. "I cannot." He blinked his right eye in a furious fashion. "Our galaxy is not this one. It is a galaxy too distant for your instruments."

"I see," said Reynolds, because he could not very well call the alien a liar, even if it was. But Jonathon's hesitancy to reveal the location of its home world was not unexpected; Reynolds would have acted the same in similar circumstances.

Richard spoke. "May I pay obeisance?"

Jonathon, turning to Richard, spoke in a series of shrill chirping noises. Then Richard replied in kind.

Turning back to Reynolds, Richard again asked: "May I pay obeisance?"

Reynolds could only say, "Yes." Why not?

Richard acted immediately. Its legs abruptly shot out from beneath its trunk at an angle no giraffe could have managed. Richard sat on its belly, legs spread, and its neck came down, the snout gently scraping the floor.

"Thank you," Reynolds said, bowing slightly at the waist. "But there is much we can learn from you, too." He spoke to hide his embarrassment, directing his words at Jonathon while hoping that they might serve to bring Richard back to its feet as well. When this failed to work, Reynolds launched into the speech he had been sent here to deliver. Knowing what he had to say, he ran through the words as hurriedly as possible. "We are a backward people. Compared to you, we are children in the universe. Our travels have carried us no farther than our sister planets, while you have seen stars whose light takes years to reach your home. We realize you have much to teach us, and we approach you as pupils before a grand philosopher. We are gratified at the chance to share our meagre knowledge with you and wish only to be granted the privilege of listening to you in return."

"You wish to know deeply of our star?" Jonathon asked.

"Of many things," Reynolds said. "Your spacecraft, for instance. It is far beyond our meagre knowledge."

Jonathon began to blink its right eye furiously. As it spoke, the speed of the blinking increased. "You wish to know that?"

"Yes, if you are willing to share your knowledge. We, too, would like to visit the stars."

Its eye moved faster than ever now. It said, "Sadly, there is nothing we can tell you of this ship. Unfortunately, we know nothing ourselves."

"Nothing?"

"The ship was a gift."

"You mean that you did not make it yourself. No. But you must have mechanics, individuals capable of repairing the craft in the event of some emergency."

"But that has never happened. I do not think the ship could fail."

"Would you explain?"

"Our race, our world, was once visited by another race of creatures. It was they who presented us with this ship. They had come to us from a distant star in order to make this gift. In return, we have used the ship only to increase the wisdom of our people."

"What can you tell me about this other race?" Reynolds asked.

"Very little, I am afraid. They came from a most ancient star near the true centre of the universe."

"And were they like you? Physically?"

"No, more like you. Like people. But–please–may we be excused to converse about that which is essential? Our time is short."

Reynolds nodded, and the moment he did, Jonathon ceased to blink. Reynolds gathered that it had grown tired of lying, which wasn't surprising; Jonathon was a poor liar. Not only were the lies incredible in themselves, but every time it told a lie it blinked like a madman with an ash in his eyes.

"If I tell you about our star," Jonathon said, "will you consent to tell of yours in return?" The alien tilted its head forward, its neck swaying gently from side to side. It was plain that Jonathon attached great significance to Reynolds's reply.

So Reynolds said, "Yes, gladly," though he found he could not conceive of any information about the sun which might come as a surprise to these creatures. Still, he had been sent here to discover as much about the aliens as possible without revealing anything important about mankind. This sharing of information about stars seemed a safe enough course to pursue.

"I will begin," Jonathon said, "and you must excuse my impreciseness of expression. My knowledge of your language is limited. I imagine you have a special vocabulary for the subject."

"A technical vocabulary, yes."

The alien said, "Our star is a brother to yours. Or would it be sister? During periods of the most intense communion, his wisdom–or hers?–is faultless. At times he is angry–unlike your star– but these moments are not frequent. Nor do they last for longer than a few fleeting moments. Twice he has prophesied the termination of our civilization during times of great personal anger, but never had he felt it necessary to carry out his prediction. I would say that he is more kind than raging, more gentle than brutal. I believe he loves our people most truly and fully. Among the stars of the universe, his place is not great, but as our home star, we must revere him. And, of course, we do."

"Would you go on?" Reynolds asked.

Jonathon went on. Reynolds listened. The alien spoke of its personal relationship with the star, how the star had helped it during times of individual darkness. Once, the star had assisted it in choosing a proper mate; the choice proved not only perfect but divine. Throughout, Jonathon spoke of the star as a reverent Jewish tribesman might have spoken of the Old Testament God. For the first time, Reynolds regretted having had to dispose of the tape recorder. When he tried to tell Kelly about this conversation, she would never believe a word of it. As it spoke, the alien did not blink, not once, even briefly, for Reynolds watched carefully.

At last the alien was done. It said, "But this is only a beginning. We have so much to share, Bradley Reynolds. Once I am conversant with your technical vocabulary. Communication between separate entities– the great barriers of language . . ."

"I understand," said Reynolds.

"We knew you would. But now–it is your turn. Tell me about your star."

"We call it the sun," Reynolds said. Saying this, he felt more than mildly foolish–but what else? How could he tell Jonathon what it wished to know when he did not know himself? All he knew about the sun was facts. He knew how hot it was and how old it was and he knew its size and mass and magnitude. He knew about sunspots and solar winds and solar atmosphere. But that was all he knew. Was the sun a benevolent star? Was it constantly enraged? Did all mankind revere it with the proper quantity of love and dedication? "That is its common name. More properly, in an ancient language adopted by science, it is Sol. It lies approximately eight—"

"Oh," said Jonathon. "All of this, yes, we know. But its demeanour. Its attitudes, both normal and abnormal. You play with us, Bradley Reynolds. You joke. We understand your amusement— but please, we are simple souls and have travelled far. We must know these other things before daring to make our personal approach to the star. Can you tell us in what fashion it has most often affected your individual life? This would help us immensely."

II

Although his room was totally dark, Reynolds, entering, did not bother with the light. He knew every inch of this room, knew it as well in the dark as the light. For the past four years he had spent an average of twelve hours a day here. He knew the four walls, the desk, the bed, the bookshelves and the books, knew them more intimately than he had ever known another person. Reaching the cot without once stubbing his toe or tripping over an open book or stumbling across an unfurled map, he sat down and covered his face with his hands, feeling the wrinkles on his forehead like great wide welts. Alone, he played a game with the wrinkles, pretending that each one represented some event or facet of his life. This one here, the big one above his left eyebrow–that was Mars. And this other one, way over here almost by his right ear –that was a girl named Melissa whom he had known back in the 1980s. But he wasn't in the proper mood for the game now. He lowered his hands. He knew the wrinkles for exactly what they really were: age, purely and simply and honestly age. Each one meant nothing without the others. They represented impersonal and unavoidable erosion. On the outside, they reflected the death that was occurring on the inside.

Still, he was happy to be back here in this room. He

never realized how important these familiar surroundings were to his state of mind until he was forcefully deprived of them for a length of time. Inside the alien starship, it hadn't been so bad. The time had passed quickly then; he hadn't been allowed to get homesick. It was afterwards when it had become bad. With Kelly and the others in her dark, ugly impersonal hole of an office. Those had been the unbearable hours.

But now he was home, and he would not have to leave again until they told him. He had been appointed official emissary to the aliens, though this did not fool him for a moment. He had been given the appointment only because Jonathon had refused to see anyone else. It wasn't because anyone liked him or respected him or thought him competent enough to handle the mission. He was different from them, and that made all the difference. When they were still kids, they had seen his face on the old TV networks every night of the week. Kelly wanted someone like herself to handle the aliens. Someone who knew how to take orders, someone ultimately competent, some computer facsimile of a human being. Like herself. Someone who, when given a job, performed it in the most efficient manner in the least possible time.

Kelly was the director of the moon base. She had come here two years ago, replacing Bill Newton, a contemporary of Reynolds, a friend of his. Kelly was the protégée of some U.S. Senator, some powerful idiot from the Midwest, a leader of the anti-NASA faction in Congress. Kelly's appointment had been part of a wild attempt to subdue the Senators with favours and special attention. It had worked after a fashion. There were still Americans on the moon. Even the Russians had left two years ago.

Leaving the alien starship, he had met Kelly the instant he reached the air lock. He had managed to slip past her and pull on his suit before she could question him. He had known she wouldn't dare try to converse over the radio; too great a chance of being overheard. She would never trust him to say the right things.

But that little game had done nothing except delay matters a few minutes. The tug had returned to the moon base and then everyone had gone straight to Kelly's office. Then the interrogation had begun. Reynolds had sat near the back of the room while the rest of them flocked around Kelly like pet sheep.

Kelly asked the first question: "What do they want? He knew her well enough to understand exactly what she meant: What do they want from us in return for what we want from them?

Reynolds told her. They wanted to know about the sun.

"We gathered that much," Kelly said. "But what *kind* of information do they want? Specifically, what are they after?"

With great difficulty he tried to explain this too.

Kelly interrupted him quickly. "And what did you tell them?"

"Nothing," he said.

"Why?"

"Because I didn't know what to tell them."

"Didn't you ever happen to think the best thing to tell them might have been whatever it was they wished to hear?"

"I couldn't do that either," he said, "because I didn't know. You tell me: is the sun benevolent? How does it inspire your daily life? Does it constantly rage? I don't know, and you don't know either, and it's not a thing we can risk lying about, because they may very well know themselves. To them, a star is a living entity. It's a god, but more than our gods, because they can see a star and feel its heat and never doubt that it's always there."

"Will they want you back?" she asked.

"I think so. They liked me. Or he liked me. It. I only talked to one of them."

"I thought you told us two."

So he went over the whole story for her once more, from beginning to end, hoping this time she might realize that alien beings are not human beings and should not be expected to respond in familiar ways. When he came to the part about the presence of the two aliens, he said, "Look. There are six men in this room right now besides us. But they are here only for show. The whole time, none of them will say a word or think a thought or decide a point. The other alien was in the room with Jonathon and me the whole time. But if it had not been there, nothing would have been changed. I don't know why he was there and I don't expect I ever will. But neither do I understand why you feel you have to have all these men here with you."

She utterly ignored the point. "Then that is all they are interested in? They're pilgrims and they think the sun is Mecca."

"More or less," he said, with the emphasis on "less".

"Then they won't want to talk to me—or any of us. You're the one who knows the sun. Is that correct?" She jotted a note on a pad, shaking her elbows briskly.

"That is correct."

"Reynolds," she said, looking up from her pad, "I sure as hell hope you know what you're doing."

"Why?" he asked.

She did not bother to attempt to disguise her contempt. Few of them did anymore, and especially not Kelly. It was her opinion that Reynolds should not be here at all. Put him in a rest home back on Earth, she would say. The other astronauts—they were considerate enough to retire when life got too complicated for them. What makes this one man, Bradley Reynolds, think he's so special? All right, she would admit, ten years, twenty years ago, he was a great brave man struggling to conquer the unknown. When I was sixteen years old I

couldn't walk a dozen feet without tripping over his
name or face. But what about now? What is he? I'll tell
you what he is: a broken down, wrinkled old relic of a
man. So what if he's an astronomer as well as an
astronaut? So what if he's the best possible man for the
lunar observatory? I still say he's much more trouble
than he's worth. He walks around the moon base like a
dog having a dream. Nobody can communicate with
him. He hasn't attended a single psychological ex-
pansion session since he's been here, and that goes back
well before my time. He's a morale problem; nobody
can stand the sight of him anymore.And as far as doing
his job goes, he does it, yes–but that's all. His heart isn't
in it. Look, he didn't even know about the aliens' being
in orbit until I called him in and told him they wanted to
see him.

That last part was not true, of course. Reynolds,
like everyone, had known about the aliens, but he did
have to admit that their approach had not overly concerned him. He had not shared the hysteria which
had gripped all Earth when the announcement was
made that an alien starship had entered the system.
The authorities had known about it for months before ever releasing the news. By the time anything was
said publicly, it had been clearly determined that the
aliens offered Earth no clear or present danger. But
that was about all anyone had learned. Then the
starship had gone into orbit around the moon, an action intended to comfirm their lack of harmful intent
toward Earth, and the entire problem had landed
with a thud in Kelly's lap. The aliens said they
wanted to meet a man who knew something about
the sun, and that had turned out to be Reynolds.
Then–and only then–had he had a real reason to become interested in the aliens. That day, for the first
time in a half dozen years, he had actually listened to
the daily news broadcasts from Earth. He discovered
–and it didn't particularly surprise him–that everyone

else had long since got over their initial interest in the
aliens. He gathered that war was brewing again. In
Africa this time, which was a change in place if not in
substance. The aliens were mentioned once, about
halfway through the programme, but Reynolds could
tell they were no longer considered real news. A meeting between a representative of the American moon
base and the aliens was being arranged, the announc-
er said. It would take place aboard the alien's ship in
orbit around the moon, he added. The name Bradley
Reynolds was not mentioned. I wonder if they remember me, he had thought.

III

"It seems to me that you could get more out of
them than some babble about stars being gods," Kelly said, getting up and pacing around the room, one
hand on hip. She shook her head in mock disbelief
and the brown curls swirled downward, flowing like
dark honey in the light gravity.

"Oh, I did," he said casually.

"What?" There was a rustling of interest in the
room.

"A few facts about their planet. Some bits of detail
I think fit together. It may even explain their theology."

"Explain theology with astronomy?" Kelly said
sharply. "There's no mystery to sun worship. It was
one of *our* primitive religions." A man next to her
nodded.

"Not quite. Our star is relatively mild-mannered, as
Jonathon would say. And our planet has a nice, comfortable orbit, nearly circular."

"Theirs doesn't?"

"No. The planet has a pronounced axial inclina-
tion, too–nothing ordinary like Earth's twenty-three
degrees. Their world must be tilted at forty degrees or

so to give the effects Jonathon mentioned."

"Hot summers?" one of the men he didn't know said, and Reynolds looked up in mild surprise. So the underlings were not just spear carriers, as he had thought. Well enough.

"Right. The axial tilt causes each hemisphere to alternately slant toward and then away from their star. They have colder winters and hotter summers than we do. But there's something more, as far as I can figure it out. Jonathon says his world "does not move in the perfect path" and that ours, on the other hand, very nearly does."

"Perfect path?" Kelly said, frowning. "An eight-fold way? The path of enlightenment?"

"More theology," said the man who had spoken.

"Not quite," Reynolds said. "Pythagoras believed the circle was a perfect form, the most beautiful of all figures. I don't see why Jonathon shouldn't."

"Astronomical bodies look like circles. Pythagoras could see the moon," Kelly said.

"And the sun," Reynolds said. "I don't know whether Jonathon's world has a moon or not. But they can see their star, and in profile it's a circle."

"So a circular orbit is a perfect orbit."

"Q.E.D. Jonathon says his planet doesn't have one, though."

"It's an ellipse."

"A very eccentric ellipse. That's my guess, anyway. Jonathon used the terms "path-summer" and "pole-summer", so they do distinguish between the two effects."

"I don't get it," the man said.

"An ellipse alone gives alternate summers and winters, but in both hemispheres at the same time," Kelly said brusquely, her mouth turning slightly downward. "A "pole-summer" must be the kind Earth has."

"Oh," the man said weakly.

"You left out the "great-summer," my dear," Reynolds said with a thin smile.

"What's that?" Kelly said carefully.

"When the "pole-summer" coincides with the "path-summer"–which it will, every so often."

"Because of the ellipse," Kelly added.

"Yes, that." Reynolds pursed his lips.

"What else is there?" Kelly demanded.

"From Jonathon's words, I think the axial tilt of his world is changing direction–precessing–rapidly."

"So?"

"That exaggerates the seasons, too. I wouldn't want to be around when that happens. Evidently neither do the members of Jonathon's race."

"How do they get away?" Kelly said intently.

"Migrate. One hemisphere is having a barely tolerable summer while the other is being fried alive, so they go there. The whole race."

"Normads–an entire culture born with a pack on its back," Kelly said distantly. Reynolds raised an eyebrow. It was the first time he had ever heard her say anything that wasn't crisp, efficient, and uninteresting.

"I think that's why they're grazing animals, to make it easy, even necessary, to keep on the move. A "great-summer" wilts all the vegetation; a "great-winter"–they must have those, too–freezes a continent solid."

"God," Kelly said quietly.

"Jonathon mentioned huge storms, winds that knocked him down, sand that buried him overnight in dunes. The drastic changes in the climate must stir up hurricanes and tornadoes."

"Which they have to migrate through," Kelly said. Reynolds noticed that the room was strangely quiet.

"Jonathon seems to have been born on one of the Treks. They don't have much shelter because of the winds and the winters that erode away the rock. It

must be hard to build up any sort of technology in an
environment like that. I suppose it's pretty inevitable
that they turned out to believe in astrology."

"What?" Kelly said, surprised.

"Of course." Reynolds looked at her, completely
deadpan. "What else should I call it? With such a
premium on reading the stars correctly, so that they
know the precise time of year and when the next
"great-summer" is coming, what else would they believe in? Astrology would be the obvious, un-
challengeable religion–because it worked!" Reynolds
smiled to himself, imagining a flock of atheist giraffes
vainly fighting their way through a standstorm.

"I see," Kelly said, clearly at a loss. The men stood
around them awkwardly, not knowing quite what to
say to this barrage of unlikely ideas. Reynolds felt a
surge of joy. Some lost capacity of his youth had returned: to see himself as the centre of things, as the
only actor on stage who moved of his own volition,
spoke his own unscripted lines. *This is the way the
world feels when you are winning,* he thought. This
was what he had lost, what Mars had taken from him
during the long trip back with the half-mad Paul
Smith in utter deep silence and loneliness. He had
tested himself there and found some inner core, had
come to think he did not need people and the fine
edge of competition with them. Work and cramped
rooms had warped him.

"I think that's why they are technologically re-
tarded, despite their age. They don't really have the
feel of machines; they've never got used to them.
When they needed a starship for their religion, they
built the most awkward one imaginable that would
work." Reynolds paused, feeling lightheaded. "They
live inside that machine, but they don't like it. They
stink it up and make it feel like a corral. They mis-
trusted that tape recorder of mine. They must want to
know the stars very badly, to depart so much from

their nature just to reach them."

Kelly's lip stiffened and the eyes narrowed. Her face, Reynolds thought, was returning to its usual expression.

"This is all very well, Dr. Reynolds," she said, and it was the old Kelly who always came out on top. "But it is speculation. We need *facts*. Their starship is crude, but it *works*. They must have data and photographs of stars. They know things we don't. There are innumerable details we could only find by making the trip ourselves–and even using their ship, that will take centuries. Houston tells me that bomb-thrower of theirs can't go above one per cent of light velocity. I want—"

"I'll try," he said. "But I'm afraid it won't be easy. Whenever I try to approach a subject it does not want to discuss, the alien begins telling me the most fantastic lies."

"Oh?" Kelly said, suspiciously, and he was sorry he had mentioned that, because it had taken him another quarter hour of explaining before she had allowed him to escape the confines of her office.

Now he was back home again–in his room. Rolling over, he lay flat on his back in the bed, eyes wide open and staring straight ahead at the emptiness of the darkness. He would have liked to go out and visit the observatory, but Kelly had said he was excused from all duties until the alien situation was resolved. He gathered she meant that as an order. She must have. One thing about Kelly: she seldom said a word unless it was meant as an order.

IV

They came and woke him up. He had not intended to sleep. His room was still pitch black, and far away there was a fist pounding furiously upon a door. Getting up, taking his time, he went and let the man inside. Then he turned on the light.

"Hurry and see the director," the man said breathlessly.

"What does she want now?" Reynolds asked.

"How should I know?"

Reynolds shrugged and turned to go. He knew what she wanted anyway. It had to be the aliens; Jonathon was ready to see him again. Well, that was fine, he thought, entering Kelly's office. From the turn of her expression, he saw that he had guessed correctly. *And I know exactly what I'm going to tell them,* he thought.

Somewhere in his sleep, Reynolds had made an important decision: he had decided he was going to tell Jonathon the truth.

Approaching the alien starship, Reynolds discovered he was no longer so strongly reminded of his old home in São Paulo. Now that he had actually been inside the ship and had met the creatures who resided there, his feelings had changed. This time he was struck by how remarkably this strange twisted chunk of metal resembled what a real starship ought to look like.

The tug banged against the side of the ship. Without having to be told, Reynolds removed his suit and went to the air lock. Kelly jumped out of her seat and dashed after him. She grabbed the camera off the deck and forced it into his hands. She wanted him to photograph the aliens. He had to admit her logic was quite impeccable. If the aliens were as unfearsome as Reynolds claimed, then a clear and honest photograph could only reassure the population of Earth; hysteria was still a worry to many politicians back home. Many people still claimed that a spaceship full of green monsters was up here orbiting the moon only a few hours' flight from New York and Moscow. One click of the camera and this fear would be ended.

Reynolds had told her Jonathon would never permit a photograph to be taken, but Kelly had remained adamant.

"Who cares?" he'd asked her.

"Everybody cares," she'd insisted.

"Oh, really? I listened to the news yesterday and the aliens weren't even mentioned. Is that hysteria?"

"That's because of Africa. Wait till the war's over, then listen."

He hadn't argued with her then and he didn't intend to argue with her now. He accepted the camera without a word, her voice burning his ears with last minute instructions, and plunged ahead.

The smell assaulted him immediately. As he entered the spaceship, the odour seemed to rise up from nowhere and surround him. He made himself push forward. Last time, the odour had been a problem only for a short time. He was sure he could overcome it again this time.

It was cold in the ship. He wore only light pants and a light shirt without underwear, because last time it had been rather warm. Had Jonathon, noticing his discomfort, lowered the ship's temperature accordingly?

He turned the first corner and glanced briefly at the distant ceiling. He called out, "Hello!" but there was only a slight echo. He spoke again and the echo was the same, flat and hard.

Another turn. He was moving much faster than before. The tight passage no longer caused him to pause and think. He simply plunged ahead, trusting to his own knowledge. At Kelly's urging he was wearing a radio attached to his belt. He noticed that it was bleeping furiously at him. Apparently Kelly had neglected some important last minute direction. He didn't mind. He already had enough orders to ignore; one less would make little difference.

Here was the place. Pausing in the doorway, he removed the radio, turning it off. Then he placed the camera on the floor beside it, and stepped into the room.

Despite the chill in the air, the room was not otherwise different from before. There were two aliens standing against the farthest wall. Reynolds went straight toward them, holding his hands over his head in greeting. One was taller than the other. Reynolds spoke to it. "Are you Jonathon?"

"Yes," Jonathon said, in his child's piping voice. "And this is Richard."

"May I pay obeisance?" Richard asked eagerly.

Reynolds nodded. "If you wish."

Jonathon waited until Richard had regained his feet, then said, "We wish to discuss your star now."

"All right," Reynolds said. "But there's something I have to tell you first." Saying this, for the first time since he had made his decision, he wasn't sure. Was the truth really the best solution in this situation? Kelly wanted him to lie: tell them whatever they wanted to hear, making certain he didn't tell them quite everything. Kelly was afraid the aliens might go sailing off to the sun once they had learned what they had come here to learn. She wanted a chance to get engineers and scientists inside their ship before the aliens left. And wasn't this a real possibility? What if Kelly was right and the aliens went away? *Then* what would he say?

"You want to tell us that your sun is not a conscious being," Jonathon said. "Am I correct?"

The problem was instantly solved. Reynolds felt no more compulsion to lie. He said, "Yes."

"I am afraid that you are wrong," said Jonathon.

"We live here, don't we? Wouldn't we know? You asked for me because I know our sun, and I do. But there are other men in our home world who know far more than I do. But no one has ever discovered the least shred of evidence to support your theory."

"A theory is a guess," Jonathon said. "We do not guess. We know."

"Then," Reynolds said, "explain it to me. Because I don't know." He watched the alien's eyes carefully, waiting for the first indication of a blinking fit.

But Jonathon's gaze remained steady and certain. "Would you like to hear of our journey?" it asked.

"Yes."

"We left our home world a great many of your years ago. I cannot tell you exactly when, for reasons I'm certain you can understand, but I will reveal that it was more than a century ago. In that time we have visited nine stars. The ones we would visit were chosen for us beforehand. Our priests—our leaders—determined the stars that were within our reach and also able to help in our quest. You see, we have journeyed here in order to ask certain questions."

"Questions of the stars?"

"Yes, of course. The questions we have are questions only a star may answer."

"And what are they?" Reynolds asked.

"We have discovered the existence of other universes parallel with our own. Certain creatures—devils and demons—have come from these universes in order to attack and capture our stars. We feel we must—"

"Oh, yes," Reynolds said. "I understand. We've run across several of these creatures recently." And he blinked, matching the twisting of Jonathon's eye. "They are awfully fearsome, aren't they?" When Jonathon stopped, he stopped too. He said, "You don't have to tell me everything. But can you tell me this: these other stars you have visited, have they been able to answer any of your questions?"

"Oh, yes. We have learned much from them. These stars were very great—very different from our own."

"But they weren't able to answer all your questions?"

"If they had, we would not be here now."

"And you believe our star may be able to help you?"

"All may help, but the one we seek is the one that can save us."

"When do you plan to go to the sun?"

"At once," Jonathon said. "As soon as you leave. I am afraid there is little else you can tell us."

"I'd like to ask you to stay," Reynolds said. And he forced himself to go ahead. He knew he could not convince Jonathon without revealing everything–yet by doing so he might also be putting an end to all his hopes. Still, he told the alien about Kelly and, more generally, he told it what the attitude of man was toward their visit. He told it what man wished to know from them, and why.

Jonathon seemed amazed. He moved about the floor as Reynolds spoke, his feet clanking dully. Then he stopped and stood, his feet only a few inches apart, a position that impressed Reynolds as one of incredulous amazement.

"Your people wish to travel farther into space? You want to visit the stars? But why, Reynolds? Your people do not believe. Why?"

Reynolds smiled. Each time Jonathon said something to him, he felt he knew these people–and how they thought and reacted–a little better than he had before. There was another question he would very much have liked to ask Jonathon. How long have your people possessed the means of visiting the stars? A very long time, he imagined. Perhaps a longer time than the whole lifespan of the human race. And why hadn't they gone before now? Reynolds thought he knew: because, until now, they'd had no reason for going.

Now Reynolds tried to answer Jonathon's question. If anyone could it should be him. "We wish to go to the stars because we are a dissatisfied people. Because we do not live a very long time as individuals, we feel we must place an important part of our lives into the human race as a whole. In a sense, we surrender a portion of our individual person in return for a sense of greater immortality. What is an accomplishment for man as a race is also an accomplishment for each individual man. And what are these accomplishments? Basically this: anything a man does that no other man has done before–whether it is good or evil or neither one or both–is considered by us to be a great accomplishment."

And to add emphasis to the point, he blinked once.

Then, holding his eyes steady, he said, "I want you to teach me to talk to the stars. I want you to stay here around the moon long enough to do that."

Instantly Jonathon said, "No."

There was an added force to the way he said it, an emphasis his voice had not previously possessed. Then Reynolds realized what that was: at the same moment Jonathon had spoken, Richard too had said, "No."

"Then you may be doomed to fail," Reynolds said. "Didn't I tell you? I know our star better than any man available to you. Teach me to talk to the stars and I may be able to help you with this one. Or would you prefer to continue wandering the galaxy forever, failing to find what you seek wherever you go?"

"You are a sensible man, Reynolds. You may be correct. We will ask our home star and see."

"Do that. And if it says yes and I promise to do what you wish, then I must ask you to promise me something in return. I want you to allow a team of our scientists and technicians to enter and inspect your ship. You will answer their questions to the best of your ability. And that means truthfully."

"We always tell the truth," Jonathon said, blinking savagely.

V

The moon had made one full circuit of Earth since Reynold's initial meeting with the aliens, and he was quite satisfied with the progress he had made up to now, especially during the past ten days after Kelly had stopped accompanying him in his daily shuttles to and from the orbiting starship. As a matter of fact, in all that time he had not had a single face-to-face meeting with her and they had talked on the phone only once. And she wasn't here now either, which was strange, since it was noon and she always ate here with the others.

Reynolds had a table to himself in the cafeteria. The food was poor, but it always was, and he was used to that by now. What did bother him, now that he thought about it, was Kelly's absence. Most days he skipped lunch himself. He tried to remember the last time he had come here. It was more than a week ago, he remembered–more than ten days ago. He didn't like the sound of that answer.

Leaning over, he attracted the attention of a girl at an adjoining table. He knew her vaguely. Her father had been an important wheel in NASA when Reynolds was still a star astronaut. He couldn't remember the man's name. His daughter had a cute, tiny face and a billowing body about two sizes too big for the head. Also, she had a brain that was much too limited for much of anything. She worked in the administrative section, which meant she slept with most of the men on the base at one time or another.

"Have you seen Kelly?" he asked her.

"Must be in her office."

"No, I mean when was the last time you saw her here?"

"In here? Oh—" The girl thought for a moment. "Doesn't she eat with the other chiefs?"

Kelly never ate with the other chiefs. She always ate in the cafeteria–for morale purposes–and the fact that the girl did not remember having seen her meant that it had been several days at least since Kelly had last put in an appearance. Leaving his lunch where it lay, Reynolds got up, nodded politely at the girl, who stared at him as if he were a freak, and hurried away.

It wasn't a long walk, but he ran. He had no intention of going to see Kelly. He knew that would prove useless. Instead, he was going to see John Sims. At fifty-two, Sims was the second oldest man in the base. Like Reynolds, he was a former astronaut. In 1999, when Reynolds, then a famous man, was living in São Paulo (for the first of three times), Sims had commanded the second (and first successful) Mars expedition.

Sims and his crew had flown an accelerated, energy-squandering orbit to Mars, carefully shepherded by psychoanalysts who found the measure of their isolation and erased their budding neuroses. Once there and right of mind, they'd begun the process of sorting out the truth about Martian life–that indigent lifeforms had existed, but were by now so thoroughly altered by the virulently successful Earth microbes that their true nature and essence could never be known. No amount of chemical analysis could peer through that cloudy act of contamination to glimpse the past.

This final, humbling answer had taken another ten years in coming, but for a few brief months Sims had been a famous man. Still, he had never accomplished anything more than was naturally expected; he had never met the threat of death. Reynolds, on the other hand, had failed miserably. Three people had died with him on Mars. He'd failed to discover the Soviet contamination.

Yet it was he–Reynolds, the failure–who had been hailed as a true hero. Sims had done his program-

matic job, nothing more. Reynolds, isolated in São
Paulo studying astronomy, found his fame enlarged
by the Sims expedition. There was often a sudden,
waiting silence when he came into a room; it never
failed to unnerve him. He received far more carefully
phrased invitations than he could ever bother to answer. (Had his distance fed the fame? He didn't
know. The past filmed over with afterthoughts.)

And maybe I'm a hero again, he thought as he
knocked on the sheet-metal door of Sims's office.
Maybe down there the world was once again reading
about him daily. He hadn't listened to a news broadcast since the night before his first voyage to the ship.
Had the complete story been released to the public
yet? He couldn't see any reason why it should be sup-
pressed, but that seldom was important. These people
never unzippered themselves–voluntarily–in public.
Still, it would be interesting to find out. He would ask
Sims. Sims would know.

The door opened and Reynolds went inside. Sims
was a huge man who wore his black hair in a crewcut.
The style had been out of fashion for thirty or forty
years; Reynolds doubted there was another crewcut
man in the universe. But he could not imagine Sims
any other way.

"What's wrong?" Sims asked, guessing accurately
the first time. He led Reynolds to a chair and sat him
down. The office was big but empty. A local phone
sat upon the desk along with a couple of daily status
reports. Sims was Assistant Administrative Chief,
whatever that meant. Reynolds had never understood
the functions of the position, if any. But there was
one thing that was clear: Sims knew more about the
inner workings of the moon base than any other man.
And that included the director as well.

"I want to know about Vonda," Reynolds said.
With Sims, everything stood on a first-name basis.
Vonda was Vonda Kelly. The name tasted strangely

upon Reynolds' lips. "Why isn't she eating at the cafeteria?"

Sims answered unhesitantly. "Because she's afraid to leave her desk."

"It has something to do with the aliens?"

"It does, but I shouldn't tell you what. She doesn't want you to know."

"Tell me. Please." His desperation cleared the smile from Sims's lips. And he had almost added: for old time's sake. He was glad he had controlled himself.

"The main reason is the war," Sims said. "If it starts, she wants to know at once."

"Will it?"

Sims shook his head. "I'm smart, but I'm not God. As usual, I imagine everything will work out as long as no one makes a stupid mistake. The worst will be a small local war lasting maybe a month. But how long can you depend upon politicians to act intelligently? It goes against the grain with them."

"But what about the aliens?"

"Well, as I said, that's part of it, too." Sims stuck his pipe in his mouth. Reynolds had never seen it lit, never seen him smoking it, but the pipe was invariably there between his teeth. "A group of men are coming here from Washington, arriving tomorrow. They want to talk with your pets. It seems nobody–least of all Vonda–is very happy with your progress."

"I am."

Sims shrugged, as if to say: that is of no significance.

"The aliens will never agree to see them," Reynolds murmured.

"How are they going to *stop* them? Withdraw the welcome mat? Turn out the lights? That won't work."

"But that will ruin everything. All my work until now."

"*What* work?" Sims got up and walked around his

desk until he stood hovering above Reynolds. "As far as anybody can see, you haven't accomplished a damn thing since you went up there. People want re- sults, Bradley, not a lot of noise. All you've given anyone is the noise. This isn't a private game of yours. This is one of the most significant events in the history of the human race. If anyone ought to know that, it's you. Christ." And he wandered back to his chair again, jiggling his pipe.

"What is it they want from me?" Reynolds said. "Look—I got them what they asked for. The aliens have agreed to let a team of scientists study their ship."

"We want more than that now. Among other things, we want an alien to come down and visit Washington. Think of the propaganda value! And right now is a time when we damn well need some- thing like that. Here we are, the only country with sense enough to stay on the moon. And being here has finally paid off in a way the politicians can under- stand. They've given you a month in which to play around—after all, you're a hero and the publicity is good—but how much longer do you expect them to wait? No, they want action, and I'm afraid they want it now."

Reynolds was ready to go. He found out as much as he was apt to find here. And he already knew what he was going to have to do. He would go and find Kelly and tell her she had to keep the men from Earth away from the aliens. If she wouldn't agree, then he would go up and tell the aliens and they would leave for the sun. But what if Kelly wouldn't let him go? He had to consider that. He knew; he would tell her this: If you don't let me see them, if you try to keep me away, they'll know something is wrong and they'll leave without a backward glance. Maybe he could tell her the aliens were telepaths; he doubted she would know any better.

He had the plan all worked out so that it could not fail.

He had his hand on the doorknob when Sims called him back.

"There's another thing I'd better tell you Bradley."

"All right. What's that?"

"Vonda. She's on your side. She told them to stay away, but it wasn't enough. She's been relieved of duty. A replacement is coming with the others."

VI

Properly suited, Reynolds sat in the cockpit of the shuttle tug, watched the pilot beside him going through the ritual of a final inspection prior to takeoff. The dead, desolate surface of the moon stretched briefly away from where the tug sat, the horizon so near that it looked almost touchable. Reynolds liked the moon. If he had not, he would never have elected to return here to stay. It was the earth he hated. Better than the moon was space itself, the dark endless void beyond the reach of man's ugly grasping hands. That was where Reynolds was going now. Up. Out. Into the void. He was impatient to leave.

The pilot's voice came to him softly through the suit radio, a low murmur, not loud enough for him to understand what the man was saying. The pilot was talking to himself as he worked, using the rumble of his own voice as a way of patterning his mind so that it would not lose concentration. The pilot was a young man in his middle twenties, probably on loan from the Air Force, a lieutenant or, at most, a junior Air Force captain. He was barely old enough to remember when space had really been a frontier. Mankind had decided to go out, and Reynolds had been one of the men chosen to take the giant steps, but now it was late: the giant steps of twenty years ago were mere tentative contusions in the dust of the cen-

turies, and man was coming back. From where he sat,
looking out, Reynolds could see exactly fifty per cent
of the present American space programme: the protruding bubble of the moon base. The other half was
the orbiting space lab that circled the earth itself, a
battered relic of the expansive seventies. Well beyond
the nearby horizon–maybe a hundred miles away–there
had once been another bubble, but it was gone now.
The brave men who had lived and worked and struggled and died and survived there–they were all gone,
too. Where? The Russians still maintained an orbiting space station, so some of their former moon col-
onists were undoubtedly there, but where were the
rest? In Siberia? Working there? Hadn't the Russians
decided that Siberia–the old barless prison state of the
czars and early communists–was a more practical
frontier than the moon?

And weren't they maybe right? Reynolds did not
like to think so, for he had poured his life into this–
into the moon and the void beyond. But at times like
now, peering through the artificial window of his suit,
seeing the bare bubble of the base clinging to the edge
of this dead world like a wart on an old woman's
face, starkly vulnerable, he found it hard to see the
point of it. He was old enough to recall the first time
he had ever been moved by the spirit of conquest. As
a schoolboy, he remembered a film about the first
time men conquered Mount Everest–it was around
1956 or '57–and watching that film, seeing the
shadows of pale mountaineers clinging to the edge of
that white god, he had decided that was what he
wanted to be. And he had never been taught otherwise–only, by the time he was old enough to act, all
the mountains had long since been conquered. And
he had ended up as an astronomer, able if nothing
else to gaze outward at the distant shining peaks of
the void; and from there he had been pointed toward
space. Thus he had gone to Mars and become famous

–but fame had turned him inward, so that now, without the brilliance of his past, he would have been nobody but another of those anonymous old men who dot the cities of the world, inhabiting identically bleak book-lined rooms, eating daily in bad restaurants, their minds always a billion miles away from the dead shells of their bodies.

"We can go now, Dr. Reynolds," the pilot was saying.

Reynolds grunted in reply, his mind several miles distant from his waiting body. He was thinking that there *was* something, after all. How could he think in terms of pointlessness and futility when he alone had actually seen them with his own eyes? Creatures, intelligent beings, born far away, light-years from the insignificant world of man? Didn't that in itself prove something? Yes. He was sure that it did. But what?

The tug lifted with a murmur from the surface of the moon. Crouched deeply within his seat, Reynolds thought that it wouldn't be long now.

And they found us, he thought, *we did not find them.* And when had they gone into space? Late. Very late. At a moment in their history comparable to man a hundred thousand years from now. They had avoided space until a pressing reason had come for venturing out and then they had gone. He remembered that he had been unable to explain to Jonathon why man wanted to visit the stars when he did not believe in the divinity of the suns. Was there a reason? And if so, did it make sense?

The journey was not long.

It didn't smell. The air ran clean and sharp and sweet through the corridors, and if there was any odour to it, the odour was one of purity and freshness, almost pine needles or mint. The air was good for his spirits. As soon as Reynolds came aboard the starship, his depression and melancholy were forgotten. Perhaps he was only letting the apparent grimness of the situation get the better of him. It had been too long a time since he'd last had to fight. Jonathon would know what to do. The alien was more than three hundred years old, a product of a civilization and culture that had reached its maturity at a time when man was not yet man, when he was barely a skinny undersized ape, a carrion eater upon the hot plains of Africa.

When Reynolds reached the meeting room, he saw that Jonathon and Richard were not alone this time. The third alien–Reynolds sensed it was someone important–was introduced as Vergnan. No adopted Earth name for it.

"This is ours who best knows the stars," Jonathon said. "It has spoken with yours and hopes it may be able to assist you."

Reynolds had almost forgotten that part. The sudden pressures of the past few hours had driven everything else from his mind. His training. His unsuccessful attempts to speak to the stars. He had failed. Jonathon had been unable to teach him, but he thought that was probably because he simply did not believe.

"Now we shall leave you," Jonathon said.

"But—" said Reynolds.

"We are not permitted to stay."

"But there's something I must tell you."

It was too late. Jonathon and Richard headed for the corridor, walking with surprising gracefulness. Their long necks bobbed, their skinny legs shook, but they still managed to move as swiftly and sleekly as any cat, almost rippling as they went.

Reynolds turned toward Vergnan. Should he tell this one about the visitors from Earth? He did not think so. Vergnan was old, his skin much paler than the others, almost totally hairless. His eyes were wrinkled and one ear was torn.

Vergnan's eyes were closed.

Remembering his lessons, Reynolds too closed his eyes.

And kept them closed. In the dark, time passed more quickly than it seemed, but he was positive that five minutes went by.

Then the alien began to speak. No—he did not speak; he simply sang, his voice trilling with the high searching notes of a well-tuned violin, dashing up and down the scale, a pleasant sound, soothing, cool. Reynolds tried desperately to concentrate upon the song, ignoring the existence of all other sensations, recognizing nothing and no one but Vergnan. Reynolds ignored the taste and smell of the air and the distant throbbing of the ship's machinery. The alien sang deeper and clearer, his voice rising higher and higher, directed now at the stars. Jonathon, too, had sung, but never like this. When Jonathon sang, his voice had dashed away in a frightened search, shifting and darting wildly about, seeking vainly a place to land. Vergnan sang without doubt. It—*he*—was certain. Reynolds sensed the overwhelming maleness of this being, his patriarchal strength and dignity. His voice and song never struggled or wavered. He knew always exactly where he was going.

Had he felt something? Reynolds did not know. If so, then what? No, no, he thought, and concentrated more fully upon the voice, too intently to allow for the logic of thought. Within, he felt strong, alive, renewed, resurrected. *I am a new man. Reynolds is dead. He is another.* These thoughts came to him like the whispering words of another. *Go, Reynolds. Fly. Leave. Fly.*

Then he realized that he was singing too. He could not imitate Vergnan, for his voice was too alien, but he tried and heard his own voice coming frighteningly near, almost fading into and being lost within the constant tones of the other. The two voices suddenly became one, mingling indiscriminately . . . merging . . and that one voice rose higher, floating, then higher again, rising farther, going farther out—farther and deeper.

Then he felt it. Reynolds. And he knew it for what it was.

The sun.

More ancient than the whole of Earth itself. A greater, vaster being, more powerful and knowing. Divinity as a ball of heat and energy.

Reynolds spoke to the stars.

And knowing this, balking at the concept, he drew back instinctively in fear, his voice faltering, dwindling, collapsing. Reynolds scurried back, seeking the earth, but grasping, pulling, Vergnan drew him on. Beyond the shallow exterior light of the sun, he witnessed the totality of that which lay hidden within. The core. The impenetrable darkness within. Fear gripped him once more. He begged to be allowed to flee. Tears streaking his face with the heat of fire, he pleaded. Vergnan benignly drew him on. *Come forward. Come. See. Know.* Forces coiled to a point.

And he saw.

Could he describe it as evil? Thought was an absurdity. Not thinking, sensing and feeling instead, he experienced the wholeness of this entity– a star–the sun–and saw that it was not evil. He sensed the sheer totality of its opening nothingness. Sensation was absent. Colder than cold, more terrifying than hate, more sordid than fear, blacker than evil. The vast inner whole nothingness of everything that was anything, of all.

I have seen enough. No.

Yes, cried Vergnan, agreeing.

To stay a moment longer would mean never returning again. Vergnan knew this too, and he released Reynolds, allowed him to go.

And still he sang. The song was different from before. Struggling within himself, Reynolds sang too, trying to match his voice to that of the alien. It was easier this time. The two voices merged, mingled, became one.

And then Reynolds awoke.

He was lying on the floor of the starship, the rainbow walls swirling brightly around him.

Vergnan stepped over him. He saw the alien's protruding belly as it passed. It did not look down or back, but continued onward, out the door, gone, as quick and cold as the inner soul of the sun itself. For a brief moment, he hated Vergnan more deeply than he had ever hated anything in his life. Then he sat up, gripping himself, forcing a return to sanity. I am all right now, he insisted. I am back, I am alive. The walls ceased spinning. At his back the floor shed its clinging coat of roughness. The shadows in the corners of his eyes dispersed.

Jonathon entered the room alone.

"Now you have been," it said, crossing the room and assuming its usual place beside the wall.

"Yes," said Reynolds, not attempting to stand.

"And now you know why we search. For centuries our star was kind to us, loving. But now it too–like yours–is changed."

"You are looking for a new home?"

"True."

"And?"

"And we find nothing. All are alike. We have seen nine, visiting all. They are nothing."

"Then you will leave here too?"

"We must. But first we will approach your star. Not until we have drawn so close that we have seen everything, not until then can we dare admit our failure. This time we thought we had succeeded. When we met you, this is what we thought, for you are unlike your star. We felt that the star could not produce you–or your race–without the presence of benevolence.

But it is gone now. We meet only the blackness. We struggle to penetrate to a deeper core. And fail."

"I am not typical of my race," Reynolds said.

"We shall see."

He remained with Jonathon until he felt strong enough to stand. The floor hummed. Feeling it with moist hands, he planted a kiss upon the creased cold metal. A wind swept through the room, carrying a hint of returned life. Jonathon faded, rippled, returned to a sharp outline of crisp reality. Reynolds was suddenly hungry and the oily taste of meat swirled up through his nostrils. The cords in his neck stood out with the strain until, gradually the tension passed from him.

He left and went to the tug. During the great fall to the silver moon he said not a word, thought not a thought. The trip was long.

VII

Reynolds lay on his back in the dark room, staring upward at the faint shadow of a ceiling, refusing to see.

Hypnosis? Or a more powerful alien equivalent of the same? Wasn't that, as an explanation, more likely than admitting that he had indeed communicated with the sun, discovering a force greater than evil, blacker than black? Or—here was another theory—wasn't it possible that these aliens, because of the conditions on their own world, so thoroughly accepted the consciousness of the stars that they could make him believe as well? Similar things happened on Earth. Religious miracles, the curing of diseases through faith, men who claimed to have spoken with God. What about flying saucers and little green men and all the other incidents of mass hysteria? Wasn't that the answer here? Hysteria? Hypnosis? Perhaps even a drug of some sort: a drug released into the air. Reynolds had plenty of possible solutions; he could choose one or all. But he decided that he did not really care.

He had gone into this thing knowing exactly what he was doing, and now that it had happened he did not regret the experience. He had found a way of fulfilling his required mission while at the same time experiencing something personal that no other man would ever know. Whether he had actually seen the sun was immaterial; the experience, as such, was still his own. Nobody could ever take that away from him.

It was some time after this when he realized that a fist was pounding on the door. He decided he might as well ignore that, because sometimes when you ignored things, they went away. But the knocking did not go away—it only got louder. Finally Reynolds got up. He opened the door.

Kelly glared at his nakedness and said, "Did I wake you?"

"No."

"May I come in?"

"No."

"I've got something to tell you." She forced her way past him, sliding into the room. Then Reynolds saw that she wasn't alone. A big, red-faced, beefy man followed, forcing his way into the room, too.

Reynolds shut the door, cutting off the corridor light, but the man went over and turned on the overhead light.

"All right," he said, as though it were an order.

"Who the hell are you? Reynolds said.

"Forget him," Kelly said. "I'll talk."

"Talk," said Reynolds.

"The committee is here. The men from Washington. They arrived an hour ago and I've kept them busy since. You may not believe this, but I'm on your side."

"Sims told me."

"He told me he told you."

"I knew he would. Mind telling me why? He didn't know."

"Because I'm not an idiot," Kelly said. "I've known enough petty bureaucrats in my life. Those things up there are alien beings. You can't send fools up there to go stomping all over their toes."

Reynolds gathered this would not be over soon. He put on his pants.

"This is George O'Hara," Kelly said. "He's the new director."

"I want to offer my resignation," Reynolds said casually, fixing the snaps of his shirt.

"You have to accompany us to the starship," O'Hara said.

"I want you, too," Kelly said. "You owe this to someone. If not me, then the aliens. If you had told me the truth, this might never have happened. If anyone is to blame for this mess it is you, Reynolds. Why won't you tell me what's been going on up there the last months? It has to be something."

"It is," Reynolds said. "Don't laugh, but I was trying to talk to the sun. I told you that's why the aliens came here. They're taking a cruise of the galaxy, pausing here and there to chat with the stars."

"Don't be frivolous. And yes, you told me all that."

"I have to be frivolous. Otherwise it sounds too ridiculous. I made an agreement with them. I wanted to learn to talk to the sun. I told them, since I lived here, I could find out what they wanted to know better than they could. I could tell they were doubtful, but they let me go ahead. In return for my favour, when I was done, whether I succeeded or failed, they would give us what we wanted. A team of men could go and freely examine their ship. They would describe their voyage to us–where they had been, what they had found. They promised cooperation in return for my chat with the sun.

"So then nothing happened?"   .

"I didn't say that. I talked with the sun today. And saw it. And now I'm not going to do anything except sit on my hands. You can take it from here."

"What are you talking about?"

He knew he could not answer that. "I failed," he said. "I didn't find out anything they didn't know."

"Well, will you go with us or not? That's all I want to know right now." She was losing patience, but there was also more than a minor note of pleading in her voice. He knew he ought to feel satisfied hearing that, but he didn't.

"Oh, hell," Reynolds said. "Yes, all right. I will go. But don't ask me why. Just give me an hour to get ready."

"Good man," O'Hara said, beaming happily.

Ignoring him, Reynolds opened his closets and began tossing clothes and other belongings into various boxes and crates.

"What do you think you'll need all that for?" Kelly asked him.

"I don't think I'm coming back," Reynolds said.

"They won't hurt you," she said.

"No. I won't be coming back because I won't be wanting to come back."

"You can't do that," O'Hara said.

"Sure I can," said Reynolds.

It took the base's entire fleet of seven shuttle tugs to ferry the delegation from Washington up to the starship. At that, a good quarter of the group had to be left behind for lack of room. Reynolds had requested and received permission to call the starship prior to departure, so the aliens were aware of what was coming up to meet them. They had not protested, but Reynolds knew they wouldn't, at least not over the radio. Like almost all mechanical or electronic gadgets, a radio was a fearsome object to them.

Kelly and Reynolds arrived with the first group and entered the air lock. At intervals of a minute or two, the others arrived. When the entire party was clustered in the lock, the last tug holding to the hull in preparation for the return ship, Reynolds signaled that it was time to move out.

"Wait a minute," one of the men called. "We're not all *here*. Acton and Dodd went back to the tug to get *suits."*

"Then they'll have to stay there," Reynolds said. "The air is pure here. Nobody needs a suit."

"But," said another man, pinching his nose. "This smell. It's *awful."*

Reynolds smiled. He had barely noticed the odour. Compared to the stench of the first few days, this was nothing today. "The aliens won't talk if you're wearing suits. They have a taboo against artificial communication. The smell gets better as you go farther inside. Until then, hold your nose. Breath through your mouth."

"It's making me almost sick," confided a man at Reynolds' elbow. "You're sure what you say is true, doctor?"

"Cross my heart," Reynolds said. The two men who had left to fetch the suits returned. Reynolds wasted another minute lecturing them.

"Stop enjoying yourself so much," Kelly whispered, when they were at last underway.

Before they reached the first of the tight passages where crawling was necessary, three men had dropped away, dashing back toward the tug. Working from a hasty map given him by the aliens, he was leading the party toward a section of the ship where he had never been before. The walk was less difficult than usual. In most places a man could walk comfortably and the ceilings were high enough to accommodate the aliens themselves. Reynolds ignored the occasional shouted exclamation from the men behind. He steered a silent course toward his destination.

The room, when they reached it, was a huge stale

space, big as a basketball gymnasium, the ceiling lost in the deep shadows above. Turning, Reynolds counted the aliens present: fifteen . . . twenty . . . thirty . . . forty . . . forty-five . . . forty-six. That had to be about all. He wondered if this was the full crew.

Then he counted his own people: twenty-two. Better than he had expected–only six lost en route, victims of the smell.

He spoke directly to the alien who stood in front of the others. "Greetings," he said. The alien wasn't Vergnan, but it could have been Jonathon.

From behind he heard: "They're just like giraffes."

"And they even seem intelligent," said another.

"Exceedingly so. Their eyes."

"And friendly, too."

"Hello, Reynolds," the alien said. "Are these the ones?"

"Jonathon?" asked Reynolds.

"Yes."

"These are the ones."

"And they are your leaders–they wish to question my people."

"They do."

"May I serve as our spokesman in order to save time?"

"Of course," Reynolds said. He turned and faced his party, looking from face to face, hoping to spot a single glimmer of intelligence, no matter how minute. But he found nothing. "Gentlemen?" he said. "You heard?"

"His name is Jonathon?" said one.

"It is a convenient expression. Do you have a real question?"

"Yes," the man said. He continued speaking to Reynolds: "Where is your home world located?"

Jonathon ignored the man's rudeness and promptly named a star.

"Where is that?" the man asked, speaking directly to the alien now.

Reynolds told him it lay some thirty light-years from Earth. As a star, it was very much like the sun, though somewhat larger.

"Exactly how many kilometres in a light-year?" a man wanted to know.

Reynolds tried to explain. The man claimed he understood, though Reynolds remained sceptical.

It was time for another question.

"Why have you come to our world?"

"Our mission is purely one of exploration and discovery," Jonathan said.

"Have you discovered any other intelligent races besides our own?"

"Yes. Several."

This answer elicited a murmur of surprise from the men. Reynolds wondered who they were, how they had been chosen for this mission. Not what they were, but who. What made them tick. He knew what they were: politicians, NASA bureaucrats, a sprinkling of real scientists. But who?

"Are any of these people aggressive?" asked a man, almost certainly a politician. "Do they pose a threat to you or–or to us?"

"No," Jonathon said. "None."

Reynolds was barely hearing the questions and answers now. His attention was focused upon Jonathon's eyes. He had stopped blinking now. The last two questions–the ones dealing with intelligent life forms–he had told the truth. Reynolds thought he was beginning to understand. He had underestimated these creatures. Plainly, they had encountered other races during their travels before coming to Earth. They were experienced. Jonathon was lying, yes–but unlike before, he was lying well, only when the truth would not suffice.

"How long do you intend to remain in orbit about our moon?"

"Until the moment you and your friends leave our craft. Then we shall depart."

This set up an immediate clamour among the men. Waving his arms furiously, Reynolds attempted to silence them. The man who had been unfamiliar with the term "light-year" shouted out an invitation for Jonathon to visit Earth.

This did what Reynolds himself could not do. The others fell silent in order to hear Jonathon's reply.

"It is impossible," Jonathon said. "Our established schedule requires us to depart immediately."

"Is it this man's fault?" demanded a voice. "He should have asked you himself long before now."

"No," Jonathon said. "I could not have come—or any of my people—because we were uncertain of your peaceful intentions. Not until we came to know Reynolds well did we fully comprehend the benevolence of your race." The alien blinked rapidly now.

He stopped during the technical questions. The politicians and bureaucrats stepped back to speak among themselves and the scientists came forward. Reynolds was amazed at the intelligence of their questions. To this extent at least, the expedition had not been wholly a farce.

Then the questions were over and all the men came forward to listen to Jonathon's last words.

"We will soon return to our home world, and when we do we shall tell the leaders of our race of the greatness and glory of the human race. In passing here, we have come to know your star and, through it, your people who live beneath its soothing rays. I consider your visit here a personal honour to me as an individual. I am sure my brothers share my pride and only regret an inability to utter their gratitude."

Then Jonathon ceased blinking and looked hard at Reynolds. "Will you be going too?"

"No," Reynolds said. "I'd like to talk to you alone if I can."

"Certainly," Jonathon said.

Several of the men in the party protested to Kelly

or O'Hara, but there was nothing they could do. One by one they left the chamber to wait in the corridor. Kelly was the last to leave.

"Don't be a fool," she cautioned.

"I won't," he said.

When the men had gone, Jonathon took Reynolds away from the central room. It was only a brief walk to the old room where they had always met before. As if practising a routine, Jonathon promptly marched to the farthest wall and stood there waiting.

Reynolds smiled. "Thank you," he said.

"You are welcome."

"For lying to them. I was afraid they would offend you with their stupidity. I thought you would show your contempt by lying badly, offending them in return. I under-estimated you. You handled them very well."

"But you have something you wish to ask of me?"

"Yes," Reynolds said. "I want you to take me away with you."

As always Jonathon remained expressionless. Still, for a long time he said nothing. Then: "Why do you wish this? We shall never return here."

"I don't care. I told you before: I am not typical of my race. I can never be happy here."

"But are you typical of my race? Would you not be unhappy with us?"

"I don't know. But I'd like to try."

"It is impossible," Jonathon said.

"But—but why?"

"Because we have neither the time nor the abilities to care for you. Our mission is a most desperate one. Already, during our absence, our home world may have gone mad. We must hurry. Our time is growing brief. And you will not be of any help to us. I am sorry, but you know that is true."

"I can talk to the stars."

"No," said Jonathon. "You cannot."

"But I did."

"Vergnan did. Without him, you could not."

"Your answer is final? There's no one else I can ask? The captain?"

"I am the captain."

Reynolds nodded. He had carried his suitcases and crates all this way and now he would have to haul them home again. Home? No, no home. Only the moon. "Could you find out if they left a tug for me?" he asked.

"Yes. One moment."

Jonathon rippled lightly away, disappearing into the corridor. Reynolds turned and looked at the walls. Again, as he stared, the rainbow patterns appeared to shift and dance and swirl of their own volition. Watching this, he felt sad, but his sadness was not that of grief. It was the sadness of emptiness and aloneness. This emptiness had so long been a part of him that he sometimes forgot it was there. He knew it now. He knew, whether consciously aware of it or not, that he had spent the past ten years of his life searching vainly for a way of filling this void. Perhaps even more than that: perhaps his whole life had been nothing more than a search for that one moment of real completion. Only twice had he ever really come close. The first time had been on Mars. When he had lived and watched while the others had died. Then he had not been alone or empty. And the other time had been right here in this very room with Vergnan. Only twice in his life had he been allowed to approach the edge of true meaning. Twice in fifty-eight long and endless years. Would it ever happen again? When? How?

Jonathon returned, pausing in the doorway. "A pilot is there," it said.

Reynolds went toward the door, ready to leave. "Are you still planning to visit our sun?" he asked.

"Oh, yes. We shall continue trying, searching. We

know nothing else. You do not believe–even after what Vergnan showed you–do you, Reynolds?"

"No, I do not believe."

"I understand," Jonathon said. "And I sympathize. All of us–even I–sometimes we have doubts."

Reynolds continued forward into the corridor. Behind, he heard a heavy clipping noise and turned to see Jonathon coming after him. He waited for the alien to join him, and then they walked together. In the narrow corridor there was barely room for them both.

Reynolds did not try to talk. As far as he could see, there was nothing left to be said that might possibly be said in so short a time as that which remained. Better to say nothing, he thought, than to say too little.

The air lock was open. Past it, Reynolds glimpsed the squat bulk of the shuttle tug clinging to the creased skin of the starship.

There was nothing left to say. Turning to Jonathon, he murmured, "Goodbye," and as he said it, for the first time he wondered what he was going back to. More than likely he would find himself a hero once again. A celebrity. But that was all right: fame was fleeting; it was bearable. Two hundred and forty thousand miles was still a great distance. He would be all right.

As if reading his thoughts, Jonathon asked, "Will you be remaining here, or will you return to your home world?"

The question surprised Reynolds; it was the first time the alien had ever evidenced a personal interest in him.

"I'll stay here. I'm happier."

"And there will be a new director?"

"Yes. How did you know that? But I think I'm going to be famous again. I can get Kelly retained."

"You could have the job yourself," Jonathon said.

"But I don't want it. How do you know all this? About Kelly and so on?"

"I listen to the stars," Jonathon said in his high warbling voice.

"They are alive, aren't they?" Reynolds said suddenly.

"Of course. We are permitted to see them for what they are. You do not. But you are young."

"They are balls of ionized gas. Thermonuclear reactions."

The alien moved, shifting his neck as though a joint lay in the middle of it. Reynolds did not understand the gesture. Nor would he ever. Time had run out at last.

"When they come to you," Jonathan said, "they assume a disguise you can see. That is how they spend their time in this universe. Think of them as doorways."

"Through which I cannot pass."

"Yes."

Reynolds smiled, nodded and passed into the lock. It contracted behind him, engulfing the image of his friend. A few moments of drifting silence, then the other end of the lock furled open.

The pilot was a stranger. Ignoring the man, Reynolds dressed, strapped himself down, and thought about Jonathon. What was it he had said? *I listen to the stars.* Yes, and the stars had told him that Kelly had been fired?

He did not like that part. But the part he liked even less was this: when he said it, Jonathon had not blinked.

(a) He had been telling the truth. *(b)* He could lie without flicking a lash.

Choose one.

Reynolds did, and the tug fell toward the moon.

THREE

2052

AFRICA

Just beyond the high, shadowless monastery wall, with the red winter sun pounding down, Bradley Reynolds sat barelegged, oblivious to any possible physical discomfort. The blistering Tunisian sand seared his flanks and thighs, but Bradley struggled to force his mind to meditate in soundless rhythm with the other dark-robed monks who formed this circle with him. Yet the others were so young. Bradley found it difficult to keep his inner eye focused upon the eternal void when his outer vision kept showing him pictures of their shining faces: smooth skin, full lips, crystal clear eyes. I was once like them myself, he recalled fondly, but I had not yet learned to serve the softness of immoderate youth.

A new force further penetrated his self-imposed loneliness. Bradley heard the swift, hard beat of whirring helicopter blades. Surrendering himself hopelessly, he glanced quickly up against the sun and glimpsed, swooping in a dwindling, descending gyre, the plump, gorged shape of the 'copter.

So now, as if old age were not curse enough, they had chosen to come for him again. The helicopter, Bradley knew, was surely his. More than a decade had passed since their last invasion here, but no devil ever waited too long before offering new temptations.

The younger monks had also spotted the 'copter

and their excited, trilling voices filled the air. In pure contrariness, Bradley sprang back into meditative silence. At first he easily isolated that other, outer world–the one containing voices, whirring blades, smooth flesh, and young skin–but as the helicopter dipped lower the blades disturbed the sand, and tiny yellow fragments splashed painfully against his brown, withered face. Grimacing, Bradley thought suddenly of the very end, when the dirt of the grave would slap his face. Perhaps only then–physical death–might he achieve the oblivion he had so long desired.

For thirty-five years, Bradley Reynolds had endured the seclusion of the monastery. When Jonathon, possessed of the knowledge he sought, had left the solar system, Bradley had also chosen to desert the human world. Had he come here to discover a truth, or only to hide himself? This question was one he had never satisfactorily answered, and he often feared that failure might be why enlightenment, though often so close, continued to elude his grasp. The sand no longer blew. He relaxed, his meditative trance exhausted. The whirring ceased. The helicopter had touched ground.

Bradley stood, leaving the remnants of the circle. Two of the younger monks already raced eagerly across the sand toward the waiting 'copter. Bradley observed them briefly, their black robes floating like the wings of weary bats. He saw, emblazoned upon the side of the 'copter, the blue and green emblem of the United Congress. A monk touched his arm as he turned. A pretty, fleshy girl, twenty, her head shaven. The daughter of a Swedish shipping merchant. He was ignorant of her given name; even now too many faces passed for him to recall one over another.

"What–what is it?" Her fear surprised him.

"A helicopter," he answered gently.

"Is it–do you think–a sign?"

He shook his head, confused. "No, it's just for

me." He patted her hand tenderly. "In a few hours, they'll be gone."

"When it came, I was thinking—in my meditation, I saw the eye of God."

Her revelation caused him to shiver. He pointed to the 'copter. "Well, that isn't God." He hurried toward the stone wall that separated the plush oasis of the monastery grounds from the harsh desert beyond.

At eighty-seven years, Bradley Reynolds still carried himself with the vigour of a man a generation younger. He thanked his years in space for that privilege. Weightlessness caressed the inner body, kept the vital organs from choking under their own weight. Still, he was not young. The moments increased when his body simply refused to respond to commands that had once been automatically obeyed. These confusions of the body led naturally to deeper confusions of the mind. Men, he believed, died for reasons of their own ultimate devising, but Bradley himself endured. The same question had first confronted him thirty-five years before: how to devise anything meaningful to serve a polished old age. Should he sit on his flanks and thighs and mesmerize his mind into believing, or should he seek, search, rummage the universe for the right sign, the one precious pebble that might reveal all in an instant? When young, he had tried the latter way; for old age, he opted for the former. Now, as death swept inexorably nearer, both methods seemed ludicrous. *I have surely failed,* he thought, for he had seen the proof of that written large in the young girl monk's innocent bewilderment: her world contained a god, and his did not. *I was too long part of that world out there.* He could not avoid its grasping embrace.

Brother Ling, white robes obliviously stirring dust, met Bradley beyond the inner gate. Bradley had loved and served Ling for more than three decades but no more knew this frail yellow man now than ever. *Why*

am I torturing myself with these bleak thoughts today?
he wondered. It must be the helicopter. He would
blame them for this pain, too.

"Yes, they've come for me again," Bradley told
Ling, knowing he wished to ask about the 'copter.

"And will you see them?"

"I—no" Then he nodded. "No, send them to my
cell."

The monastery had been erected from the ruined
monument of an ancient Moorish temple, the stone
battered by age and yet preserved by the deadly same-
ness of the desert environment. Each night Bradley
climbed to the highest point of the eastern tower and
watched the stars. The gesture was meant as a
farewell, a way of departing the universe he had once
occupied and of entering another; but the next night
he always came and watched again.

"They should let you rest, Brother Bradley."

"Maybe—but they won't."

"They feel you are needed out there."

"No one man is ever needed, Brother Ling."

His cell, of course, was kept bare. A clean blanket
lay neatly bundled in one corner. Bradley sat in the
middle of the floor. With the door left open. He allowed his bearded chin to drop weakly to his chest.
He smiled. Automatically he had adopted the tech-
nique that had worked well before. There had been
no real need to come here; he could have remained
outside and met them there. But this was his ground
—his retreat—and he drew strength from the encroaching
emptiness. When they came and found him, a bent
old man squatting upon the stone floor of a monk's
bare cell, they understood immediately that they
would fail.

This time only one man came. Bradley saw the
shock upon his face and read his thoughts: *Can this
be Bradley Reynolds? The first man on Mars? The man
who talked to aliens? The man we need to save the*

world? Bradley fondly remembered the occasion, twelve years before, when Vonda Kelly had come. He recalled her visit above the others, for she had spent a night attempting to convince him to return, even resorting to sex. Brother Ling had chastised him thoroughly for his failure to resist her. But old age didn't sap a man down there. What it did was make it easier to concentrate upon the less physical aspects of existence.

"Dr. Reynolds, I—"

"No, just Bradley. The other name–it's no longer mine."

"Sir, my name is Carr, and I've been delegated to request your presence—"

"No. I am never present anywhere except here." Bradley saw that his game had already been won. This man, Carr, as forgettable as any minor bureaucrat, hesitated. With no place to sit, he shifted nervously on his feet. Beneath his gaze, Bradley sat firmly rooted to the floor and held the full advantage.

Carr finally made up his mind. "I have a subpoena."

Bradley held out his hands. "Arrest me."

"I'm sure *that* won't be necessary." Carr ignored the outstretched wrists. "We seek only your testimony. Since the entire matter hinges on the question of practicality, your authority could easily tip the balance."

Bradley, who had not scanned a newscast in thirty-five years, asked, "What are you talking about?"

"Why, the Alpha Libra signal. The Puzzle."

Bradley felt himself losing control. There was something threatening in what Carr said. The words seemed to vibrate with a meaning far beyond their obvious incomprehensibility.

He tottered, uncertain. Curiosity at last emerged victorious. "You'll have to explain that to me."

"I can show you." Carr removed a photograph from a wide coat pocket. "This is it."

Again, Bradley held back, but there was no way, with the photograph already cold in his hands, that he could not look. "A communications grid," he said at once.

"You mean you really hadn't seen this before?" said Carr, amazed.

"When was this received?"

"Two months ago."

"And has it been deciphered?"

"Only this portion." Carr indicated one corner of the photograph. "We believe this is their plantary system. And this–this must be their home world."

"It's a giant," said Bradley.

"That's the problem."

"Then they must be—" He gave a mighty shrug, as

though throwing off a heavy weight. "Who can say?"

"We want to find out. Your testimony–a meeting of the Science and Astronautics Committee–it *could* make all the difference."

There was no need to ask how. They'd made a mistake, but how could he explain? Carr sought his testimony, his support, his weight, but the man they wanted was no longer here: Bradley Reynolds, the legend, the spaceman, a creature from another time. How could Carr be made to understand that to the older Bradley, the aged monk he now faced, that younger Bradley was the same: a face seen dimly through a cluttered string of pale memories, a yellowed photograph, a strange and distant piece of tattered history? He could understand some of the things that younger man had done, but he could never slide smoothly into that firm body or experience the same light, springing thoughts. His eyelids now were purplish and wrinkled, his nose fleshy; his skin had acquired an odd olive cast. We are more than simple passengers inside the hull of a body, he thought. The flesh shapes us, contorts us, spins us about, points us in whatever direction the corpuscles, arteries, glands dictate. The fact that the course plotted by his body had shifted with time did not seem a significant one. The mind within learned, forgot, sifted among details and memories without ever knowing how the body–always silent, always supreme–had weighed them before bringing these things to consciousness. The mind suffered illusions; the body, none. "I am too old," he told Carr.

"Too old to talk?"

"Yes. Because it's not me. I'm not that man anymore."

"But the old people worship you now."

The others before had told him that, too. The aged and dying, their numbers so swelled and their isolation so rigid that they had developed a worldwide subculture of their own–Bradley Reynolds was their reigning hero. Why? To them, drawn into a possessive fest of the tired, the used, and the antique, he shone as a distant, bright beacon, the man who had done it all and then cast it aside.

"Let me alone."

"I'm afraid I can't take no for an answer. This involves the whole future of the human race."

"I didn't say no. I said let me think."

The force of Bradley's rage forced Carr back toward the open door. "Until when?" he called from the corridor.

"I'll let you know by nightfall," Bradley promised.

But it took longer, much longer, for he was forced to ponder the beliefs and practices of thirty-five years. He sat still upon the floor of his cell and used the methods of the present to examine the ambitions of yesterday. Studying his own naked forearms, as gnarled as ancient elm, he tried to capture, then follow, the chain of a single rational thought. Despite the hard stone beneath his buttocks, the world seemed to melt; the air rippled with unseen activity. Events repeat, return, he thought–events and people and ideas form and reform, unravel and then curl again, swirl into circles, return endlessly. One should not fear a return to the past. All things properly flow without natural limits. Exploration remains an endless task. But Bradley did not feel this could be all; there was some thrusting point to events, some direction in time and human life. He did not accept the vision of man as merely an animated mustard seed, born to grow and die and endlessly stamp out another image of itself. Biology's idiot repetition could not serve as a symbol for humankind. There had to be a vector.

For long, long hours he sat in the shadowed, chilled cell as winter rain spattered the unseen grounds beyond. Angry dark clouds boiled up from the horizon, while restless birds twittered and called. He felt awash, drowning in the sweet, heavy air of Africa.

Then something budged him. It was late, near midnight. The answer came to him in a flash of insight. It could have been enlightenment but was only:

A planet. A giant world. Bands of light and colour.

Jupiter, Bradley recognized, and seeing that, the myriad fragments fell neatly into place and the totality of a solution lay open to him.

Bradley smiled.

If the Alpha Libra signal was necessary to human existence, then the nexus of any serious study of the puzzle must be Jupiter. He would appear before the Congressional committee. He would speak idealistically at first. Man was not alone in the galaxy. The marvellous things to be learned from another intelligence. Then, when he had their attention, he would swiftly recommend the establishment of an orbiting laboratory around Jupiter, where a permanent party could attempt to mine the secrets of that mysterious world.

If they refused him, he would return here to the dank silence of Africa.

If they accepted his suggestion, then he would go himself. They could not deny him. He knew of the misnamed Anti-Senility Acts that forbade discrimination because of age. He would use their own political laws against them. No other man living could possibly stand better qualified for service in space than Bradley Reynolds. He was too old–perhaps–but they could no longer use that charge against him.

Bradley stood. The end was too close for staying here. The time had come to complete the circle of life. How better to die than by doing, thinking, seeing what was old and what was new? Fatigue would eventually drag him down, but only the rough and abrasive edges of life could rub him toward fresh awareness. Were all the mysteries to be solved by sitting, flanks numbed, on this cold stone floor? For some, perhaps–for Brother Ling or that wide-eyed girl–but not for him.

As Bradley moved toward the open door, his legs responded automatically to the commands of his mind. He walked without stiffness or pain.

At the door, he paused briefly. I have lost nothing here, he thought. I have learned. Learn first, then act. The moment had come to spring forth again.

He found Carr seated uncomfortably in the main chamber, where he cast suspicious, almost frightened glances at the rows of squatting, silent monks. Bradley said, in a clear voice, "I'll be going with you as soon as you're ready."

When he spoke, only Brother Ling looked up.

FOUR

2060

JUPITER

There is a story about two friends, who were classmates in high school, talking about their jobs. One of them became a statistician and was working on population trends. He showed a reprint to his former classmate. The reprint started, as usual, with the Gaussian distribution, and the statistician explained to his former classmate the meaning of the symbols for the actual population, and so on. His classmate was a bit incredulous and was not quite sure whether the statistician was pulling his leg. "How can you know that?" was his query. "And what is this symbol here?" "Oh," said the statistician "this is pi." "And what is that?" "The ratio of the circumference of the circle to its diameter." "Well, now you are pushing your joke too far," said the classmate. "Surely the population has nothing to do with the circumference of the circle."

—Eugene P. Wigner
Symmetries and
Reflections

I

She hung suspended in the void of space, dangling from the umbilical of the airhose, floating like an embryo contemplating the feasibility of birth.

Inside the bubble of her helmet the sharp, singsong voice of Bradley Reynolds pierced her careful serenity: "I don't mean later, Mara, I mean now. You know damn well you're violating every regulation written. Particularly working alone in an outer bay."

She did not intend to let him ruin it—not quite yet. She answered distantly, "Who wrote these regulations, Bradley? Not thee, not me, not—"

"But we have to follow them."

"Thee, perhaps." She giggled sharply, knowing that would irritate him. "But not me. I follow a higher law."

"Your own."

"So?"

He went on, but she ignored him. Tugging at her mooring line, she rotated back toward Jupiter. What a grand and glorious sight this was. Mara could no more hop to turn her eyes than she could have ignored the visage of God standing at her elbow. Wasn't Jupiter a god in its own good right—a massive oblate sphere blotting out an improbable chunk of black sky? The atmospheric belts churned slowly, blending orange and pink, splotches of white at their boundaries. The Great Red Spot crept past the limb at the western edge of the South Tropical Zone, but the most remarkable sight lay between two equatorial belts, where they merged in a solid yellow band, speckled occasionally with misty white spots. An acquaintance on the Orb, a dull astronomer, had pointed out this sight to her. An extraordinary event, he'd claimed, yet what on this remarkable globe was not at least improbable? She would have liked to float out here forever, watching the giant planet swirling through its ten-hour day, strange features blending and flowing beneath her eyes. Not normally a mystic, Mara reminded herself that her universe was one populated with firm and certain objects; Bradley and the Christers fretted about the unseen and unknown.

But Jupiter? Here the boundaries blurred, the categories shattered. They knew so little. . . .

"Mara, please." Bradley again, a flinty edge to his voice. "I won't accept responsibility. If you don't care for yourself, then respect the equipment. If that shuttle gets loose it could prang itself sliding out across the top of the Orb."

She detected a note of bemused detachment in his voice. Whatever bothered Bradley? He seemed like an actor only gingerly involved in the role of his life. Yet she answered him seriously. "It's berthed with elastic lines on retrieval coils. I'll be back soon."

"No." His tone remained dry and even. "I'll come out and drag you back myself."

"Bradley, your heart."

"I'm coming."

"You're threatening."

"So?" She swore she heard a distant chuckle. "I'm not bluffing."

If he was—and she thought so—he provided no means for detecting that. "All right. Damn you, Bradley. I'll come."

"Then hurry." He was triumphant.

"I will." She saw no reason why these petty rules included her. Since she wasn't a member of the orbital crew, she regarded herself as a free person. Bradley Reynolds? Commander or not, she owed him no allegiance. There was nothing to fear out here. No gigantic monster came swimming past to gobble her up in great foaming jaws. She had come to Jupiter to live free from the asylum on Earth. If she died, so what? One human life gone from four billion. Even among the five hundred denizens of the Orb, her life could not be counted a significant factor.

She drifted idly. The Orb—that was a stupid name. It wasn't a sphere, it was a tin can, a lazy spinning cylinder. A few hundred metres above her head—she glanced up—was the pancake of storage water which blocked the sleeting high energy protons from the Van Allen belt. Orb came from orbit. A dumb way to pick a name. . . .

"Mara. You're stalling."

"No. I said I was coming."

"Then—" He was deliberately patient. "—let's come."

"I was thinking." She calculated the distance downward to the Orb's spinning top. Her shuttle was in berth six, which just now was a full diameter away across the Orb. Reaching it was much like catching a horse on a merry-go-round, only she couldn't run alongside and match velocity. It was too difficult to turn in a circular arc using attitude jets alone; she had to jet downward toward the Orb and intercept it just as berth six passed. If she missed, there were hand-holds to clasp for crawling. She gauged the times and distance with some relish; it made an interesting cal-culation–fun. Better than zero-gee squash.

"Keep my supper hot," she told Bradley. "Your lost little girl is coming home."

Giving the jets a burst, she coasted toward the grey metal top of the Orb. Berth six slid along and, when she was sure she had it right, she flipped over, point-ing her feet toward the deck. Impact was satisfying; she missed the berth by only a few metres. She went hand over hand to the edge of the berth, then glanced downward at the shuttle moored securely in its slot. Swinging over the edge, she looked around for the air hose connection. Her suit air was okay; it had a metallic oily taste that bit her throat. Spotting the hose on the other side of the berth, she leaped deftly across.

Zero-gee manoeuvring was fun, a challenge, using eyes set in a line parallel to the ground to negotiate three dimensions. It was necessary to keep in mind that up and down were no less essential than side-ways. This world was a larger one, somehow more real.

She snagged the hose and made the transfer to ship's air. But she wasn't quite ready to quit. No, before going in, she wanted one more look at the giant planet. She cursed Bradley for shattering her peace. She felt restless; her throat was scratchy; her period was due in three days. On impulse she kicked upward, drifting suddenly free from the berth. The Red Spot loomed larger now, like an open sore before the scab forms. The sight made her feel instantly better, free again. She drew her knees up as far as her skinsuit would allow and turned a free-space tumble. She laughed aloud. What about Bradley? She could hear him whining now. What could she do to please him? The possibilities were enormous. Sing a little song, perhaps a tap dance in zero-gee. Or maybe she should simply thumb her nose at him, then do a pratfall. Or she could—

Something tugged at her, then gave way.

She vectored to the left. A push had—

The air hose. She understood now: it had snapped. Which meant–quite simply–that she was dead.

Her ears popped. She automatically reached behind her and snatched at the wildly flapping hose. She caught it with one hand and pinched it closed. She tried a tentative breath. Nothing. Her lungs refused to expand.

She thumbed on her attitude jets. Taking a quick sighting on berth six, she fired. The Orb swam up fast, too fast. She began a turn to land, trying to manoeuvre with one hand while holding the hose with the other. *I am dead,* she suddenly reminded herself. She landed on one foot, slamming the deckplates. A flash of pain burned her leg. She spun away, glancing off the shuttle's bumper, and smacked into another face of the berth. A rushing, roaring sound swept through her head. *Am I dead now?* she wondered.

Where was her suit bottle? She had forgotten to put it into its desk clasp and now, as she glanced frantically around, it was nowhere to be seen.

Bradley shouted incoherently in her numb ears. If she heard him, she guessed that meant she must not be dead. He would be seeing it all on video. She was providing a show after all: the severed hose flapping, snarling on itself; the girl clumsily ricocheting around the berth—

The air bottle was gone. She cleared her thoughts, struggling. That left only the hose. She couldn't snag the end of it. The hose whipped around like an enraged snake. She searched for the cutting laser. It was on another face of the berth, moored securely. She kicked across and spun over to take the impact on her back. The laser was a small, precise instrument she could operate with one hand. Snatching it out of its clip, she thumbed it to operational mode. Her ears throbbed with pain. Lightly, she moaned.

Now the hose. Again she kicked, drifting languidly for the air hose socket where it joined to the Orb. The hose snapped and lashed. She ignored it. The roaring in her ears pounded like great waves in a storm. Her chest was burning inside. The world moved with a warm, lazy slowness. Now there was time for everything–the job, another look at the dancing pink bands of Jupiter, more.

With an effort of will she snatched at the air hose and brought the cutting laser next to its socket. She pressed down. A thin yellow bolt shot out, slicing the hose. The amputated hose blew away in a gust of wind. She could see the gas; it made the running lights ripple. So strange–a supposedly invisible gas. Purple flecks brushed the corners of both eyes, forming crazy, almost intelligible patterns. She tried to concentrate upon the colours but . . .

No. She pulled the hose around from the back of her helmet and sliced it off at arm's length. She threw herself forward, jamming the stub of her helmet hose against the socket extending from the hull, fighting to force it into the hole, battling the stream of air. There was a reason for doing this. It was important. Something from far, far back in time. It—

Her ears popped. The purple darkness thinned, blew away. She held the hose on the socket with both hands and breathed in quick short gasps. She drifted, anchored to the hose socket.

As soon as she could, she told Bradley to shut up. "I'm all right. Can't you see that? Now–please–get somebody out here. Save me."

Bradley Reynolds was convinced that Tolstoy was right–events make the man, not the universe. For a time he'd thought that those unnerving star-worshippers had been the prime vector in his life, sealing his story when they rode their jewel-like chain of explosions out of the solar system. Then he'd become convinced that the monastery was the most important factor. Now he was here, ninety-five years old, encased in an artificial satellite, a tin can orbiting Jupiter. And so finally he'd given up his faith in his own self-determination. He wasn't a maker of history, though God knew he'd been in enough of it. No, he was an unwilling passenger in the river of time. His only conscious choice, on Mars and with Jonathon and in Africa, had been to float, not sink. It was folly to strain, to try to reach some distant shore, some mirage of the mind. The flow itself was the destination.

He looked at his office. Thin pine panelling. Lightweight frame desk. 3-D of the surf crashing in Baja. The low hum of machines was a constant force. His thoughts never ran to completion.

Odd, that Jonathon and his kind were responsible for his being in this desiccated place. Earth's giant antenna systems had been built to regain communication with Jonathon, but that quickly faded when the aliens quite plainly did not want to respond. So the immense phased arrays went into search mode, seek-

ing leakage radio signals from some other nearby civilization. After all, the presence of aliens meant life
was probably common in the universe. There must be
others.

Old logic poured into new bottles and sold as a
research project. Luckily, it worked. The Alpha Libra
Puzzle was picked up almost immediately. And various forces it set in motion plucked Bradley out of
Africa and plunked him down here. Elected commander of the Orb, dispatching atmospheric probes,
scrutinizing the icy Jovian moons. Amidst thin pine
panelling, implausible yet of a human scale. And he
also played housekeeper to a mad genius. Bradley reminded himself, as his office door popped open.

"Bradley, you—" she began.

"Sit down, Mara." He pointed to a chair opposite
the desk from him.

She shook her head, refusing, as always, to sit. Of
course, Mara was damn pretty: the quality of genetic
tampering necessary to produce her would hardly
have been satisfied with an ugly wart of a girl. But as
he sometimes thought, perhaps that was their key
mistake as well. She was too perfect. A hint of ugliness,
a sagging lip or crooked chin, might have taken some of
the edge off her.

"This room is incredible," she said, waving at his
many artifacts. It was a subject she never hesitated to
bring up; it had become almost a ritual between
them. Approaching the desk, she fingered a statue of
Krishna, caressing the metal. "Buddha on a bad
day?" she asked, smiling quizzically.

"You know damn well." Elsewhere in the room,
the Buddha was much in evidence; and on the wall
above his head dangled a silver crucifix.

"I asked because I thought that's what you were,
some kind of Buddhist."

"I'm a man. Any possible answer interests me."

"But what about the question?"

"That interests me, too."

"Not me." She shook her head, let the statue drop back into place in the low-gee field, and turned away to gaze at the bookshelves directly behind as if trying to choose a title. She snickered at several volumes. He wondered if she would now proceed to chide him for reading fiction when there were so many facts–she would name several as examples–of which he remained ignorant.

But she turned without a word. "Somebody tried to kill me," she said flatly.

He let a silent moment filter past. "You're sure?"

"I don't make mistakes. Before I came back I tried cutting that air hose twice myself. It isn't exactly made of paper. I recovered the severed portion. It was extruded, as though somebody had weakened it."

"You can't fly around and stretch it indefinitely, you know."

"Sure. But I say I wasn't pulling it that far out of equilibrium. Somebody rigged that hose on purpose. I want you to find out who."

"Any suggestions?"

She shook her head. "Nobody specific."

He couldn't help laughing. He rocked in his chair, letting his eyes slide past her as she grew angrier. Finally, calming himself, he said, "I could name five hundred suspects. We might eliminate me and you. Perhaps Corey. Should I arrest the remainder?"

Her nostrils flared. "Don't be such an asshole."

"I imagine most of them have motives, Mara. Good ones, too."

"All of them?" She seemed genuinely puzzled.

He nodded. "Yes."

"They don't like me?"

"Let's say they find you supremely irritating."

"It's not just a stray Christer or two? A few fanatics?" She suddenly frowned, self-absorbed.

Bradley decided to be kind. "You must understand that most people in the Orb are research scientists. Quite a few are prima donnas themselves. It's an occupational hazard."

"And they don't like smartass kids, even with my credentials."

"You don't make it easy."

"No, but—" She suddenly loomed over his desk, shaking a fist. "I want you to find out who was around the air lock when I went out. You have to check into this. I want to know who did—"

Bradley shook his head wearily. "No."

She backed off. "You won't?"

"I don't give a damn. If you hadn't violated a key regulation going out by yourself, you wouldn't have been in danger. I can't stop you from being stupid, but you have to accept the consequences. If you'd died, I'd have made a check, for my own information. But you didn't die. The case is closed."

"You callous old bastard."

"And you're grounded." He kept his voice deliberately calm and even. "Whatever you want to call it. From this moment, you don't leave the Orb. You can work in the tanks. Everybody else draws hydroponic duty and I'm sick of letting you be our miraculous exception." He reached toward the intercom on his desk, fully intending to call the gardens.

But a hand fell firmly on his. "Don't, Bradley."

He met her gaze. "Why not? I'm commander. If you don't like me, depose me."

She released his hand, smiling blandly. "Then call."

He didn't move. "What do you mean?"

"Call." Her smile remained rigidly fixed. "But if you do, I'm quitting."

His hand twitched tentatively. "You're bluffing."

"No, threatening. I won't scrub tubs for anyone. I came here to be excited, thrilled. If that doesn't happen, I go back to Earth."

"So? Why should I care?"

"Because on Earth I testify. I say it's a gigantic waste of time, nothing is being accomplished. Shut down the Orb."

All Bradley could manage was a pained headshake. "I must have even-handed discipline on the Orb. I can't have one set of rules for you, another for everyone else."

She laughed. "That's what I was told in nippy grade school. It's bullshit."

"Nippy?"

"That's me. Nippy for people who have been nipped, manipulated, genetically tampered with"

"You're tuned for intelligence and creativity, Mara, not hand-eye coordination. You're only somewhat above average in that department."

"You don't still think that accident out there was my mistake."

"Probably. Space can be deceiving; the eye can measure distances quite the same way. If you'd bother to finish your training as we suggested, you—"

"Spare me the advertisement."

"No, advice. I wish we had some humility therapy I could prescribe."

"Save that, too. All I wanted was to see Jupiter. It's your fault. You people never give it a glance."

"We can see it any time on 3-D screens."

"Screens, my ass! Five decks below our feet there's high vacuum and, beyond that, Jupiter. If you'd move your office to the full-gee level and cut a hole in the floor, you could see it."

"Full gravity is bad for me." Saying it, Bradley thought he could feel the gentle partial gee tugging at his arteries, slowing the loyal slosh of his blood. "And anyway, the view isn't all that impressive when it goes by every eighteen seconds and you're standing on top of it."

"Then you ought to experience it directly. That's

what I want. I spent most of my life walled up with computer teachers and books and biodapts peering at me. I hardly knew there was anything else. It took me years to realize I had to stop being an obedient rat running through a custom-tailored maze. The trouble with being a manip is you never really get a chance to spread your legs wide to the world."

"I thought you'd done quite a bit of that."

"No more than what I had coming." Mara smiled expansively, an unexpected burst of raw delight. "I've been weighed and found wanton."

Bradley experienced a sudden dreamlike vision of her coupling soundlessly somewhere, legs akimbo, smooth skin sprinkled with shadow. The endless beat of biology. A woman's salty musk stirring up through his nostrils, quickening the pace. The human being as a particularly efficient method for transmitting RNA. Long chain molecules coiling, embracing, squeezing phosphorous and hydrogen into spiders and salamanders. The infinite, crooked paths of evolution; to understand it takes St. Paul and Paul Tillich, Pauli and Paul McCartney. God invented the orgasm so we would know when to stop.

He realized a long silence had passed. As he started to speak, his desk monitor beeped. He flipped a switch automatically and behind Mara doors opened: pterodactyl wings. A man poked his head through the doorway. "Meeting's already started, Bradley."

Mara deliberately removed the six-inch black cigar from her hip pocket and carefully stripped the plastic wrapping paper. Done, she crumpled that into a ball and tossed it aimlessly past a shoulder. Then, taking the cigar in both hands, she laid it lengthways between her lips and delicately moistened the outer leaf of tobacco from end to end. Slowly she thrust the tip into her mouth, bit off the point and spat that out on to the floor.

Then she lit a match.

At last Tom Rawlins reacted. "Bradley, I protest. Can't we at least keep the air in here clean?" Next to Bradley, Mara most enjoyed testing Rawlins. He was a fat, pompous man more or less in charge of the recovery booster systems. Once or twice he had actually seemed to know what he was doing.

She pulled on her cigar, stifling a need to cough. "I want to relax."

"And poison the entire Orb," Rawlins said.

"Prove it." Mara flicked an ash.

"What?"

"I said prove it. Poison the entire Orb—then show me how."

"But I couldn't–I can't–just—"

"I can." Mara quickly laid the calculation out for him: Orb air volume; cycle rate; average human exhalation; flow within the meeting room. "Even if all of us were smoking, nobody would get poisoned." She blew a thick cloud of blue-grey smoke in Rawlins's direction.

He turned beet red, not a pretty shade. Bradley rushed into the breach. "Now, Tom, we all know she is. Allow her some eccentricities. We'll survive."

"Suffocated," said Rawlins.

Mara repeated her concluding figure, then let loose a second smokescreen.

Everyone was present: a dozen men and herself, the lone woman. And Corey, too, whatever it was. She found it amusing that, with all the talk on Earth of final sexual equality, whenever one probed to the upper reaches of any group or profession, the faces invariably turned out to be bearded. The only likely exception was whoredom, and she thought that might be changing, too.

There were times when she wondered which irritated them most: that she was so quick, so imaginative, so young–or that she was a woman. A perfect man they might have accepted. But then, how much of this was due to her own self-consciousness, causing her to misread these men? She smiled inwardly at this subtle prick of self-knowledge; the world was subjective and even internal visions were blurred.

She spat. Even soaked in good bourbon, these cigars, three years removed from Havana, tasted like rat's piss.

"Let's take it in turn," Bradley said. "Inform us of your present progress and what, if anything, you've recently learned. When that's done, we'll try to put it together. Tom, you lead off: the booster systems." Bradley sat in the middle. In a largely futile attempt at cosiness, the room had been decorated in a spiral rainbow swirl, a style now out of fashion Earthside. Still, it was a welcome contrast to the womb whiteness of most of the Orb. They met here once each Earthweek in an attempt to make sense out of their mission. For a time, Mara had ceased attending the meetings; nothing ever happened here. Only recently had the pleasure of taunting Tom Rawlins drawn her back.

Mara paid no attention to Rawlins's dissertation till the tone of many voices grew abruptly animated. She listened to a few lines.

"A good engineer ought to know better than to mess with a glassblower's tools."

"He had to get the job done!"

But it was nothing. Mara wrote off the sudden electricity to the gradually increasing barometric pressure. Odd, she thought, the others could sense it. They were such sensitive animals, reacting to the slightest change in pressure, but they had no direct perception of it. The Orb pressure varied through the work day, to promote productivity: a mood music of the atmosphere.

Idly, she glanced across the room and noticed the large green and yellow rendering of the Puzzle. Frowning, she fingered a stray wisp of brown hair. The thing started with irritating simplicity. A transmission of simple on-and-off dots, numbering 29 by 53. It was just like a textbook example: 29 and 53 primes, so the natural impulse was to break it down into a 29-by-53 grid. And out popped the Puzzle. A large object in the upper right-hand side, probably a star, and below it a string of seven planets. The three nearest were apparently terrestrial in size, with the outer four probably Jovian class. It was the fourth and largest planet that had that funny little line extending from its heart and leading to the left, arcing out in a semicircle that embraced the rest of the message— all indecipherable. So they thought they knew what the squiggle meant: whoever sent the message resided on that planet. And there—that mysterious world—was clearly Jovian type.

Thus, the Orb. Understand life on Jupiter and therefore understand the alien message.

A sound enough idea. But, some problems: as yet no one had managed to find any life on Jupiter or seen how any hypothetical beings down in that churning atmosphere might ever build a radio.

A radio broadcast it was, though. It waxed and waned with a 16.3-hour cycle, presumably as their planet turned. A localized source on the surface, then. There was a slight Doppler shift in the frequency, with period of 15-74 years. A reasonable phenomenon: as their planet performed its own Newtonian waltz about its star, it moved progressively toward and then away from us along its orbit.

Given our knowledge of stellar spectra, and the finely observed luminosity of Alpha Libra, the astrophysicists could pretty near guess Alpha Libra's mass. Applying Kepler's Laws to the unseen planetary orbit, it turned out that the radio source was about 7.2 Astronomical Units out from the star —just about right for a gas-giant-type planet like Jupiter or Saturn.

All this, without ever deciphering the signal.

Which proved impossible.

"Any new ideas?" Bradley now enquired.

Arthur Vance, a linguistic expert, had one, but before he'd spoken more than a dozen words, Mara had taken his idea, comprehended it, analysed it, and rejected it as not only invalid but also misleading, a dead end. Still, Vance talked on. Her mind wandered.

Puffing on her cigar, she stood up, making no effort to conceal her distracting motion, and went to where Corey, in its box, sat on the floor. More than one well-meaning soul had mistaken Corey for a piece of furniture–a four-by-four steel box resting on a pair of wide wheels, with an assortment of tack-ins and sensors extending from its top and sides. An animated safebox. A blank television console. But Corey was the only other manip aboard, her brother –or sister.

"I intended to come see you today," Mara told the box. Her voice sounded deliberately loud. Vance continued talking, outlining a syntactical strategy. "I ran into some trouble outside."

A pair of lights flashed on top of the steel box. The voice murmured, like the purr of a happy cat. "They tell me you almost died."

"An accident." She shrugged.

"But some tell me the line was servered on purpose."

"Wishful thinking, maybe. Why would anyone do that?"

"They dislike you, Mara. This cramped Orb breeds much hostility. You are too good for them."

"Could be." She didn't smile.

"Do you know the identity of this one person involved?"

"Not exactly. I've narrowed it to five hundred possibilities. Bradley said it wasn't him. I know it wasn't me or you. I guess it was one of the others."

"We must expose the one and—"

"Damn it!" This was Rawlins. Apparently, after Vance had finally finished expressing his banal idea, Rawlins had had one of his own. "If you're not interested in this, Mara, why don't you go outside and let the rest of us talk?"

She turned slowly and met his eye. "I've already analysed Vance's idea. He wants to interpret the signal as a coded ecological scheme, based on the different layers in a Jovian-type planet's atmosphere. Okay, maybe ammonia flow rates are all these things know. But Vance has tried to blow a kernel of truth into a sort of intellectual puffed rice. It won't work. I know, I've already tried it."

"Mara," Bradley said, "at least you could let him—"

"He can blab on his own time, not mine."

"Then get out of here." Bradley spoke with a definite snap to his voice. "Right now."

"I won't—"

"Now," he said softly. "I mean it, Mara."

She glanced at Corey. A light on the side of the box flashed a quick, dancing red pattern: their private code. Without a backward glance, she turned and went through the door. The box wheeled after her.

"Idiots," she said out in the corridor. "Goddamn fools."

"Bradley was very angry."

"Or wanted to appear that way. He's a pretty fair politician when he thinks about it."

"I thought he was beyond such earthly matters. He seems a very mystical, deeply religious man."

Mara said in a singsong voice, a fair parody of Bradley. "If you can think about it without laughing, the question of existence becomes a very real one."

Corey made a noise like laughter, a dry barking rasp.

"You're getting better at that," Mara said.

"Yes, oscillating the verbal output has an oddly

pleasurable effect in neutral terms. It releases something."

"You've got it, then. Come on. Let's go down to your room and play chess. I'm bored."

"You'll beat me."

"Maybe not this time," she said.

I let them call me Corey, but never say I am man or woman. Mara alone, she knows which, but has sworn never to tell. I move my king's knight forward, leaping through space regardless of barrier, and capture her pawn. Light, airy, I fall upon the square. A contest of remorseless geometry, savouring of Euclid. It erases other memories. Born alive in this box, my first waking memory was a low whimper of some woman crying, "My God, my God, what, what—?" I understood at once–the words, that is–but their full meaning has escaped me forever. We place a ten-second limitation on our moves, but Mara does not require even that. I am aware that she commences each new game with the results of the last clearly ingrained in her mind. Any move I may make–whether intelligent or otherwise, rational or mad–she has taken into account. Still, we exist much in love, for we are too much the same. I go to work for my government, my existence veiled in mystery. The experiment that failed is called Corey. I work with the dolphins. Their intelligence, I am told, lies open to mine, but mostly they are stupid. Some whales seem brighter, but soon they are extinct, and who knows? Mara vaults her queen clean and swift the length of the board, swooping upon my undefended bishop. I could kiss her. No, I could not. Such tactics are not destined to be mine in life. My love melts. Eight seconds pass–and so I move. Spliced into these sliding moments an image comes to me; I have noticed her unclothed body many times, for nobody hides anything from a steel box. We are siblings. "Check," she says, so I move. A Pascal defence. "Checkmate."

II

"Well, *Jesus,* Dr. Reynolds. I just don't want to do it."

"I'm afraid we haven't much choice."

Kurt Tsubata shook his head vehemently. "She doesn't know which end to hold on a soldering iron. To let her go out in a *shuttle*—"

Bradley shook his head. "It's not a matter of "let". I'm afraid Mara possesses considerable leverage. We've pretty well got to go along with her."

"But it's *dangerous*. It's—"

"She has been practising." Bradley saw that his attempt at reassurance had failed: poor Tsubata looked bleaker than ever. "And she has mastered at least some of the mechanics of the thing. She has a strong, agile body. She does rather well in zero-gee calisthenics."

"And she wants to work outside."

"Yes, but I'm afraid that's not the end of it either." He lowered his voice. "She doesn't just want to work in one of the repair bays."

"Oh, no."

"Yes, she wants satellite maintenance. It's why I'm talking to you."

"Jesus Christ!" Tsubata appeared ready to explode.

"She does know electronics." Even to Bradley that sounded very lame.

Tsubata grimaced, struggling to recover. "I did ask for help."

"I meant to give you someone else, someone who could help. Maybe later."

"Well, these storms are coming more often now. Most of the funny stuff, the really big ones, seem to be happening near the poles. Those flights take longer. I'm getting worn out by them."

Bradley knew enough not to speak. Tsubata was talking himself into it. After a moment of silence, Tsubata looked up and said, "She won't go funny on me?"

"Oh, no. She may be—" Bradley rummaged through his memory for the slang word. "—manip, but she's quite emotionally stable. Odd, eccentric, yes. She's been bred and tuned for mental quickness. Dexterity. Imagination. She's not unduly unstable or she would never have been allowed out here. Most manips can't qualify for Earth orbital work, I understand."

Tsubata made a sour expression. "I still don't like it, Bradley."

"I didn't ask you to like it."

The long-distance shuttle, the *Rather Not,* had its permanent mooring in the hollow centre of the Orb. A four-legged strutwork held it in place against the gentle centrifugal tug, so it remained fixed over a repair berth. Mara clipped onto a mooring line that ran to the *Rather Not* and adroitly pushed off from the Orb's inner wall. Tsubata watched her movement with a critical eye. After a moment of coasting she flexed and turned so that her feet pointed toward the shuttle. She squirted her jets and slowed perceptibly. As an extra fillip, she unclipped from the mooring lines a few metres away, and landed catlike on the tail section.

"Good enough. Don't move till I get there." Tsubata said over suit radio.

"Okay." Mara watched him swim easily across the twenty metres between them. He probably wanted her to mess up the manoeuvre; it would be easy to document if he had a friend watching on 3-D and would make a good first entry in a file. She knew enough about organizations to guess that, if Tsubata wanted to get rid of her, he would have to build a thick folder of instances to prove incompetence.

As Tsubata moved toward her, Mara glanced around and attached her suit tie-line to the nearest pipe. Most shuttles she had seen were different, each thrown together from cannibalized spare parts that came to hand. The *Rather Not* had a few customized pieces and the magnetic shielding coils were considerably larger, but otherwise it was like the others–all bones and no skin. The pilot couch was located at dead centre of gravity in the middle, surrounded by struts, tanks, pipes, hauling collars, and storage lockers, all placed to obscure as little of the view as possible. A large ion engine was mounted behind the couch in grey housing. It was lumpy but balanced; it wouldn't go into spinover if a pilot made a wrong move.

As Tsubata touched down she glided away from him, perching on top of the pilot couch backrest.

"I told you not to move." Tsubata came after her.

"You're going to have to give me more latitude than that. I know you're not exactly tingling with anticipation to see me out here, but that's the way it's got to be."

Tsubata said nothing, waving a hand to dismiss the subject. "First, I'm going to make sure you know what every piece of equipment on this shuttle is for."

Mara had expected to know most of it, but there was a bewildering maze of detail. There were systems for fuel feed, a pipe complex regulating attitude jets, three different superconducting magnet configurations for screening against Van Allen belt particles, two overlapping electrical systems, navigation index, vector integrater, multiple communications rigs, an emergency high-gain antenna for work when the Orb and shuttle were not in line of sight, gyros, radio, hauling apparatus, repair parts, life support–all this had to be integrated so that a change in one system didn't cause a malfunction in another. In the next three hours Mara gained considerable respect for Tsubata and his work. He made it clear to her that a shuttle could not be run by the book; like most human creations, it demanded intuition, craft, and a certain seat-of-the-pants shrewdness.

It wasn't until two days later that Tsubata considered her competent enough to take the *Rather Not* out on a routine flight.

She works outside now, far from me. In the hours when the others sleep I wonder about this. They do not think I am a person in here, no real human things like hands, a face, legs and hair and the winking of an eye. They never think of me sitting next to them in a bar and trading funny stories. Slap them on the back, slap me on the back, hail fellow well met, good buddies. No. They are told I have guts and lungs and blood and slimy ropy things inside. And my brain. Yes, they keep Corey because of that brain. I calculate, store data, analyse, and give readout in swift, sharp human terms. But Corey is an idiot savant, they say, when they think of him (me) at all. I know Laplace and Lagrange, can integrate over four variables simultaneously, truncate a curve and give numerical solutions for the least squares fit, all the things Mara can do but faster in some ways, and easier. So they keep Corey, ship her (me) here to play her brain trade. Keep quiet, too. Far away from Earth and the ones who think it (me) is but a foul mistake. Once a man comes to interview me and partway through (when the others burst into the room) he is shouting, raving frantically, struggling vainly to tell me something. I never understand what has happened, but the scene comes again and again in the long humming nights when the frail and fleshy men sleep and stink. I have never quite understood what Mara says about these screaming men and what they want of me. Yes, I wonder yet.

And now Mara is not here so much. Outside, like an ordinary beast, she labours. With her body. I seek to imagine the pleasure she derives from movement, coordination, being able to touch and feel. Some distant sense of this joy reaches Corey, but only as a grey shadow of feeling, nothing to resemble the jolts of electrical stimulation they supply him. When they tap Corey with the images, the raw sensation of pleasures manufactured on Earth especially for her, Corey knows it is not the things men and women talk about privately. There are no satiny-skinned bodies, no heaving, thrusting rhythms. The tapping network provides only calm, restful inputs. Things flow smoothly when Corey has the tapping; I feel muzzy and blurred and easy. There are times when I sleep, though only briefly. Best of all, after tapping, I cast away my prison of dreams when sleep does come. The bright yellow visions do not appear; the woman's voice lies silent. Sometimes he (she) sees Mara, but that is all.

And Mara is different from the others–she is like Corey. On Earth they say there should be no more, but I am sure that is a lie, for the fragile flesh comes cheaply and perfection is an eagle sought upon the highest summits. I see more clearly. I hear the soundless sounds. Corey is a metal man, and that is a taste like no others; the absence of other tastes, the essence. But I am yellow guts, too. A box that talks. Mara comes to see me less now. I see the others more. They chatter, sweat, fart, black shadows of beard sprouting in oily skin, lines of age, pink flesh splotches, sagging breasts. They are not Corey (he) (she) (it). Perhaps they are not Mara, either.

She backed the shuttle cautiously out of its berth, clear of the mooring lines. They still carried the angular velocity of the Orb, so she gave a quick burst of the lateral jets to slow them. They moved away from the Orb's inner wall. The tin can seemed to spin faster and faster as she applied additional side thrust.

"Inertial frame check." She spoke over her suit radio in crisp, clipped tones. In a moment the bridge responded that she was at rest with respect to the centre of mass of the Orb. She was cleared to begin her ascent out the top, but first she waited a long moment to get her bearings. Out this far from the inner wall, the Orb struck her more than ever as a large can. The sides whirled by at a dizzying speed, running lights streaking past and leaving yellowish traces on her retina. The large central cylinder of the Orb seemed darker now that they were out of the shuttle berth. She could see no stars. Both ends of the Orb were plugged by pancake sacs of water. As she watched a few viewports passed, glowing with soft light. In one a woman glanced at her ceiling port, out into the bay, smiled and waved.

"That's right, take your time. The motion is disorienting." It was the first kind thing Tsubata had said to her. She nodded before remembering that in a skinsuit the gesture was concealed.

"Has Monitoring cleared us?"

"I'll call. Keep your eyes on where we're going."

"Right." They coasted on a clean straight line toward the top of the Orb. Safety neons splashed pools of light over the skins of two large cruisers moored at the centre of the can. They were kept here to prevent radiation damage to them. The running lights were intense, but blackness swallowed them. Bounded everywhere by motion, shadows shifting beneath the restless pinwheeling lights of the Orb, the scene still carried a curious dead stillness about it. Overhead the pancake turned softly in the great night; Jove's pink light reflected off the grainy skin. As they came level with the top of the Orb, Mara gently eased on the decelerating jets and they came to zero velocity hanging in the narrow hundred-metre slot between the Orb and the upper pancake. Mara had a sudden chill perception that she hovered between two great grinding mechanical teeth, endlessly spinning, a looming immense machine framing the giant planet beyond. She shook her head, puckered her lips, giggled slightly. It was a trick of perception; she blinked and the Orb stood taut and bright beneath the shuttle.

"Let's go." Tsubata waved his hand.

Mara thumbed the rear jets. The shuttle accelerated out, slipping between the lips of the Orb and the pancake. In a moment they drifted clear and she remembered just in time to cut in the superconducting magnets. She checked power levels in all three magnet networks. Glancing to the right, she spied the distant silvery crescent of Callisto. The can orbited a constant distance behind the large moon, which swept the volume relatively clear of high-energy Van Allen particles. Riding in the wake of Callisto's broom, the Orb still had to shield with metres of water on all sides.

"Over to Monitoring," Tsubata said. Mara punched a key on the pilot's dash. Shifting, the shuttle murmured beneath them. An unseen hand tilted their axis, pointing them out of the Orb's orbital plane. A hum, as the ion engine cut in. A slight low-impulse thrust.

"Satellite 106 is quite far northward," Tsubata said. "I've programmed a fast elliptical orbit. Rendezvous in five hours."

"What's wrong with it? S-106, I mean. I haven't had time to finish that stack of manuals about satellite maintenance."

"Some components are below operable voltage levels. The Faraday cup measurements aren't reasonable either."

The shuttle drifted; Mara relaxed. "That's not surprising. Not with the radiation levels as they've been lately."

"The Faraday cup should tolerate the high dosage rate. It hasn't."

Mara turned back to the dwindling Orb: a mere glinting facet of light. As she watched, an observation dome refracted Jupiter's pale yellowish-pink glow, focusing it into a momentary brilliant point.

"What do you do out here during these long flights?" Mara asked, turning back.

"Sleep, mostly. Watch the radiation counter."

And talk as little as possible, Mara thought. She briefly considered forcing a conversation, bombarding him with intimate details from her fascinating life. A strange urge gripped her to pry open this silent man. But the vastness of space smothered her desire. Out here, mere words seemed petty, somehow futile.

"What do you think of the storms?" She forced herself to speak, say something, a human grunt hurled against the fast encroaching blackness. She gestured downward, where a dark band broke and eddied into bright orange swirls. The pattern grew more turbulent toward the north pole. Here tiny whirlpools whipped and churned at the edges of the band.

"The people in astrophysics think a lot of electromagnetic energy is being dumped because of something happening in Jupiter's core. That's just a theory. The planetary magnetic fields are shifting around some."

"Changing fields, lots of high-energy particles–quite interesting."

"There's a rise in radio noise as well." It was the first note of real interest Mara had detected in Tsubata's voice. A demon for work but little else. Out here, he smiled happily, at peace and rest. "We've got time." He fished in his pouch and handed her a clipboard with a maze of circuit diagrams on it. "This is S-106."

She could follow the pattern well enough, though the Faraday cup arrangement looked awkward to her. It was a simple particle-detector, designed to count the number of high-energy electrons or protons sucked into a small metal grid.

Mara sighed. Twisting in her seat, she faced Jupiter once more. It seemed to have grown vaster now that the Orb was engulfed by darkness behind. She stared at the swelling storms. Tsubata heaved up from his seat and moved hand over hand to check the shuttle. Mara saw faces superimposed upon the shifting bands of Jupiter. She smiled. Now who were these?

Twenty minutes from rendezvous, on command from Monitoring, Mara spun the shuttle end for end. A small dot grew at their backs, swelling into a silvery box that sprouted sensors and a microwave dish. To Mara it seemed incredibly old, small, less than two metres across and pitted.

"How long has this been out here?" she asked.

"Four years or so."

"Then why the damage?"

"There's a lot of junk orbiting Jupiter. Enough micro-meteorites to form a small world, probably."

She stared at the satellite. "It looks like a real relic. Think I'll make a closer check."

She sprang directly out of her seat, twisted to get the proper angle, and tapped her manoeuvring jets.

Tsubata cried, "Wait!"

"I might as well do this one." She neared the satellite.

"But you're not qualified. You're supposed to be observing."

"I'm a lousy looker." Coasting closer, she gave a burst of air and came to a full stop beside S-106. Tsubata was still saying something but she ignored him easily, swimming around the box, locating the right inset cabinets, and then quickly pulling out several shelves of circuitry. The Faraday cup configuration was easy to extract; she slipped the pins free and temporarily bypassed the rest of the network. "This one's really been pounded," she said. "There's a dime-sized hole in the circuitry. So much for the subtleties of electronics."

Tsubata still pouted. "That was a dumb thing to do, Mara. You could have jammed those boards—"

"But I didn't."

"If you wanted to be a technician—"

"I do. But I'd rather be a hammer than a nail."

Tsubata shut up. Mara freed the board and carefully applied her jets to coast back toward the shuttle. She remembered her training and kept the jets pointed away from S-106, to avoid tumbling it. She reclipped her mooring line and handed Tsubata the board. With an impatient gesture he handed her a replacement part.

"You take this over and put it in," he said. "But I'm coming with you."

"Fine."

They installed the replacement together. Tsubata slid his analysing devices into place and ran through a sequence of checks. There were still intermittent shorts and an overload index beyond normal. He told her to return to the shuttle. She composed two piercing retorts and then decided to let the point pass; she wasn't sure she could handle the necessary repairs alone and something said Tsubata had been pushed exactly as far as he would go.

On the shuttle, she watched him follow through a detailed inspection. Tsubata worked with quick caution, the studied grace of a professional. She realized she could learn quite a bit from this man and observed his actions intently.

"All right, that's it," Tsubata said decisively. He coasted back to the shuttle, dropping beside Mara. She reached for the controls to begin manoeuvres but he stopped her.

"That was a bad mistake you made. I could get you removed from this job on the strength of that alone."

"If you try—"

He raised his hand. "I'm not. Your diagnosis was correct. You didn't solve the problems, but I never expected that."

"Then I—"

"Shut up." She did. "I'll keep working with you.

But no more stupid stunts. You're fast, smart. I know that—everyone does. But you can make mistakes. Don't ever forget that."

"I–I won't."

"Now let's go."

On the long ride back, casting through a smooth, stately ellipse, Tsubata did not refer to the incident. Mara appreciated that; it showed a sense possessed by few ordinary humans. Instead, they spoke of other things. Both slept at times. Waking first, Mara downed the compressed dinner she'd selected. It was nutty, crisp, dry; she ate with pleasure. *I handled him exactly the right way,* she thought.

Corey comes late for the dinner hour. I do not eat in the manner of ordinary flesh but receive my fat, protein, artificial elements directly through a murmuring package on my back. Corey goes to dinner hour to see, talk, listen. He is a silent monkey trapped in the steel box of humanity, as sly as any hermit. I learn through observation what people are, not merely what they say. She squats on the floor beside her sister, Mara. Excellent sensors slash through the clattering noise to probe the conversation. The entire table is Corey's to inspect.

BRADLEY: Kurt tells me you're doing okay.

MARA: Well enough.

TSUBATA: She's quite dextrous.

BRADLEY: That's good, though it doesn't help much with why she was sent here.

MARA: I'm dextrous there, too. I've tried various special keying methods to break it down. It's not a simple decoding problem.

VANCE: That was obvious years ago.

MARA: That's why I had to check: what's obvious to you may not be so obvious to them. I don't think the Puzzle can be solved until we understand the life form that sent it. There's a hidden assumption there. Some reason we can't decode the signal.

BRADLEY: (sighs) *Corey sees that he is old in a way other people are not.* I still don't see how anything alive in that atmosphere can build solid devices. Without land, how can they—?

VANCE: That's elementary. We've been through it.

MARA: But you haven't understood it. If you had, it would be over, solved.

VANCE: You can't know that. We may be entirely wrong. It's not my field, but maybe we're misinterpreting that line. Maybe the signals don't come from that big planet.

BRADLEY: If they don't, then we're wasting a great deal of money out here.

MARA: They do.

VANCE: It must be nice to be so certain of everything.

BRADLEY: I'm certain of nothing, but I've worked with dolphins. So has Corey. Unless we find life on Jupiter, that's as close as the solar system comes to our hypothetical life form. There isn't much I can generalize about. The dolphins had a substantial forebrain and broadly expanded cerebellum long before we did. Fifteen, twenty million years ago. Their complex storytelling culture evolved; it's amazing. They never knew a damn thing about technology.

MARA: Or the whales. They were intelligent–all the analysis shows that–but you wiped them out. They couldn't protect themselves against a few technological Ahabs.

BRADLEY: They used their brains for other things, better things.

MARA: What's better about dying?

BRADLEY: The whales used the ocean surface as a resting place. It was where they breathed, worked, mated, gave birth. We caught them where they were most vulnerable. They never learned how to deal with the threat.

MARA: So we can't generalize from that. Anything on

Jupiter can't know there is such a thing as a surface. The ammonia is hundreds of kilometres thick.

TSUBATA: But we've never rejected the moon hypothesis. To me that's always made more sense.

BRADLEY: Perhaps. I've just looked at some of the reports from Ganymede. The environment looks hopeful, if you can imagine a life form evolving at 150 degrees Kelvin. Actually, Titan is a better bet.

MARA: Have they worked out the radioactive transfer mechanisms in the Titan atmosphere? The convection between layers should be enough to drive a pretty substantial ecology.

BRADLEY: Yes, but it doesn't. There's no life on Titan.

VANCE: As far as we know.

MARA: What about those crystal structures?

VANCE: Well, they don't move around. They do seem to exchange material between each other, but it's not what you could call an ecology.

MARA: He didn't say ecology—he said life. Bradley, I thought those crystal things were dependent on the cold trap at the poles, where the methane and ammonia stacks up. That leaves water as the only volatile condensate abundant at 150 degrees Kelvin.

TSUBATA *(softly humming):* What kind of music is that?

MARA: Rossini. Look, I agree the moon hypothesis isn't a bad one. But why doesn't the Puzzle show any moon at all? It seems improbable they would fail to distinguish between satellites of planets and the planets themselves.

TSUBATA: Maybe they feel it's obvious.

VANCE: Why?

TSUBATA: To things living on a moon, a planet like Jupiter must seem vicious, hostile. We, on the other hand, spend far more money studying Jupiter than Titan. Preconceptions dominate everything.

VANCE: This dessert is dreadful. I still think even beings on a moon would recognize a distinction. They'd know that some planets could be the same size as moons.

MARA: But the terrestrial-type planets in the Alpha Libra system are probably too close, burned to a crisp. It's like Kurt said–preconceptions dominate.

COREY: Perhaps they deceive us–purposely. *(The Box speaks rarely, only when necessary.)*

BRADLEY: Then why send the message at all if you're going to lie? It's pretty clear they're responding to our early UHF transmissions, or the DEW-line radar pulses that got out of the atmosphere. I doubt they've ever contacted another civilization. It's unlikely–we're so close.

COREY: My point, exactly. Too close. We come and visit–we are too strange. So they say they live in a gas-giant world, knowing it is hard for us to enter the deep atmosphere. A smart move.

VANCE: Why? If they're intelligent, they should desire contact.

COREY: With you? They break down your television and see you bang-bang shooting each other. White man hates black and ordinary hates nippie. What about aliens?

BRADLEY: Then why call us at all?

COREY: Perhaps that is the real puzzle.

Bradley nods carefully and Corey sees that his hint has been caught. For a moment I filter my input and see them drop away, becoming tiny, as though I now watch from some high, secluded sanctuary–an alien vantage point. They do not realise, even sister Mara, that I see so clearly and well. Bradley speaks calming words, knowing there is discordance within Corey. But what kind?

BRADLEY(finishing):—would be the point of making the rest of the signal–those miles and miles of taped message–so hard to decipher? They may be secretive, but I don't think they're whimsical. What's the time?

TSUBATA: Three clockwise.

BRADLEY: I've got an appointment. Be glad to get out of this high-gee level, anyway. It takes months off my life.

COREY *(done):* The obvious is not always untrue, Dr.
Reynolds.
But they shrug off his final remark, fearing the dis-
covery of implication. Mara's eyelashes flicker and she
glances at the box without appearing to do so. Stillness
descends like spring snow. They stand, chairs scrape,
spoons and forks clatter. Activity slowly swirls; they break
camp. Mara slips among them. They shuffle in a herd,
Bradley at the fore, Tsubata at the flank. My box whirs,
whines, whirs.

<h1 style="text-align:center">III</h1>

Slumped in a chair, Bradley peered across the neat,
flat expanse of his office and waited for the door to pop
open. In one fist he clutched the crumpled remains of
the message from Earth which only moments before had
been thrust into his hand. It was a damn shame, he
thought. Only yesterday, at the dinner hour, he had
glimpsed a degree of genuine humanity in Mara he had
not previously thought existed; it kept peeping through
lately, at the most unexpected times and places. And
now this–the message–that would ruin it. He sighed softly
to himself. He had called them both. Nobody else would
want to tell them.

It bothered him that the message had not affected him
more deeply, in a less personalized way, but the Earth
seemed such a distant place, its churning problems of
population and discontent, mutual fear and hate, of far
less interest than the crystals of Titan. He often believed
that he would not likely be returning; he expected to die
somewhere out here. They had taken Tunisia away from
him but he had erected a new monastery here beside
Jupiter–this office. *Is it that I no longer care?* he wondered, fingering the message. *Has my heart grown cold*
and encrusted as the decades stretched past? Or is it only
that I've grown stingier with my sympathy, that I care as
much as ever, but about fewer things?

He thought he cared about Mara and Corey, though

he did not like them. These genetic freaks, these nippies—
he considered their very existence an abomination. A
medieval attitude perhaps, but based fully on his felt belief that the human race, in mass, could hardly be im-
proved or bettered. He had spent the last fifty years of
his own life trying vainly to wreak some improvement in
one solitary soul (his own) and he was far from sure that
he had succeeded. Mara an improvement? He did not
think so. Intelligence was a virtue whose importance
shrank as one grew old. And Corey? He shivered at the
thought.

It went back to a young woman he had known in his
last years at the Tunisian monastery, Catherine
McClair, a devout and learned Christian, who confided
one still, silent afternoon that the Messiah had come to
Earth.

He took her hand lightly in his, exulting in the smooth
pink softness untouched by age. "Which do you mean?"
He anticipated her joke. "There are several."

"No, none of those." Her lips were painted red, an
ancient fashion; her hair, drawn formlessly back, revealed an oval face. "Christ was God incarnate. I mean
man incarnate."

"You'll have to explain that to me, Cassie."

She never sweated, hidden in her olive cowled robes;
the desert heat rose dry and crisp. "God created man,
don't you agree?"

"At times, yes."

"Then you must also agree that man's highest aim
must be to reverse the process, to create God."

"No."

"And that's been done. By manipulating—"

"Not those freaks, Cassie!" His hands shook from the
shock of his horror; until this moment Bradley had envied this woman. He wanted to help her. "I'm not completely ignorant. There's one of them in Houston. A
thing in a steel box. It isn't even a man, Cassie. How can
you call it a god?"

"And Mara?" she asked.

"Who?" He remembered Cassie's father was a geneticist. Could her ideas have come from him?

"Father knows her. Mara is the one that worked. They've kept her penned up until now. The fools can't comprehend the wonder they've created. But she's it, Bradley. Mara is—she's godly."

He sometimes wondered how many prospective Catherine McClair's might live on Earth. Is that why someone had been so eager to send Mara way out here to Jupiter?

The office door popped open and Mara entered. Corey, clicking in its box, came, too.

"Make this quick, Bradley," Mara said. "Tsubata and I are going out in an hour clockwise."

Bradley glanced at his desk, the scrubbed surface, the eighth avatar. High upon a barren bookcase Shiva also danced, chaos under control. He had tried to stock this room so that any possible spiritual mood might find solace. Nothing gripped him now, Christ or Buddha. This problem was wholly secular, like sex.

"I'm afraid I have some painful news for you, Mara, Corey. I received this message a short time ago." He gestured toward a chair.

She reached out in a practised motion and plucked the message from his hand. In a flash, she had read it. "I've expected this." She handed the message back.

"And what do you intend to do?"

She grinned. "Haven't you got that backwards, Bradley? It's you who's got to act."

He knew that was true. "Mara, I'm going to have to—"

She ignored him bluntly, whispering at the box. "We've been stripped of our human rights, Corey, deprived of citizenship. The Earth has finally decided that a superman isn't really a man. We're state property now. They made us, they own us."

When the two of them spoke so intimately, Bradley

felt lost, an alien in a land where the language was not his own. "Mara, this is serious. Genetic experimentation has been forbidden. There's some sort of religious revival occurring on Earth. I'm afraid I've been ignoring the news lately."

Corey hummed with sudden information: "It is the Christian revival. Man created in an image of God. Manip a desecration, blasphemy. Fourteen votes in recent United Congress election."

Mara lit one of her long cigars, puffing calmly. She stared at the growing ash, then let it drop, studiously observing as the mass shattered into grey fragments. "When the elephant has slipped inside the Arab's tent, it's too late to cry no vacancy."

Corey whirred. Laughter?

"What's so funny?" Bradley asked.

"Your thinking is too slow." Mara abruptly dropped into the waiting chair and threw her booted feet upon his desk. "What's the present nippie–I love that word–population on Earth?"

He saw no alternative to playing her game. "A few hundred."

"Three hundred seventeen. And do you know where they are, where they work, live, think, defecate? Give it some thought, Bradley. Are they peasants, engineers, programmers, poets, painters?"

"They're involved in high science, I suppose."

"And the highest of high sciences?"

His master in Tunisia had lectured similarly; force the student to uncover his own sources of wisdom. "Isn't that a matter of opinion? Physics? Biology?"

"Christ, Bradley." Another ash fluttered down. *"War."*

"War?"

"We control your arsenals. They won't work without us. Do you think we're stupid, blind to probabilities? This has been foreseen."

"You're talking about some form of nuclear blackmail."

She grinned. "Now you've found it. Shocked?"

"Appalled is more likely." He leaned across the desk, meeting her high blue eyes. "Blackmail is effective only when you're prepared to have your bluff called."

"We are."

"Mara, you won't blow up the world." There was a tingling silence between them. Bradley felt a welling sense of dread.

"Who said anything about the world? Pick a city. Then two. Leave us alone or we'll blow them up one by one." She snapped her fingers. "Governments are created for only one purpose: to maintain order. Study Chinese history someday, the dynastic cycle; it's all there. We'll win." She stood up, point proved, victory achieved. Corey hummed at her heels.

"Wait, Mara," he called.

She paused. "You disagree?"

He spoke truthfully, with sadness. "I don't care."

"Then what?"

"I'm restricting you, both of you, from this moment. I don't want you to leave your quarters."

She bristled, glaring, her wall of complacency shattered at last. "You bastard, you tried that before."

"But I mean it this time, Mara. It's my duty to maintain order here on the Orb. I can't let you outside—not now."

"Don't you trust us?"

"It's not you, it's the others. This order—" He meant the message. "—is like a licence to kill. We have our Christers here, too. I don't want to take the risk."

"It's not your risk, it's mine."

He shook his head, smiling grimly. He had never seen her so angry, so human. "I think you'd better study some Chinese history, Mara. Or Confucius. The leader's responsibility for his flock." He waved a hand at the trinkets of his office. "I don't intend to have you cost me the mandate of heaven."

"You won't get away with it."

"I have."

* * *

Mara reached out and with a single wide sweep of her hand sent the chess pieces toppling loudly to the floor. She stared at the mess she had made.

Corey hummed. "I assume you have elected to conclude our contest abortively."

"That bastard Bradley. Three full days now." Her voice sounded tired and weary to her own ears. "I'm sorry." Reaching down, she began to retrieve the scattered chess pieces.

"Perhaps you are being unfair to Bradley. I have ventured into the corridors. There is an ugly atmosphere flowing there. Hate rushes with the wind."

"There isn't any wind on board the Orb. And that's not hate–it's fear. Some of them have relatives in Tokyo; more have friends. In a few days, *blooey*. Then they'll learn."

Mara's room was a cluttered, jumbled place. Stacks of papers, charts, books tilted precariously upon a low table. There were two beds, a filthy oven, the table that held the chessboard. Music shrilled lightly from twin overhead speakers–a jazz quintet. The rectangular certainties of the room seemed blunted by the clutter, leaving it musty and airless.

"What is this?" Corey had discovered something of interest upon the second bed, a sheet of paper curled between two huge books–T'ang annals. The box loomed above the rumpled sheets.

"It's what you think." Mara had replaced the chess pieces exactly as they'd stood before the sudden wave of destruction. She should be winning in four moves. "I drew it from memory. With all these dog days, I needed something more than chess to fill my mind. I thought I'd solve their Puzzle." The sheet of paper was the grid. "That ought to prove something."

Corey rumbled back toward the chess table. A new recording suddenly spun: *Verklärte Nacht*, an old favourite. Corey said he never learned to decipher music; to him it remained random sounds.

"But what can it prove?" said Corey. "They admit our intelligence."

"But not our power." Mara let her king's knight pounce. "I solve the Puzzle, refuse to tell. Then what?"

"They will force you."

"Torture? Sticks in my fingernails, a hot iron up my ass? I'm too stubborn. They give me my freedom–a guarantee–then I'll tell."

"But what's to prevent them from reneging later?"

"Bradley. He's honest."

"Then they'd depose him."

"I–" Corey was making her feel petty. She sighed, aware that he was correct.

"But you haven't solved the Puzzle, have you?"

"No, but—" She strengthened her voice. "—I will. You ought to know, studying the dolphins and whales. They were extinct before we knew just how intelligent they were."

"You should watch your pronouns." The game had continued; Corey moved his king with sad desperation.

"Huh?"

"When you refer to the human race, sometimes it is they and sometimes it is we."

"I often think of you as he and she rather than it."

"But you know the truth."

"Do I? Besides, it was a nippie who solved the puzzles of dolphins and whales. Since I've been here, I haven't really tried. I've romped and played, a hedonist of the spaceways. With my full energies, I can crack it. I already feel I'm closer than Vance and some others." Her queen darted forward; she played black. "Check."

"How?"

"By getting into their minds, slipping inside their skins. The aliens, I mean. If I know how they think, then I'll know what they sent. Jupiter would help by spilling his secrets. Without that, it will be hard."

"There may be none."

"Checkmate."

"Another game?"

"If you wish."

"No." She folded her hands upon the finished board. "I want you to tell me some things about the dolphins."

"Such as?"

"What we were talking about before." She reached for a cigar. For the first time, she smoked for pleasure, not because the habit irritated others. "Tell me how they think."

"You may not understand."

"Try me."

Her questions dart like milling wasps, stinging my memories, sucking dry my knowledge. I fear the depth of her perceptions. Mara is more than them, greater. She can see.

COREY: They think in curves, high spanning arcs. Men, including us, are limted to straight, flat lines. Some say this is the result of the linear nature of our speech forms, but I blame the shape of our world. We exist solely on the surface. Subjectively, the earth is a two-dimensional place. The ocean bears three. Thought follows environment. An intelligent microorganism will never know the moon.

Mara demands knowledge of the content. What do they think about? I proceed with utter caution, selecting my pronouns with careful malice.

COREY: They think largely in terms of themselves, emotive thought, introverted. Because of our ability to create and use tools, much of our thought is devoted to such extraneous objects. Our artifacts dominate us. We are smothered by them, drawn outward like serum from a hypodermic. In the dolphin vocabulary there are more than a hundred distinct words dealing with some different aspect of the spiritual sensation produced by leaping from the water and hanging briefly suspended in midair; there is no word for *work, puzzle, thing,* all extroverted concepts. The whales were more sophisticated. Their speech ran to pure sound. Songs without words, symphonies of noise, pure communication. How did they think? Similarly? That we shall never know.

Engulfed by my colourful digression, Mara wishes to hear more of the whale songs.

COREY (grinning): The form was primarily a storytelling vehicle, a wordless opera. Not simple folktales, either. As far as we have determined, some of their songs run weeks in length, with the plot complications of Dickens, the intricate levels of Joyce and Mann, the poetry of Homer. And these are songs.

MARA: I'd like to hear some.

COREY: I can arrange that.

I hasten towards the door. Something wells up inside me. I flee from her maddened thoughts like a dark medieval knight pursued across the field of battle by some fiery, voracious dragon. Inside me the pulsing yellow fat coils, spasms, coils.

Bradley's proscription left her free to roam at will in the residence quarters. Still, Mara moved carefully through the long corridors. With the horizon so close at hand it sometimes seemed near enough to be touched, the chances of running into someone by mistake were too strong. Twice in her quest she darted into strategic doorways to avoid being seen. Once Bradley himself hastened past. Tom Rawlins danced angrily in his wake, hands flashing like knives. "That stupid bitch!" he cried. *I wonder who?* thought Mara.

Kurt Tsubata semed more surprised than displeased to see her. The amber lines of his face deepened, as seen through the door slit.

"For God's sake, let me in."

"I thought you were restricted."

"To the quarters, that's all."

"I have seen Corey."

"Kurt, let me in. Please. Now."

"Oh, sure. I'm sorry." He showed her to the one soft

pillow that intruded upon the hard, angular vacancy of the large room. A few scattered books–technical journals–peeped from the wall slots. The overhead light was harsh, brutal. Tsubata shown like a ghost. Mara dropped down.

"I need a favour."

He seemed amused. "From me?"

"Yes."

"What? Bradley's head?"

"Not this time. I want you to take me out."

"But I thought—"

"That's right. You're not supposed to." She could have lied, fed him a good story, but she was too tired for that. Twenty straight hours of study had drained her energies–twenty straight hours staring at the Puzzle. "I want to see Jupiter."

He snuggled close to her on the pillow, two shipwrecked sailors perched upon a precarious lifeboat; the floor swept away from them like the endless sea. "I can take you to the screens."

"That's not good enough." She moved closer, tilting her head to see his face. "I'm trying to solve the Puzzle. Laugh if you like."

"No, I won't. How can I? The Puzzle's beyond me."

Humility: "Me, too. So far. To solve it I want to learn how these beings think. I can't do it cooped up inside my room."

He considered, drawing back from her, nearly slipping from the pillow. "You're asking a lot of me." What did he do in this room, alone? No books, no music, surely not chess. He rarely socialized. "Bradley could have me dumped. I'd spend my tour cleaning floors, scrubbing toilets."

"It's not Bradley. It's the others. They're the ones who are afraid of me. Of Corey. That's why I want to solve the Puzzle."

"So they won't be afraid of you anymore? So they'll like you?"

If he wanted it that way . . . "Yes."

Tsubata was not a fool. "It may not work. There are rumours, stories trickling from the bridge. Your people on Earth–they are doing something, causing trouble."

"The trouble was not our idea, Kurt." She went toward him this time, snuggling. "We just want to be left alone."

"I have a mission scheduled in five hours clockwise. Another satellite is blinking. If you want, you can come."

"Five hours. Fine." She was proud of her seductive charm. "That should be just right." She reached for his hand to draw it toward her breast.

Tsubata stood up suddenly, shaking his head. "Mara," he said, "I don't want to go to bed with you."

She withstood the shock, meeting his gaze with little anger. He was trembling now. "Why, Kurt? I thought that's why you said yes."

"I know."

She persisted. "Well?" She stood beside him.

"I'm afraid . . ."

"Oh?" There was no triumph in her voice; it trembled.

"You're not human," he said, watching the floor.

*Mara returns with a second scent. Corey sniffs sharply.
"He refused?"*

"Oh, no." Her hands dart, removing the outer skin of cloth and plastic, exposing the flesh, the double-scent. "We're leaving in three hours. I want to get clean."

"You have done it with him."

She glances at me. "Ah, yes."

"I see. I see. It is like . . .?"

"I can't quite describe it, Corey really." She glides toward the shower stall; the scent will be excised, forgotten.

"As I understand it, the process ends in a terminal, exhausted state. Working together, along a mutual train of explorations, the two eventually reach the same conclusion."

But Mara is turning beneath the drumming of water and

*does not hear me. Corey wheels toward the door. The cor-
ridor outside rushes close to his face. But in the ruddy light
he has no face. Corey rumbles, groaning uphill.*

Bradley eyed Tom Rawlins. There wasn't anyone in
the Orb he disliked more, but he had taken pains to disguise the fact.

Uninvited, Rawlins dropped into the chair, crossed
his legs, locked ankles. He lunged forward, indicating
the high stack of messages piled in one desk corner.
More distantly, Krishna surveyed the scattered mess–
man as a paper-creating animal. On the wall, the Buddha winked his third eye.

"What's the situation on Earth?" Rawlins asked. "I
hope there's been no compromise."

"No, it's the same. The manips will destroy Tokyo
unless their citizenship is returned. The United Congress
says no. Stalemate." He couldn't resist an irritated barb.
"Is that what you want?"

"I want them dead."

"Why?"

"Because they're wrong. Because God never
meant—"

Bradley cut him short with a rare display of anger. His
face flushed. "You didn't come here for that," he finished, more calmly.

"Then you don't know." Rawlins seemed pleased by
that.

"What?"

"That damn woman, that thing. I just now heard and
came straight to you. If the word gets around the Orb
there'll be hell to pay."

Bradley wished he smoked, anything to penetrate this
man's dim, dull skull. "What word, Tom?"

"She's skipped out on you, Bradley. Gone out on a
shuttle with Kurt Tsubata."

The truth, after such suspense, flopped badly. "Is that
all? The way you were hinting I was afraid she'd raped
your mother."

"More likely Tsubata," Rawlins sneered. "So what do you intend to do about it?"

"When?" Bradley's stomach rumbled audibly. He had to remember to take a meal. The pills never satisfied after the third day.

"Why, *now* of course."

"Now, nothing. When she comes back, I'll do something. Spank her. Tweak her nose. Who cares?" He knew his fatigue was showing. "With all this going on—" He tapped the stack of messages, "—you're acting awfully trivial, Tom."

"But don't you see? It's all the same thing, Bradley. She's *one* of them. Do you think she'd hesitate a *minute* to blow up Tokyo, kill millions?"

"Is that why she went out on the shuttle?"

"She told Monitoring, after she left, she wanted to look at Jupiter. It would help her solve the Puzzle. Can you beat that?"

"It's our mission, Tom."

"I want her brought back right away. I want her not just restricted but quarantined. I've talked to the others. We're all agreed."

Anger was an emotion Bradley rarely experienced any more. Either age or meditation had purged it from his system. He missed it. *Act without thinking, do it now*, he mused. The mythical ideal. Zen archery; split the target. Anger cleansed in a way that sorrow, love, joy could never equal.

"Now you listen to me, Rawlins. This isn't a military garrison. I'm not the captain of the guards. I'm an administrative officer, freely elected and chosen, subject to immediate removal. Nobody tells me what to do. Not you, not Mara, not any others."

"But she's not even human!"

"Yes, she is. In fact, I think that's her problem. She's too human: arrogant, irresponsible, selfish. She does what the rest of you would do if only you possessed a fraction of the confidence she has. I don't like Mara–I don't like what she is. But call it human. She is."

Rawlins stood up, his legs unwinding. He spoke with care, plainly caught by surprise. "You mean that, Bradley?"

"Yes."

"And when they blow up Tokyo?"

"That has nothing to do with the Orb."

"This is the end for you. You know that?"

"Tom, get the hell out of here."

Bradley gave Tom Rawlins three additional minutes after the door had slammed behind him, then moved away from his desk. He checked the outer corridor before proceeding. When he entered Monitoring, he found Leigh Duffy, a biophysicist, on duty.

"Can you raise Kurt Tsubata's shuttle?" he asked her. "I want to have a talk with him."

"And Mara?" The woman smiled.

"The thought did enter my mind."

IV

Tsubata turned the shuttle. The newly repaired satellite looped behind. Mara turned her gaze back to Jupiter, sighing.

"Do you mind if I sleep?" Tsubata asked from beside her.

"Mind? No."

"I wasn't sure if it would disturb you."

"The opposite, actually."

"I knew a very brilliant man once, I was very young. Next to you, until I met you, he was the only one I'd known. I thought you might be the same."

Jupiter's oblate form blocked her view, the bulging waistline of a plump satisfied giant. The savage electrical storms of recent weeks stirred the dappled bands; the north polar region churned with an awesome fury. It's just like me, she thought. Neither Father Jupiter nor I is ever fully at rest. "I don't understand, Kurt."

"He was odd. You see, he was a professor at the university and I was only an average student. He would often come to my room. All day, sometimes all night, we would talk. It was rarely me. Just him. Talk and talk and talk. Any subject you can conceive for hours. Then, suddenly, he would stand and shout."

"Yes?"

Tsubata laughed. "He had found his answer. Whenever he had a problem he came to me. Somehow, in the talking, the solution would come. I don't know how. It worked."

"Sleepwalkers. Einstein was one, too. I sleep better alone."

"I'm sorry for that."

"No," she corrected hastily. "I don't mean that. Thank you, Kurt. For asking I mean. That was very considerate."

"I thought it might be important."

"Yes, thank you."

He slept.

Jupiter danced and swirled. The stars glittered, unhindered. She had always been alone. After birth, a couple had been selected to raise her. They were stupid and their son, four years older, had made her life a torment. Once he slipped a frog inside her brassiere, which sounded like a warm, funny childhood memory, but she had hated him for it. The man she recalled only as high, bushy brows, speckled with grey, and a voice that chattered a mile a minute. A biologist, teacher, Nobel candidate. The woman talked constantly, rattled by fear. Mara learned early she could inspire terror, but fear bred hate, and at fourteen she went away. She never saw her parents or brother again. After them there was no one else. At eighteen she told the world she was her own person now and nobody could control her movements. Jupiter groaned upon its high axis. She studied the shifting features. A photograph freezes life; the eye permits it to flow. Some faceless man captured her virginity. She took drugs, slept with other women, gambled, drank, stole money. Life ran stale, bread kept uncovered too long. At twenty-six she ran away to Jupiter. Where else did this plump pink giant, prince of Sol, spin?

There were tears in her eyes.

Reality, she was understanding, lies here. So many claim–Bradley would–that the phenomenon is internal. A lie. Utter horseshit. The human body smothers reality, keeps it trapped. Emptiness is free: outer space. *My God,* she thought, *if there is an answer, where else can it be?*

The void.

In time, the yellow dot of the Orb expanded to assume the familiar concrete form of a tin can. Tsubata slept. She let him. Inactivity dulled her senses; she thrived upon the constant stimuli of daily change. It would be good to bring the shuttle home alone.

Hesitantly, she contacted Monitoring. Twice already Bradley's voice had chirped uninvited in her ears. She had ignored him, impersonally, simply. In time, both times, he had gone away.

A woman physician, Norah Mann, stood duty. She answered Mara's call.

"Is Bradley Reynolds there?" Mara asked.

"Yes," said Norah Mann. "Do you want to talk to him?"

"God, no. Tell him to go to hell."

"He says he doesn't want to talk to you, either."

"I bet."

"He'll talk to you when you return."

"Tell him I can hardly wait." The Orb dominated her forward view, the ugly seams and stitches in its unburnished hide. Mara exchanged the necessary data with Norah Mann.

"You're getting very close," Norah said.

"Yes." Mara cut the engine. She reached for the manual steering controls. Tsubata snored lightly in her ears. The job was a mechanical one, the berth a ring to be captured.

She pressed the controls requesting a burst of air.

Nothing happened.

Automatically, driven by universal order, the shuttle continued its rigidly elliptical course. Mara calculated swiftly, jamming the controls. At this rate she would miss the Orb entirely. The blankness of space loomed ahead. *No, no,* she thought.

Puzzled, keeping calm, she released the controls, then tried again. A slight turn would possibly suffice.

Nothing happened.

Norah Mann shouted frantic questions. Bradley's voice could be heard rising in the background. Mara ignored both of them. She jabbed an elbow at the sleeping man beside her. "Kurt, something's gone wrong."

He came alert at once and she could tell by the way he moved that he understood instantly the danger they faced. Stupid? She doubted his IQ totalled half hers.

Without a word he reached past her and gripped the controls.

They no more responded to his touch than hers.

"Is something broken?" she asked. "Damaged? Can't you do something? We'll miss our berth." The orb seemed directly beneath them now.

Tsubata said, "Jump." Reaching down, he unfastened the straps that held him. He gripped the chassis with one hand. "When we're so close you can smell the hull, then do it."

"But can't they come after us, pick us up?"

"Do you want to wait for that? I said jump." Tsubata leaped, quick and clean. Mara followed. Together they slammed against the hard, pocked hide of the Orb. Mara struggled for a handhold, gripped something, braked her own motion.

The shuttle drifted on past the Orb. Within moments, it was lost from view.

Jupiter, unmoved, continued its stately spin. For a long minute, Mara saw nothing else.

A voice ran in her ears, soft, unexpectedly calm. "You

two hold on out there. I'll have someone out in a few minutes."

"Fine," said Tsubata. "We'll wait, Bradley."

"I hope Mara won't get bored. She doesn't seem to like staying in one place."

"I'll be fine, Bradley."

"Maybe you won't disobey my orders anymore."

"Oh shut up, Bradley."

"I was only making a suggestion."

"Well, don't."

I'll see you shortly, Mara."

When Mara once again reaches her room, where I stand poised beside stationary chess pieces, Bradley Reynolds bustles behind, his exterior welcoming smile (directed toward me) meant to conceal a maelstrom of interior agitation. "Corey, how are you? We just got Mara back."

"I am glad."

"Well, you ought to be," says Mara, "because it was damn close." She blazes with anger—also fear—but both emotions lie buried so deep that actual tears, as if bearing grief, rush to fill her eyes. It becomes difficult to perceive her words, flowing as they do with such savage swiftness. I am not important here. It is Bradley who dominates her attention. He flops on the second bed and casually studies Mara's replication of the Puzzle.

"Mara, you didn't come close to being killed. There's no need to cry murder. Wait till something really happens, then explode."

Her finger shakes as if bearing a life of its own. "You said so yourself, Bradley. The shuttle was tampered with."

"Tsubata said that, not me, and he won't know for sure until we recover the craft."

"I know. You know. It happened before."

"You weren't in any real danger."

"No, but what if it had happened earlier? Kurt said that too. A freeze-up in the lateral pipes. If the blowback in-

jured one of us—guess which one?—that far out, hours from the Orb . . ."

"But it didn't happen." Standing, Bradley approaches the chessboard. "A fascinating game. I haven't played it for years."

Mara grabs his shoulder, turns him. Her flesh touching his. The thin garment he wears barely blunts the physical contact. "It must be the same person. Someone wants me killed. And they won't quit."

Bradley softens. The muscles that hold his jaws and cheeks grow weak. Both arms stretch forward from his body to touch Mara upon the shoulders. Corey can be ignorant as if it is not present. Steel box. Furniture. A vacant television cabinet. "You shouldn't have gone out on the shuttle, Mara. I warned you it would be dangerous. I was protecting you, not them. Look, if you took a walk through dark Calcutta and did not return alive, whose fault would that be?"

"Then blame me, damn it." She draws triumphantly away. "I told you why I went out there."

"To solve the Puzzle," he says precisely.

"Yes."

"But you didn't."

"No, but I will."

"I believe that."

"Then believe this, too: someone on the Orb wants to kill me."

"If it's true, then it's up to you to be careful until this thing has run its course."

"What course? Look, Bradley—" She waves disparagingly at the room in which so many games have been played. "—I can't stay cooped in here with Corey. It's not me you should be worrying about. Find this man and stop him."

"And if I can't? I'm not a detective. Your own people on Earth are right this moment threatening to murder ten million people. Next to them, your life is minor, Mara."

"The attacks on me began before that. I'm not responsi-

ble for them. Jack the Ripper was a human being. Jesse James was an American. Do you want me blaming you for them?"

"I still think you should stay here." His long, fleshy hands return to their prey. He holds Mara close, his eyes reaching toward hers. "Let me look into this. I'm up to my ears in trouble now but I can do something. If the attack was deliberate, it had to be someone who knew you were going out, who was able to tamper with the shuttle. I'll ask Tsubata who he told."

"He promised to tell no one."

"Let me talk to him."

Mara laughs shrilly. "And narrow your list of suspects? What was it the last time? Everyone but you and Corey? How many this time? A mere three hundred, two hundred, just fifty. Only fifty people within the adjoining few metres who want me dead. I feel good now, Bradley. I really do."

"I think there'll be fewer than fifty, Mara."

Corey here shuts down. It is the best he can manage simply to maintain the basic functioning of his system. Often inside her box it becomes so very dark like this. Light is one phenomenon denied Corey since birth. Others speak of the raw sensation of heat against skin. A winter's bliss. Mara may be talking. Bradley may reply. Corey hears nothing. Within her box she returns to the moment of girlhood birth and relives that experience. Breath comes slowly. A whine. A cry. A shriek. Born, life, born. He cries to his dolphins and hears their clicking clacking chatter. One sleek beast swiftly glides through still blue water then leaps, unhindered, toward the high lilting sun. For Corey nothing shines. (He) (She) (It) Corey expires. Corey?

Mara gazed anxiously at the dark, silent, motionless steel box. "What happened?" she asked Bradley, not for the first time. "He can't be dead."

"I wouldn't have any idea. We'll just have to wait."

Norah Mann's dusky blue uniform stretched taut, an abstraction detailing her bones but only a hint of flesh.

She crouched beside Corey. It seemed odd when she produced a stethoscope from a valise and laid it against the side of Corey's box. Mara laid a hand upon her lips to avoid giggling. Did Corey even have a heart?

At last Norah Mann turned away, replacing her tools. "No, it's alive," she told them. "I don't know what's wrong, but it's not dead."

"You're certain?" Mara asked.

"As much as I can be. I'm no expert on steel boxes. None of us are. But the brain waves are sharp, clear, very obvious, even stronger than a deep sleep. Strong C delta signature. The other bodily signs, those it seems to have, are quite normal. If there is something physically wrong, I can't discover it."

"And you don't think we should call another doctor?" Bradley said.

"If you want. I don't think it would do any good. It would take someone who had known that thing since it was built—born. The whole structure is just too odd. Have you ever seen an X-ray?" She reached for her valise.

"That's not necessary." Norah Mann was young, pretty, very dark. Bradley didn't seem to trust her. *The prejudice of age?* Mara wondered. *God, can he have that against me, too?* "What do you recommend?"

"Stay with it, I suppose. In case anything does occur. I can come here every few hours to run additional analyses. I can't think of anything else."

"I'll stay," Mara said. "This is my room. Besides, that way Bradley will be kept happy, too."

"And you're fine?"

The question puzzled Mara. Why did this woman want to know that? "Yes, I'm fine."

"I ask—" She seemed suddenly embarrassed. "—because I was there when that accident happened."

"I remember."

"Do you? I know I hadn't met you before."

"Few people on the Orb have met Mara," Bradley said.

"Which undoubtedly pleases them."

"Oh, no," said Norah Mann. "Don't think that. I can't speak for everyone else, but I've been dying to meet you. Just think–you know so much. Why, you could talk to everyone all at once and that way nobody would get bored. One trouble with the Orb is that everyone is such a specialist and there are so few in each category. It's hard for anyone to find someone to talk to. You can't even use the weather. We don't have any here."

"That's nice of you to say," Mara said.

"Well, it's true. Everyone anticipated your arrival, but then you came and just seemed to disappear. You got involved with the Puzzle, with them—" She indicated Bradley with a surreptitious tip of the jaw, the Orb power elite. "—and we hardly saw you."

"Maybe I can change that," Mara said.

"Oh, we'd be glad. You're different. Out here everything becomes so similar, monotonous."

"Even when my people are threatening to blow up the world?"

"That's not you," Norah Mann said, with apparent sincerity. It was pleasant to hear words unshadowed by implications.

"I don't know who else."

"The ones like that." She pointed at silent, still Corey. "You–you're not much different from the rest of us; just smarter."

During the two days which had passed since Corey's strange withdrawal, Mara had not once left the quiet precincts of her private room. She replaced the phone, turned away from the wall, and told Kurt Tsubata, "Bradley said he'd come."

"Now?"

"Yes."

Tsubata smiled admiringly. "You could have convinced me, too. But—" He touched the drawing of the Puzzle; it lay beside him upon the wrinkled second cot.

"—is there really something here?"

Mara crossed the room and sat down, edging cautiously past Corey. "I look at it this way, Kurt. What's the Puzzle all about? It's communication, that's what. They're speaking one language and we're speaking another. Who could be better fitted to solve that than me? I don't speak the same language, either."

"It sounds like English to me."

"It is and it isn't. I mean nothing against you, but there's no way you or any other man can possibly understand the inner workings of my mind. And I'm not half so weird as something like Corey."

"Because you're intelligent?"

"That's part of it."

Because you never had a mother or father?"

"That's minor. No, it's just because I'm different—that's the only way I can put it." She smiled. "If I could describe it better, then there wouldn't be any problem in the first place."

Bradley arrived with surprising swiftness. The lines in his face appeared to have widened and spread the last few days. For the first time since meeting him Mara felt the true effects of this strange man's immense age. He had always seemed fifty, no more than sixty; now he had soared near one hundred.

"Just before I left the office another signal came through. The deadline has been extended again."

"What deadline?" Tsubata asked.

Bradley frowned with irritation. "The one her nippies have established for destroying ten million people."

"They won't do it," Mara said. "You were right all along, Bradley. It's just a bluff."

Her words failed to console him. He crouched upon the floor, the high shadow of the chess table looming grey above him. It was not an impressive pose; he seemed a weary man. "If I were them, it wouldn't be."

"You'd blow up the world to save yourself?" Mara asked, astonished.

"Yes." He nodded sadly. "To save my people."

"Well, it won't happen." Her own voice was hushed. "You said there'd been a delay."

"We'll see." He stood suddenly, mechanically. "But you didn't call me here for that."

"No." She reached toward the cot, gripped the Puzzle paper. "It's this. I've had an idea."

He nodded. "So you said. Well, what?"

"I—" She could see this would not satisfy him. "—I really don't want to tell you now, not yet. I don't know enough. It comes from something Corey told me once. About the dolphins."

"I know about the dolphins."

"Yes, but that was only the beginning."

Barely a flicker of interest had crossed his features. She guessed Bradley was tired of the arguments, the constant political infighting. Tom Rawlins still wanted Bradley removed as commander; strangely enough, Rawlins often proved a powerfully persuasive man. "Kurt," said Bradley, "do you know anything more about this?"

"Not a thing. I wasn't here when she had the idea."

Bradley shook his head. "Mara, this really doesn't seem so urgent to me."

"But that's not all." Mara felt her voice rising and fought to subdue the pitch. "I want to ask your permission. My idea. I don't want to leave it here. I want to go out."

Bradley frowned blankly. "That's impossible."

"Are you saying that," asked Tsubata, with unexpected force, "or is it Rawlins?"

Mara was more tactful. "It's absolutely necessary, Bradley."

"No, it isn't. If it was, you'd tell me what it's about. If I dared to let you leave this room, they'd lynch me as soon as fire me. You've gone out before–with Kurt. It's never helped."

"She wants to go farther than that this time," Tsubata said.

"To Jupiter," Mara said. She took a deep breath, then let the words explode with a rush. "A glideship into the atmosphere."

Bradley shook his head in stunned surprise. He looked at Tsubata, not Mara. "Now one of you is mad. What can you find that way that an unmanned probe can't?"

"Life. Intelligent life."

"You'll be burned to a crisp, Mara."

"Then let me go," Tsubata said. "Mara is important. It will hurt the Orb if she dies. But I'm replaceable. You can risk me."

"Not for nothing," Bradley remained unshaken on this certainty. "Mara hasn't shown either of us why a death is necessary."

"Because—" Mara began.

She was interrupted by a hum. A growl. A buzz. Corey glowed with sudden life. His voice purred. "Then let me go instead."

Bradley spun around. Mara's heart fluttered: high, birdlike, swelling with suspicion.

"You can let me go," Corey said, "because my life is worthless to everyone. I am the thing in the box, a metal man. If I do not perform this feat, then who else ever will?"

"Me," said Mara.

"Someone," said Tsubata.

"No, Corey." Bradley nodded with abrupt decisiveness. "He's right. It's got to be him."

V

Bradley lounged, letting things happen with an easy rhythm of their own.

His desk was uncluttered (with a good computer system, paperwork is rare) so he propped his feet up on it, taking the slight pressure of weight on the knobby end of his spine. Bad for the posture, he remembered. Margo Landau (biochemist; sixty-eight; possessing a special talent for holding him just so, legs akimbo in the weakened gravity, as he comes to his shuddering aged release) would tell him so, nag him gently. But as he neared one hundred he had been old nearly half his life, whereas Margo was just beginning, scarcely past the skinned knees of childhood, really. Margo was precisely what he needed to keep him in touch with others. He was reasonably sure that was why she was assigned to the Orb; everything here was calculated. Being with her resembled those chance moments when accidentally pressing fingertips and thumb together, he felt the padded throb of his own pulse, the interweaving beat of all warm things.

He reached out and snapped on his view-screen. A blue smear of light warped and rippled, then abruptly froze into a 3-D scene from the Orb axis. Small spots of green, orange, red, yellow that he knew were suited men slowly nudged a large booster into its rack. The boosters formed a pentagon around the spidery braces of Corey's entry vehicle, the *Aurora*. The sleek glideship was spineless, so the high-influence arc lights washed it in repeating patterns of stark light and dappled shadows.

Bradley thumbed over to higher magnification. He picked out Mara's suit by number. Beside it glided the awkward box of Corey. She was showing him her shuttlecraft. Anything to keep Corey occupied, Bradley thought. And the box manoeuvred itself well when free of Mara's mothering hands. Its burnished metal sides seemed grainy and solid beneath the arc lights, more substantial than the glittering colourful humans around it. A machine amidst its own kind. Indistinguishable in many ways from the shuttle, the boosters or the glideship itself.

Something caught at Bradley's sense of things; a frown flickered momentarily across his creased brow. He watched Corey adroitly spin itself, fire a lateral burst of air and coast to the underside of the shuttle. Mara followed somewhat more awkwardly. The two floated back and forth across the metal strutwork, two phosphorescent invertebrates swaying in the wash of a vacuum sea. Yet one was at home there, one would not attract the eye of anyone trained to care for humans alone.

Bradley sighed, wondering why he had not seen things so clearly before. It was always the invisible that damaged you the most. *Confusions, delusions, contusions*, he thought wryly.

He sat back to study the screen and unconsciously knotted his fist into a ball. He flinched; a cold hard spark of pain shot through his hand. It ebbed quickly, seeping through his fingers and burning away a layered numbness in his arm. Inflamed cartilage. Aching worn tissue, crying out. Bradley shrugged it off and reminded himself to tell the Orb's physicians if they asked. But only if they asked. He had things to do here, the moment he had prepared was coming to fruition. He did not want to undergo any medical song and dance at this juncture.

Bradley rubbed absently at the crow's feet streaming from the corners of his eyes, and thought about Corey. He knew he had the habit of lowering his eyelids as he thought, letting his face droop into the folded creases it naturally had. Concentration made him seem sleepy to others, which in turn was sometimes useful. Giving the appearance of an old man nodding off in the midst of an argument relaxed the opposition, made them careless. He had learned that trick decades before and it never failed. But for the moment, with no one to see, he relaxed instinctively and concentrated very hard on Corey and the mission that lay ahead.

The descent into the atmosphere was necessary; everyone had known that for some time. Automatic guidance systems were inadequate to the supersonic, raging winds of the Jovian belts. Direction from the Orb by radio link was impossible; the time delay would make the craft hopelessly sluggish. And Corey wanted to go, sought the sacrifice, whereas no human aboard the Orb did.

And perhaps it was best for that metal to go now, into

the deep ocean of gas. Better for him to take that path than the one he had been following.

Bradley would let him go, would say not a word.

The decision made, he took a gulp of coffee. It had an odd, silvery taste, like the flavour which filled his mouth when he drank orange juice soon after brushing his teeth. He sat for a long moment integrating his understanding of this situation with what he knew before. It was an elaborate dance he oversaw here, a volatile mixture of talented, idiosyncratic people. The entire Orb was a spinning can of prima donnas. It had taken him months to understand how governing and leading such a group was possible, and it had never been easy. At first he was depressed, because he had little appearance of authority. But then, perhaps that had nothing to do with the gift of command. You cannot order a man to have a new idea. Nor can you let him drift forever, bumping at random into the thoughts and abrasive skins of others.

Click. He switched over into another internal line, this time a tracking survey of the hydroponics warrens. A few figures moved among the leafy fronds and well-tended green crops.

Click. "—module won't configure until seventy seconds after we've had zone separation. The fuelled cells cut over at that time, to avoid overload. If—"

Click. A close view of the sleek glideship. Men feathered cables at the nose. The shifting light gave everything a sense of movement.

Click. "—compatibility has to depend upon temperature gradients through the whole package. We've got the thing shirtsleeved now, but I'm not sure—"

Click. A view of the assembly bay. Men and women moved with quick, brisk efficiency. Bradley thumbed up the sound and picked out several languages being used in different parts of the bay. But the words seemed less important than the sound, to him.

Click. A video from Earth. An entertainment for

those off shift. Two men argued hotly, gesturing, voices rising. Waves arched, curled, caved into white foam behind them. Their sentences were thick with slang; Bradley could not follow the logic of it.

Click. "—connections won't seat right. I don't know who designed this, but the vibration will—"

A hand camera peered into a quilted forest of printed circuits. Snouted pliers tore loose a wire and turned it into the reddened light. "Supplex won't go here, the manifold will trigger early, too many precursors—"

A green button winked on his console. He switched to com-channel and found himself looking at Rawlins, the man's deceptively smooth face knitted into lines.

"One of my men just pointed something out to me," Rawlins said quickly, the words spilling out. "Corey's going to have override on the glideship, isn't he?"

"Of course. He takes control. He has to."

"No, I mean even while he's still in near-orbit with us."

"Yes. Might as well give him as much practice as possible. He has to do all that by seat of the pants, you know." Bradley kept his voice mild, flat.

"What if he uses it against us?"

"How?"

"Smacks it into the Orb, how else?"

"Unlikely. That isn't Corey's motivation. He may be dangerous, but not to us."

"That sounds like a bunch of garbage to me. How do you know the motivations of a thing like that?"

"I don't, not totally. I have to sense the way he feels."

"That's a hell of a way to run a laboratory."

Bradley refrained from telling Rawlins that he dealt with everyone that way. In fact, it was the only way to run *this* laboratory.

"You're not going to do anything, then?"

Bradley smiled, wishing that were enough for Rawlins. He was sorry he sometimes lacked the presence to hold a silence for very long, and finally broke it, saying, "There's no need. Don't worry."

"I suppose you know about that hidden com-line Mara planted?"

Bradley shook his head. "That's your department."

"Damned right it is. And one of my men caught it right off. Mara patched into one of the telemetery channels. We found it connected through the cable shaft to a rig in her room. And there's another lead-in to her suit radio."

"So she could talk to Corey without going through Monitoring?"

"Yeah. Well, we cut that one right away, I'll tell you that."

"Good."

"Don't want these manips talking to each other where we can't hear them," Rawlins added with a decisive, conspiratorial air.

Bradley understood Rawlin's ploy. If he let the statement pass he would be implicitly accepting Rawlin's division of the world. Mara and Corey on one side of an invisible line, Bradley and Rawlins and everyone else on the other. In group and out group, the old illusions.

Still, Rawlins and those like him had been useful. Their mere presence drove Mara in a way nothing else could. Perhaps Corey too.

"You can always justify terminating an unauthorized line," Bradley said wearily. "As far as I'm concerned, that's all there is to the matter." There, that was probably enough. Justification for the action, but no overt support. Rawlins would be kept dangling, wondering if Bradley would give him enough backing for a strong move against Mara and Corey at some future intersection. And in turn, Rawlins's persistence would seep through somehow to Mara and hone her wits that much more. The dynamic equilibrium between the two would go on, each driving the other.

Bradley murmured a goodbye to Rawlins and

switched off. He needed time to think, to integrate all the changing variables into a coherent whole.

Rawlins, still preoccupied with his fantasies about manips, still tied to the strings of Earth. Vance, smart but edgy. Mara and Corey and the news from Earth. Tsubata. Margo, shepherd for his dimming but persistent passion.

Everyone mattered, everyone entered into the bracketed terms of the equation. Events themselves were coefficients, heightened by exponents. And most of what was happening in the Orb was beyond analysis, escaping a clean and precise dynamics. So he had to go by feel alone, instinct and sometimes whim.

And who could trust his judgment in such a place? Bleached corridors, dry and distant from the human landscape . . . There were times when Bradley wanted the brush of cool sea air on his face as badly as he had ever desired anything. A shimmering urgency would fill him and he would for blazing moments hate the Orb, this place made by men alone, this hollow spot beyond all nature. These instants receded eventually, dwindled, blurred. But he knew he could not stay here forever. The job had to come to some summation or, Bradley knew, he would lose his taste for it.

Click. The boosters were in place. Obliquely angled beams came together in precise sockets.

Click. An orange flower bloomed where two men played a hydrogen torch on a fabrication divot.

Click. Running indexes of data slid down the screen like rain, softly lit from behind by yellow car headlights. As Bradley watched the numbers jumped, moved, told new tales.

Click. "—verify corrections as incoming adjustments, not log them directly. In real time that gives—"

Click. The relay news squirt from Earth. Another ocean, another welter of detail.

Bradley swirled his coffee, scanning the news for its import. The liquid stirred and rocked like a flexible black coin at the bottom of the white cup.

Click. In a biological laboratory a young woman made an adjustment at the side of the hooded biological sensors package. Suited figures stood by to carry it out.

Click. The sun, rotating by, burned a clean hard hole in the space around it.

Click. Jupiter hung below.

Click, Click, Click.

Once freed, the bird glided slowly upward. The revolving pancake overhead had been pulled aside and now the bay-mounted sensors of Monitoring could see down the bore of the Orb into free space. A circle of stars spun serenely in the night.

"Don't you wonder if he will make it back?" Bradley said to Mara. He had been waiting for her to say something, to show some response to Corey's leaving, but all she did was scribble on a pad of paper.

"I think he probably will," Mara said, distracted. Around them the quiet sounds of Monitoring went on, cloaked in a dim ruddy light. In sound-deadened console pits the staff followed *Aurora's* slow exit.

"What are you doing?" Bradley said at last.

"Anticryptography, picking at the Puzzle." She glanced up at him impishly. "Why, do you think it's improper for me to ignore Corey's leaving?"

"No, but—"

"Let me set you a problem. Something to distract you. It's going to be quite a long energy-consuming ellipse he rides down, you know." She pencilled some numbers across the page:

$$8\ 5\ 4\ 9\ 1\ 7\ 6\ 10\ 3\ 2$$

"Problem for the student: What is the ordering of the numbers?"

Bradley pused his lips. "I'm not good at this sort of thing."

"Try anyway. You went to school when people still

took years learning arithmetic, didn't you, before modern education even started?"

"You might say that."

"I *would*. You're really impossibly old. How does it feel?" She said this with simple, open curiosity.

"How does it feel to be old for what seems like forever?"

"Not the same. You've been young, too."

"Have I?"

"Sure, I've read about your times. You grew up when people had those love-ins and be-ins, didn't you?"

"I'm not quite that old. I came along just in time for the famines."

Mara smiled. "You're stalling. Try my problem."

"I give up. I lost all my intellectual fibre years ago."

"Nobody's got it right away so far. Even Vance. The point is that there are numbers, but they aren't arranged according to a scheme that has anything to do with arithmetic. You have to step outside the normal context of the system to see it."

"8, 5, 4—oh, I see. Alphabetical order, in English."

"Right." Mara seemed strangely pleased. "So I'm trying to learn to think like that. To step outside contexts."

Bradley noticed that Vance was standing beside him. How long the man had been there he could not tell.

"You got that faster than I did," Vance said very evenly, without inflection. "Took me over two minutes."

Bradley smiled and said something noncommittal, but he noted the small lines around the young man's face. He knew Vance's file, and recognized in him the type of dutiful good boy who became a natural target for Mara's teasing. Bradley saw at a glance that Vance's only defence was forbearance, and the inner conviction that in the end he would succeed. He would solve the Puzzle himself.

Bradley smiled again, and made a small joke that set

them laughing. Heads turned on the bridge; this was not a place of merriment. Bradley waved them back to work. He felt a welling sense that the dynamic tension he wanted was working, that the forces within Mara and Vance and the others would finally prove true. One of these two present very probably would solve the Puzzle, and it was almost certainly not going to be the calm, steady, competitive Vance.

VI

Despite her light, airy manner, Bradley noticed that Mara could not stay away from Monitoring very long. As the *Aurora's* ellipse lengthened toward its intersection with Jupiter's atmosphere, she spent longer and longer times scribbling and watching the main display screen. The room buzzed with its own hivelike activity. Bradley rested. The gravity was stronger here, and after a while his joints began a familiar ache. This, more than anything else, reminded him that return to Earth would be painful, perhaps impossible. There were people older than he on Earth, but they were in immersion tanks now, kept alive by their own buoyant wealth. He might make a decent living of it on the moon, and the government would surely do what it could for him—he was still, he knew, a revered figure back there—but that would be clear erosion of what he already had. Here he lived on the cutting edge of events. Here he had a place, here there was some hope that he could still play a role.

That, he thought, was the crucial question. Animals lived ten times their period of growth to maturity; now that humans did, too, society had to be redesigned. He was only the first of a swelling horde of incredibly older people. Eventually the ways of great age might dominate all mankind.

An aide nudged his elbow. "There'a priority item on the coded relay from Earth, sir."

"Bring me a summary."

"It has to be in private, sir." The man was proper,

correct, absolutely unwilling to take any risk.

Bradley glanced at *Aurora*'s elongating path. "I'll stay here a few more moments."

Mara strolled casually by. "Anything new?"

Her face was absolutely impassive, so Bradley knew instantly something was wrong.

"No," he said, and left.

Rawlins was already waiting when Bradley arrived back at his desk. He silenced the man with a gesture and sat down to read the decoded message. It was simple, abrupt.

Assassination teams on Earth had caught most of the manips unaware. A special Emergency Committee had acted. They calculated the gamble and thought it worthwhile.

The attacks were mostly successful, and even those manips who escaped did not trigger their nuclear devices. Some of them were on the run. Others were simply holed up in their caverns, waiting out the play of events. No cities had been vaporized.

The communiqué dwelled on this, called the manip threat a gutless provocation. Bradley smiled at this. He remembered full well how, only days before, the entire Council had fretted and worried.

But that was not all. Appended to the news release were orders, spelled out in the rigid bureaucratic prose he had never fully understood. They wanted Bradley to do the same—kill the manips under his charge, as soon as possible. No warning. Report when the act was finished.

"I've got some men who can do it," Rawlins said intensely.

"Oh?"

"I'll call them."

Rawlins's voice was guarded and hesitant. He clenched his hands, and Bradley could see the muscles in his forearms bulge slightly.

Bradley leaned back, luxuriating in the lower gravity.

He folded his hands across his rumpled blue workshirt and stared at Rawlins for a long time. He did not like overt shows of authority, so he gave no immediate order. His stare proved effective enough; Rawlins met it, then looked away, then danced his fingers nervously on his chair arm.

"I'm not going to do it, you know," Bradley said. "We can't reach Corey anyway."

"Mara, then. Thank God we got that steel freak out of the Orb."

Bradley let Rawlins's sentence hang in the air for a long moment.

"Mara is no danger."

"What! You've got an order in your hand to—"

"I decide what my orders are."

"You slow-witted bastard. That girl—"

Bradley tuned out Rawlins's jumbled words. These smatterings of thought were not worth answering, and to declare anything more now would involve him deeper with Rawlins. He needed psychological separation from this small, turbulent man. Once again the balance of forces within the Orb was shifting and new vectors emerged.

When Rawlins paused for breath Bradley said simply, "Please get out."

Rawlins's face compressed into tight creases, the nexus of straining cords of muscle in his neck. "You're in collusion with them, aren't you?" He said in a low fierce whisper. "You told them to set up that extra telemetery line between *Aurora* and Mara. You—"

"No, I didn't. And I'm surprised you think it's cut."

"We *did* cut it. My men—"

"That was probably a false trail. Mara knew you would turn up that line in a routine check. If she really wants to talk to Corey I'm pretty sure the two of them have devised a well-concealed transmission path."

"Then we'll goddamn well splice that one, too. We can comb this—"

Bradley knew Rawlins had a clear edge now, and time

alone would deliver the Orb into Rawlins's hands. Once Bradley disobeyed an order from Earth, there were enough people on the Orb to eventually force him out of office. But time was everything here; nothing could really be done as long as *Aurora* was in flight. But when the staff had time . . .

Bradley decided to blunt Rawlins's urgency. He slumped down in his chair, wheezing audibly, and let animation seep out of his face. He licked his lips where the mottled brown shaded into florid pink, a studied gesture. He let his mouth sag slightly and his head trembled.

"Well, well, all things in time, I'm sure. You do talk, I can't quite follow all that you say." He got the odd rising note just right; the note wavered and broke as he reached the end of the sentence. "Odd, we used to say, how the only muscle that never tires is the tongue."

He blinked owlishly and looked aside, seemingly distracted. Rawlins, thinking himself unobserved, smiled in secret superiority. That last line, so much an old man's remark, tinged with homely advice and delivered with no true sharp edge, was enough. Rawlins would wait out the *Aurora* flight, biding his time. After all, a relic like Bradley could be outmanoeuvred at will. There was no need to amass political capital.

"I still think—" Rawlins began carefully, selecting his words.

A red light winked on the desk console. Bradley leaned forward with an old man's fragility and answered the message. It was Tsubata. "Mara's out," he said abruptly. "She went through the lock fifteen minutes ago. She's beyond the pancake now."

"What!" Rawlins was on his feet now.

"Don't send anyone after her," Bradley said quickly. "Sit tight—you know that phrase? It means do nothing."

"If that bitch—" Rawlins slammed his fist on the top of the console.

Bradley looked up at him evenly, thinking. "I hadn't

guessed that part," he said. "I didn't think they were that good."

"What? Guessed what?"

"An extra connection into *Aurora* was obvious. But it's clear why Mara has gone outside. She's getting beyond our clutches in the best way she knows how. It means she and Corey are tapping our coded line to Earthside." For the first time since events had begun to unfold, Bradley felt a welling fear.

As the cusping point nears Mara beeps me over the second line, the one still active. I hear the squirt from Earth; one more point plotted in the analytic continuation of their evolving animal line. Corey does not choose to even revolve his opticals and take a fix on the crescent Earth; he is safe from them now, sucked into another gravity well. So he converges, tangentially.

Insertion begins. Mara's message bisects Corey and he carries two conversations at once. The Orb wishes to know intimate details of the entry; he shares with them the singing octaves of atmosphere as they rise outside Aurora's *skin. Mara wishes more; she wants to know the thoughts of Corey on matters of human aims.*

He thinks, begins to speak, and then the acceleration falls upon him with a sudden peak of thirty gee. The world slows. Encapsulated in tightly packed circuits, immortal silicon and germanium, he is able to withstand any conceivable acceleration. Corey the warm moist engine is compressed, knows agony.

The spidery limbs fall away. The heat shield reddens and blisters. Aurora *creaks like varnished wood and with polynomial precision I carve the hydrogen sky. And think of Mara.*

There are some pictures (I) (he) retains of (her), a thing about the curve of her buttocks and the way they intersect the upward thrust of her thigh as she walks, scissoring the air. There is something there Corey cannot resolve. But Mara is different from the others and something in the

*way she tosses her head back and the hair curls down
brown and soft over her forehead, something in that tells
me she is like me and understands, she pricks the inner
side of dendritic impulse. Together we see the humans.
There are moments when the light shines brightly through
those creatures and I can see what they are doing even
though they do not know what they must be about.*

*It is so simple when you have seen the anthropological
books, read the data from Africa and Asia, seen the way
they evolved in tribes and towns. They act as a group,
always conscious of what is expected of them. But if you
are metal man, or an oily twisted woman, what is expected? I am the only metal man. They say the taste of
metal in a mouth is the absence of other tastes, but I know
otherwise. An instructor of mine once said, after going to
the dentist, that—he must have been joking here—the
taste of gold and silver alloy is like what Corey tastes. But
food flows through my blue veins. I do not feel it. I do not
have molars to be capped and bridges to be shaped across
the yawning spaces where teeth loom like mountains. I am
sliding yellow guts, not a metal taste. Even Mara, once,
whose nose wrinkled when she first saw me—so odd, so
odd, a box that talks—*

The heat shield flares red and Corey orders it to die.
The cinders fall behind. Automatic sequencing begins.
With a pop that strums through my circuits I feel the tug
and shift as the first drogue parachute deploys. I fall more
slowly. Telemetery from Orb confirms I am through the
pure hydrogen sheath, and now opticals see the pearly ammonia cirrus rushing up from below. The infinite enveloping blanket accepts me. Through the Intersoll layer, where
idiot probes have gone before me. Navigating, I twist. I
slide.

I cut a path through the ice crystals, three hundred kilometres down. Ammonia hydrosulphide. Thump—and the
second parachute billows behind, a white flower slowing
me as it sucks in the thin gas and billows into a hemisphere
the size of the Orb. I am falling at a kilometre a minute.

Mara beeps that she is in the shuttle, the connections are good. She flaps free of the Orb. She is safe there, I am falling here. She says she can remain there for days, no longer, there are not enough supplies. But there she can think and she will hear me through our clandestine relay mounted atop the spinning pancake.

All converges. Alpha Libra waits.

"Of course I'm outside the Orb, why shouldn't I be?" Mara said lightly. But Bradley caught the thread beneath her words. "Time to work. Time to think. Time to spend without being disembowelled by Rawlins and the like."

"I've called them off for the moment," Bradley said.

"Ponder the lilies, Bradley. They toil not, neither do they spin. From here the Orb spins quite clearly. Impressive, if you didn't know what was inside."

"The storms are getting worse. The radiation hazard—"

"Is quite a bit less than the danger from a casual knife thrust inside the Orb, I'd say."

"There are only a few you'd have to worry about."

"A few? How many is that? I was doing some reading, Bradley. Did you know the basic number of units a human being can perceive directly is limited to four? We immediately know one or two or three or four, but when it comes to five we break it up into four plus one or two plus three. We don't have an instant perception of higher numbers. We have to convert into arithmetic. What was so special about four in our evolution?"

Bradley felt a sudden flash of perception. She was thinking, not just running from danger. Perhaps the calibrated intersection of forces he sought could still happen. "Well, things have to cut off somewhere. It doesn't make sense to have an animal perceiving, say, 1,564 intuitively. That's cumbersome."

"Quite an orthodox answer. Maybe true. But . . ."

"Bradley," came Rawlins's harsh rasp, "is this your

idea of dealing with an emergency situation?"

"Shit. Get off this line, Rawlins."

"She could put that shuttle on automatic and fly it into the Orb."

"Quite right. What level and sector are you in?"

"Why, uh, A-17."

"Good. You're in charge of evacuating the entire A level. Do it immediately. Take as many nonshift people as you can find and secure the area."

"I didn't—"

"Move it."

There was a click and a hovering silence held for a moment. "That was rather slick," Mara said.

"I don't think Rawlins can act and think at the same time," Bradley said, suddenly tired. "Do you have enough air? You probably had to leave pretty quick—"

"I could use some."

"I'll send Tsubata out with some supplies. I'd advise you to come in pretty close to the Orb and use it as a partial radiation screen."

"Quite a mother hen, aren't you?"

"Precisely."

I Doppler on the rising heat formation and jet leftward, correcting, correcting. Above Aurora *floats the hot hydrogen balloon that keeps us buoyant, fed by the fusion percolator. Turbulence swirls about me, in Mach numbers rising and falling stochastically. All is the way the stimulations told it. I am comfortable, wrapped in warmth, waiting. The ammonia hydrosulphide tapers off in concentration and my moistened perceptors begin to find water ice among the swirling clouds.*

Infrared radar sounds the layers of pressed atmosphere below and brings back odd spotty resonances. They appear as pips of light that broaden, diffuse, then reshape themselves. In the hydro-helium atmosphere the distant cloud banks, purpling at the base, come sharp and clear.

Corey bids itself to fall. The fusion reactor mutes, the

balloon above me cools and I drift steadily down. I slide down the slopes of Jovian winds. The capsule rocks gently, babylike, in this mother of all planets. My instrumentation booms lean out into the howling eddies: sampling and measuring and pouring raw data back to the Orb as though I am a great heart, pumping a message through some swollen body.

The water content around us rises. (He) (It) feels a persistent pressure from below as his underside warms. The water becomes more plentiful. I chew the air. Here the sun is dim and I see by infrared, occasionally blinded by brief forks of lightning. The Orb tells me the storms continue and I register magnetic turbulence at many wavelengths. Ammonia snow falls upon me and vaporizes with a hiss. But for my sensors there would be no up, no down; I am suspended. Gales blow me a steady three hundred kilometres per hour to the west.

I first feel the throb on channel 107. A high infrasonic warble runs through me. It rises, steadies, lowers, then beeps and twists and slides away. I replay it, skewer it with analysis. The Fourier transform shows a smoothness my ear could not find. Frequencies melt into one another. Harmonics pile, cascade, blur into a lifting rhapsody. There is no coda; all stops at once.

I drop a robot probe. It tumbles downward into the thickening, scalding winds. It slips sideways as it falls and gives good angular separation from me. With two microphones I quickly measure the phase lag and find the source —it lies below me some twenty kilometres. It is hot there, but perhaps I can reach that zone.

Corey eases the purring of his fusion engine. He spills a bit of hot hydrogen gas from the balloon above him and the gondola begins to sink. He listens, ponders. The Orb angrily demands details and Corey swiftly spews back reams of data.

The high warbling sound comes again. Corey holds himself silent and lets the notes ripple through him.

A gust blows Corey to the side and the gondola cables

wrench fiercely, shuddering. I fire retrojets and negotiate the turbulence.

Adroitly I dance. Lean and lithe and young, I glide.

When the trouble is past, Corey's attention shifts to the sonic warblings. They return, stronger than before. But mired in these acoustic tremors, Corey notes a new phenomenon: the random rumbling of magnetic flux around the gondola now betrays a new coherence. Corey begins a cross-correlation analysis. From the stuttering noise he coaxes a clear, smooth harmonic line. It flips, complicates, spreads in dark harmonics. Corey notes a correlation with the acoustic signal. They are synchronized, though not the same.

As Corey sinks deeper into the hot, dense gases he ponders the growing signal. Now it overrides the magnetic fields of the planet itself. Are these the Alfven waves, flexing along magnetic field lines? But the signal is too strong for that. It is not a small perturbation. And if such waves are made near here, they must travel across the planet, everywhere, bringing these strange songs to all of Jupiter.

Corey feels the welling heat around him. The song draws him down . . .

Bradley looked up from the console sandy-eyed, fatigue seeping through him. "I don't have time to go back to my office for another of our little chitchats," he said sourly. Rawlins and the men behind him bristled visibly. "Say what you have to right here."

Rawlins glanced around at the crewmen in Monitoring. "It's a sensitive issue."

"There's a man down there feeling his way through the lower cloud decks," Bradley said. "My concern is him, not your fantasies."

"I've been elected to head this delegation—"

"I thought I sent Mr Tsubata to tell you to stay with the others. It's important we keep everybody off level A who doesn't absolutely have to be there."

"That's done," Rawlins said impatiently. He folded

his arms and glowered at Bradley. "But we can't just hole up in the safe parts of the Orb forever. I'm here with these men to demand that we lay down the law to Mara."

"What law?"

Bradley knew he had to make a show of authority here, but somehow the energy wasn't in him. He briefly contemplated placing Rawlins under arrest. But that would not stick for long and, anyway, he didn't want to exhaust all his political capital in one shot. No, he would have to depend on Mara.

"—is a renegade, and we—" Rawlins was saying something, but Bradley hadn't been tracking. He set his jaw into a stern line and waved Rawlins into silence.

"I agree, I agree. Why don't you talk to Mara yourself?" He thumbed his console over to an external circuit and punched into Mara's com-line.

"What is it?" her voice boomed angrily through the console speaker. "I can't listen to Corey and work and gab with you at the same time."

"We want to negotiate with you, Rawlins began.

"Oh, Jesus."

"We know you feel hostile toward us," Rawlins said smoothly. "And, admittedly, you do have an edge. You could ram us."

"Get this primate off the line, Bradley."

"We know you're different. We accept that." Rawlins's voice edged higher. "We sympathize with you, believe me. We may not know what it was like, not having real parents—"

"Hah! Have you disconnected your cerebellum, Rawlins? So I'm unlucky, not having "real parents"? It wasn't enough that somebody tinkered with my head, huh? I should have taken genetic roulette the way the rest of you were made?"

"Mara—"

"And I could've had a mother who really loved me and would guide me through life, tell me how to marry a rich man with a weak heart?"

Rawlins shifted uneasily and glanced at the men around him. "Perhaps if we came out to parley, could meet at some point away from the Orb—"

"Come out here and I'll knock you ass over entrails."

The speaker gave a distinct metallic click. Bradley smiled wanly and looked at each of the men in turn. It was an old device, but it worked; each pretended to be looking somewhere else.

"I think your negotiations are concluded. And I'll thank you to get back to your posts."

Corey dives. The insulating cup beneath me reddens with each descent until the overload circuits pop and I must return to the cooler upper reaches. Thin wafers float near me. They are waxen smatterings of complex carbon compounds. Ammonia, water, chlorine. Variable temperature, vicious updraughts, a persistent drifting current to the northwest. I swim, evade trapping vortexes, persist through cycling eddies.

As I search for the warbling signals time slides by. An Earth day passes. (Absurd measure of duration; nothing Earthly matters here.) I eat, listen for faint whispers, talk to Mara. She is isolated three kilometres from the Orb. Suspicious. Watchful. She laughs at Rawlins, but at times admits that she fears him. It is well for her to be apart from the Orb now. She needs separateness to work. That is the way she solved the northern African irrigation problem: total isolation, reassembling the worn facts into a form the engineers did not perceive. In the end Mara is always alone.

I swim through clouds of sleeting hydrocarbons. No free oxygen here. In the years before idiot robot probes had reported this, before they tumbled helpless into the heat deck below. Now I float through these low-energy chemical agents where the scientists are sure no animal life can persist. Active creatures require higher-energy reactions. So, too, do the voices from the Orb point out that the wavelengths I have observed in the warbling voices here are immense—hundreds of metres long. Far too large for any animals. So they are natural phenomena, and the Orb bids me to explore, measure, perceive this interesting event.

In the soft waxen snowfall I navigate, and the sonic ripplings come again. This time the magnetic pulse is large, not a mere fluttering on top of the noise spectrum. I follow it to the southeast, downward, muting my fusion reactor to drop swiftly. In this misty torrent infrared and opticals are blind, but the microwaves bring back granulated pictures I can perceive. Ahead small points flicker and dance. I approach. They are below me but I do not know how far.

Corey emits a sharp spike of microwave energy and waits for the rebounding echo. Range is only forty kilometres; she increases her fall. The steep descent takes him through a froth of white hydrocarbons as though she skis down alpine slopes. The gondola sways and creaks. A jolting bump comes as she falls through a pressure differential. The points below swell into grainy blobs.

Suddenly the clouds disappear and Corey sees that he has emerged from the face of a vast milky wall. A vortex churns here, swirling the cloud banks in long circular arcs a hundred kilometres in diameter. At the centre is a clear crystalline cylinder arcing up into heaven, a floor below of misty red. The infrared opticals swivel left, right, up—and Corey sees the source of the warbling.

Below float things like ball bearings. They seem motionless, suspended in the beautiful clear ammonia. They are small and give off a hot white sheen. An echo burst shows their true dimensions; they are at a range of nine kilometres and appear at least half a kilometre in diameter.

Immense spheres. A consequence of the vortex? The ribbed cloud banks on all sides churn slowly as Corey sinks. The spheres have not moved. Then she notices a small point: the spheres do not rotate with the majestic cloud barrier around them. They are still. Humming, Corey drops further toward them. As she approaches their design breaks and they move in strangely hyperbolic paths. They form a net. They are manoeuvring to Corey's stimulus. In this vast waxen tunnel they manoeuvre. They are alive. Like Corey.

* * *

"Jesus," Bradley said.

He thumbed over to Mara's channel. "Mara, talk to him. He won't pay any attention to us. Tell him to stay away from those things until we've had a good look at them."

"Ummmm. I think I'm beginning to make some sense out of this, Bradley."

"Call him!"

"Okay."

The line went dead. Bradley waited long moments. Around him the bridge stirred as technicians shouted back and forth at each other. They were recalibrating optical and microwave sensors to study the odd, rusty-brown balls Corey had found. There was a high air of revelry on the room, and Bradley knew he had to insulate himself from it. Technical matters he could leave to his staff; Corey was his problem. And Mara.

Her line hummed again. "He's backing off, he says."

"Good. I want him to get a good look at whatever those things are, and then boost out of there."

"Up above the cloud deck?"

"No. I mean lift free. Ignite the fusion motor and come back out."

"He's still got two more running days on his mission."

"He's done enough."

"You'll get an argument. From Corey for sure, and probably from me, too. But never mind that. Put me on to Vance, will you?"

"He's here." Bradley handed Vance the microphone. The young man took it with a slight hesitation, as though it were a snake that might bite.

"Vance here."

"I've got an idea we might work on. I think the Puzzle might be based on a different topological referent." Mara's voice lacked the usual cutting, illusive edge she took with Vance. Bradley leaned forward eagerly.

"Well, I've tried some—"

"I know, I did too. The point is there are too many choices to make, no way to single out anything. But those spheres—they have to be creatures, don't you agree?—made me think. They're probably bladder fish or something like that."

"Where's the bladder? I'm not even sure they're alive."

"Under high pressures a spherical shape is a good idea. Least surface, most volume. Best internal support against pressure differentials on the surface."

"Maybe . . ."

"I don't know why it didn't occur to me before. It's an obvious solution. Mother Nature didn't have to go that far on Earth, that's all. It was more profitable to make fins and teeth at the ocean bottom, and anyhow life on Earth never got away from bilateral symmetry, left and right."

"Okay, maybe. We'll check with the biologists. But—so what?"

"Imagine living down there. You're perfectly round. Your surroundings are just clouds and variable flows of gas and water vapour. If you float there's no real sense of up and down—not a sensitive one, anyway. Now, suppose you're Euclid. What kind of geometry do you make up?"

Vance smiled. "Well, I suppose—Lobachevsky. Riemann. Geometry on a curved surface."

"So how would you count things?"

"Well, in angular units, I guess."

"What *we* call angular units—that's the point. To them, angles would be the *natural* set of numbers. A simple choice would be to set pi equal to one."

"Sure, but—"

"Never mind trying it; I did. It doesn't work. So our friends must be a little more sophisticated. After all, the first chunk of the Puzzle is in ordinary rational numbers. That's how we could decipher it. But look at the picture —that circle arcing toward the left. Couldn't that mean that the code was shifting from ordinary linear number systems to a different topological notation?"

Vance frowned. "I suppose so. But which one?"

"I don't know. There are lots of places we could start."

"We can try algorithms. There may be some fundamental identity our notation system has in common with theirs."

Vance sat frozen, rapt. Bradley leaned over and watched the young man write quick clear notes on a pad.

$$e^{i\pi} = -1 \qquad f(\theta) = \sum_n a_n \sin n\theta$$

"I don't follow this," Bradley said.

"We'll go through it in detail later, Bradley," Mara said hurriedly. "Look at it this way. We measure the angles in a triangle one way, and we count apples another. Using one and two and three and so on seems natural to us, and angular coordinates—degrees, radians—aren't. But the Alpha Libra signals may have it the other way around though. They live in a universe of clouds, with no straight lines anywhere. So they sent the first part of their message in simpleminded notations, but then switched to 'natural' ways of talking when they got down to serious business. The metric of curvature is arbitrary—"

"Skip it," Bradley said. "Vance, patch her into the computer if she needs it. You two work together. I'm going to talk to Corey."

They beg me to desist. They are, of course, mere tinny voices—even Mara. Disembodied, like me.

But I need them. There is much to study here; I need time. I jab quick spurts of energy from the fusion reactor and the hydrogen balloon above heats and swells. Corey jerks upward with a brutal, swooping lurch. Up, through velvet currents. The gondola creaks like rotten wood and

Corey's body is pressed, sandwiched by many gravities. He feels the clotted pump of blood through him. He (it) (she) wonders if this heart, this brown clenching organ, is spherical as well—a rosy ball pumping at the centre of life.

Below, the mingling creatures recede. They still perform their elaborate waltz. The revolving cloud walls of the cyclone taper and draw nearer as I rise.

I flick my opticals and receive the image from atop my rising balloon. Above, a faint swatch of dark shows that there is nearly a clean break in the cloud cover. I can almost see the stars. But it is at least a hundred kilometres above, and I have no intention of going there.

I flow, steady. I balance delicate momenta in the swirling turbulence. There's a joyous pang to these movements; I pleasure in them.

I study the beings below. True, they move with ponderous slowness. They seem more like drifting seaweed, at best grazing cattle. They do not dance, quick and spirited, as I. They have never seen the stars, even in this deep cyclone pit that lances through the bank of cloud. They know only this confined world.

Corey pauses, receives the squirt from Mara, and ponders it.

Mara has sliced through, clean to the centre. She senses what it is like here; she has seen through my eyes. On a curved surface there are no Euclidean certainties. Triangles do not sum to 180 degrees. How this shapes the mind I do not know, for I am still closer to men than to these tranquil cud-chewers below me.

I monitor them. The magnetic field still shows their flux and rush. The high keening note washes over me again. I begin to analyse, compute, break the signal down into its component parts.

And I stop.

Perhaps this is not the core. Mara sees more clearly because she is not obsessed with details, as am I. I must relax and let things emerge of their own.

So doing, the bass rippling notes from below course

through me. I am loose and floating. I am running cool and smooth. The notes merge and I sense a song at last. It is a quiet strumming message. Calm. Serene. It echoes through my enclosure, finding there a ceramic certainty. The swollen harmonics gather new forces.

Instinctively I respond. Corey swings his radio boom to focus. My signal is thin and weak, but at this near range—

They hear! They echo my call. A long rumbling signal flexes through the magnetic lines around the gondola. It is a giant hand clasping me in the welling whiteness of this alien air. It is greater than anything I know.

VII

"I don't like the signals we're getting from him," Bradley said. He paused but Mara said nothing. "The messages are intermittent and some of them don't make much sense."

"Corey never made a great deal of sense," Mara said distantly. "But I see what you mean. I'll talk to him."

With that she broke off the connection. Bradley switched rapidly through several communication lines and listened to the thread of technical data that Corey was sending back. The spheres below him showed no signs of following to greater heights. They had registered the alien ship, to be sure, but their interest seemed weak; they would receive Corey but not follow.

Mara seemed unconcerned. Bradley knew she was working and this, for her, masked all other concerns. If she had concentrated her attention on it she might understand what was happening to Corey down there. There was so little time, though.

Bradley looked around the bay of Monitoring. There were staff members standing about, just watching, who did not belong there. The entire Orb was focused on Corey now. The biologists were filtering through the microwave, infrared, and optical signals for clues to what the spheres might be. Everyone was convinced they were living. Probably they fed off the ample hydrocarbons in that deep, dense layer.

And Vance seemed to be making progress with the computer search for a mathematical transformation.

And Mara, the essential unknown Mara, working alone, ignoring Corey, isolated with a writing slate and a computer link. Brushing aside Rawlins like a hopeless clown, though in fact he could be quite dangerous. Eventually he must be; Bradley knew Rawlins could be deflected for only a while.

"Bradley? I've got–no, wait, forward this to Vance." Bradley spliced the call into a recorder and forwarded it directly to Vance in Computing. "Tell him that series of alternating symbols on the left might be a conformal representation. Try a Lee sequencing in 3-space."

"That's all?" he said.

"It's enough."

"From Earth I hear—"

"Who cares?"

"They're going to have our heads over this."

"Quite literally, in my case."

"But you've got results. That will mean something."

"Not much, with them."

"Maybe."

"Dealing with politicians is like pissing into the wind. You never get anything back that you want."

"I'll keep trying."

"Ummm? Do."

She hung like a diluted point of light three kilometres from the Orb. Everything spun–Jupiter, the crescented moons, the frantic Orb. Mara alone was a point of stillness.

She wrote small squiggles on the erasable slate, and paused. In her helmet her breath made a dim, persistent syllable, the only punctuation to the clinging stillness. She sat in the pilot's couch, head bowed. In a small cramped handwriting she made more notes. The problem seemed to slip away and then came floating back to the edge of perception.

She sat for four hours without moving, staring at the slate.

Then she stretched, yawned, made a few more notations. She thumbed on her link to Computing and punched in instructions. Static crackled in her earphones. She called Corey on their private line and spoke in a muted whisper. Corey responded and promised to make the manoeuvres she sought.

Mara waited.

It begins to rain curling loops of hydrocarbons. Dollops of paste fall past Corey. They billow whitely around me in long filaments, as though spun from spools.

The gondola yaws as I take it down. We flip through the gnawing winds and fall below the misty hydrocarbon snow. The cyclone vent tunnels deep below me and the restless globes seem almost to float above the distant floor. Thirteen kilometres away the clouds revolve tirelessly. The ammonia cirrus is patchy, translucent, the veins of darker blue form faint tributaries beneath the skin.

I send the signal Mara asked me to. The spheres below reply; magnetic fields weave and shift. I study them in the optical, the microwave.

"You were right, Mara. There are long acres across their surfaces. Regular. Rectangular. Inside each band is a pattern of pentagons."

"That's how they broadcast. They form electrical current distributions over their surfaces. Otherwise a perfect sphere could not radiate anything."

"Their surfaces are antennas?"

"They're linked into the magnetic field, Jupiter's natural field, in that region. So when they ripple currents on their surfaces, the field lines carry the signal away."

"Thus they speak to each other. And to me."

"That's not all. Jupiter is rich in radio energy. They're

linked into that. They probably feed off it, as well as chewing up those waxy hydrocarbons you see. They eat radio waves, the same way plants consume light."

"They are coming nearer."

"Together?"

"Yes. There are six of them now. Average diameter one point three six kilometres. No, one point four one–they are expanding."

"Probably have sacs inside. They fill up with gas, just like you, then heat it and rise."

"Toward me."

"Better back off."

"I've got it," Vance said. He slapped a photo output in front of Bradley. "That transformation worked. I've got a decipherable message out of the next six thousand units in the Puzzle."

"What does it say?"

"Mathematical theorems, mostly. Seems to be building up basic concepts of length and angle. There's some sort of talking about motion and the idea of differential processes."

"Tell Mara."

Bradley turned to the bridge officer. "How far down in that cyclone pattern is he?"

"Pretty far, at least forty kilometres. We can't see the top of it. The topside-skimming satellites have got a Doppler on him. He seems to be falling, but there are a lot of unknowns in the data. He hasn't said anything lately. I can't get a damn thing out of him."

Bradley scratched his head and felt a seeping fatigue. "I think we ought to order him up and out."

They rise toward me with surprising speed. I hesitate, thinking it an illusion. But no, they execute an intricate gavotte even as they soar toward me.

I fire my fusion heater to maximum. It throbs above me in its separate cradle. My gas balloon heats and I lift away from the gathering globes.

*It is not enough. They float closer in the watery light.
Intricate patterns race across their dappled curvatures.
Their song races through me with a surging new
amplitude. I am caught up in it.*

*It is clear that I cannot escape them. No matter how
fast I rise, intersection must come within a few moments.
Can I evade them? I could dart to the side, using the remaining fuel in my lateral chemical rockets, or I could
begin the countdown for the fusion ramjet. No, there is no
time for the ramjet now. Should I weave away from them?
I do not know. The song fills my head with awesome
power. I do not know.*

"—I've calculated the total oscillator strength from a
large number of spheres. It's really impressive." Mara
paused and Bradley bit his lip in concentration. Vance,
sitting beside him, seemed lost in his own private calcu-
lations.

"So you don't think those spherical creatures communicate locally by rippling the magnetic field?" Bradley said.

"Well, it's a possibility. The important point is that
the signals from Alpha Libra *could* be made that way.
We know Jupiter gives off huge radio bursts every once
in a while. We've been listening to those radio thunder-
claps for over a century now. The point is, that's just
noise. But suppose some life form could tap that source
of energy. The same way a small transistor modulates
the output of a large power supply, say. They could im-
press a signal on it, maybe even direct it toward a particular spot in the sky."

"I suppose it's possible . . ." Vance began.

"It wouldn't take many of those spherical creatures to
do it, if they were intelligent. I calculated the total oscillator strength for a bunch of spheres, evenly spaced
around the planet. They could harness an immense
amount of radio energy and modulate it at will." Mara
spoke quickly, precisely.

"So there need not be any technology on a Jovian-type planet after all," Bradley said. "It could simply be use of a natural mechanism."

"That's the idea. Those beings down there, or whatever lives on a gas-giant planet in the Alpha Libra system, don't know beans about electronics. But they sense electromagnetic forces as a part of the ebb and flow of life. They know only fluxes of things. No chemistry, no physics–but they're so big they don't *need* to know."

"I have some objections—" Vance began.

An officer touched Bradley's shoulder. "Message from Corey. He's taking evasive manoeuvres."

"I'm slipping to the left, Mara. They don't seem to be able to move sideways as easily as up and down."

"They probably drift on the winds, more like balloons than fish."

"Mara, they're calling to me. There is something about the way the sound comes . . . Mara, Mara, what do I do?"

"Dodge. Charge your ramjet."

"It takes a minimum of five minutes."

"Head for the cloud banks. They might lose you there."

"The winds are fierce here. One of the globe creatures is coming nearer. Mara, they sing to me. I feel it through the magnetic flux. You humans do not have this input, it is so, so *different.*"

"Run for it, Corey!"

"I am, I am, but–I am a bisected being, Mara. So different from you. Both of us humans have changed but you, you are so much nearer them."

"Yes, but concentrate on what you're doing, Corey."

Through the crackle of static Mara strained to catch the tone of Corey's voice.

"I have always envied you. Your closeness to the humans."

"Goddammit, you're human too, Corey. Different, but human."

"No, I am something else. Like these creatures who are drawing up behind me, Mara. Their chords speak to me. To the second half of me, the part that envied you."

"Run, Corey!"

"I cannot run. I have no legs. I am the metal man."

"Goddammit, you—"

"That is why I damaged your air hose. And sabotaged your shuttlecraft."

There was a long humming silence.

"You did those things?" she said.

"You are the same as me but you had so much *more*."

Mara felt her throat contract until she could scarcely speak. "Corey, I—"

"I knew I would never return to Earth. I would never last out this scientific expedition. I envied you. I loved you. There was a way you had of undressing before me, Mara. Your nipples were like blind eyes. They never saw me. But I–I knew I would never live out this time between us. And I want us to go together, Mara, I am a man–a male."

Bradley leaned back at his console.

So he had been right. It was Corey. Apparently Corey didn't know he was broadcasting on open channel. Well, it didn't matter. Something was going to happen down there.

"How, how did you do it? I thought you had no mechanical ability."

"I look like a drifting piece of equipment. I went out the lock and moved slowly, so the men assigned to observe the centre of the Orb would not notice me. I waited. I sliced your air hose. I learned your shuttle and what to do to it."

"Fire the fusion ramjet!"

"Three more minutes to prime it. Three more, Mara."

The swollen globes filled the screen. Bradley leaned

forward, squinting, and watched the granular surface beat an elaborate cross-hatched pattern.

In the whale, he knew, sound comes from the nasal cavity and is focused by the fat deposits in the forehead. *How do you make these complex electrical signals play over your surface?* he wondered. *Are you like the whales —intelligent, but so alien we can never understand? If Corey is strange to us, how much stranger are you?*

VIII

"They are too close. I have tried the ramjet. It will not fire."

"Try again."

"I will–I–no, nothing."

"Corey, dodge them, dammit!"

"No, they are upon me. They sing, the melody is so . . . so intricate. It swells and falls, it has something I cannot describe."

"Corey!"

"The big one, it is so near. And we go together, Mara. You and me, we go together."

Bradley thumbed quickly over to Mara's com line.

"Mara! Pay attention! Jump."

"What? Corey says—"

"Jump, dammit!"

She had a sudden understanding. She undid the pilot's couch belt and pushed off from the shuttle. There was a clacking buzz of static in her ears and someone shouted over suit radio. She flicked on her manoeuvring jets and accelerated away.

There came a convulsive spark of pain in her left leg. She doubled up, clutching at it. Below she could see the shuttle, silhouetted against Jupiter's crescent. The rear section had splintered into fragments. A liquid-air bottle bloomed outward soundlessly. The debris rushed at her, a cloud of buzzing hornets. The awful cold stabbing in

her vision and then a darker violet film came between
her vision and then a darker violent film came between
her and the shuttle below. Something rasped against her
faceplate. There was a shattering impact against her
shoulder and the enveloping purple darkness swirled
around her.

They are hard upon him.
Corey fires his remaining manoeuvring fuel and lurches
to the southwest. Behind him the globes move surely,
smoothly, on great curved trajectories.
He dodges. For a moment he stills the fusion heater and
slides down the flat face of the wind. Still they draw closer.
One comes ahead of the rest. It is the largest and from
it comes a deep bass chord that vibrates through my small
crucible. It sings of migration, or mating, or some un-
fathomable purpose. In the eggshell light the enormous
creature floats with liquid grace.
A thunderclap seizes me, tosses me high. I am sucked
into new eddies. My circuit breakers overload–pop. There
is an acrid frying smell. In the burnished light I see the
large globe filling my view. Lacy strings of phos-
phorescence dance over its surface.
The fusion ramjet has not been brought to optimum,
but—
Between steel cables above me a brassy, twisted light-
ning forks. Many of my subsystems fail to respond. Servo
controls are sluggish, drowsy. A high panic seizes me.
I fire the ramjet.
Nothing.
Nothing happens.
I revive the backup system, integrate it with onboard
autopilot.
I fire again.
Still nothing.
I am drifting now, fuelless.
Around me, now forming an hexagonal figure, the
globular brothers sing. They call to me in their magnetic

voices. They swim in this strange sea: dolphins, whales, unbound. They carol of separate joys, each blurring into the basic pain of our separation from the centre of things. Their holy hymn consumes me. Searing flame dances at my sensors. There comes a loud booming cry. The bronzed lightning forks, surrounds. Turning, I—

IX

Bradley waited outside the air lock. The emergency medical team has rushed in to treat her as soon as she came through, carried by Tsubata. Norah Mann said the wounds were not too serious. There was no permanent damage.

Rawlins had come by for a moment, blustering, officious, wanting to place Mara under immediate arrest. Bradley had said some things–precisely what, he could not remember–using words more for their impact than for their meaning. That seemed to drive the other man, and the few who trailed after him, first into a grim silence and then, finally, back to their posts.

A young man came over to Bradley, murmured a few words and went away. They had found the fragments of Corey's ingenious trap; a small radio receiver, a minute chemical charge, barely enough to implode a spot in the liquid-air bottles. One last gift from the dying.

Bradley waited, hands held behind him, and blinked back the sandy feeling in his eyes. For some reason his downward vision was clotted, darkened. He could not resolve the seams in the deck. He knew people were gathering around the bay, watching him, waiting for news of Mara. He heard their whispered conversations, but he could not make out any detail. Yet the rising busy stir of these people, his people, warmed him. He wondered, with idle rationality, how many words were spoken each day inside the Orb. Millions, surely. Most of them trivial, almost all wrong in some sense, but every one vital. The universe outside did not care for words; that was not its language. It did not sense the verbal net each person cast out to others. So the Orb was an odd hollow point spinning amidst a great necessary vacancy. A place, a sense of shelter.

The lock doors parted. Mara was stripped to her briefs but she stayed upright, leaning on Tsubata's shoulders, and hobbled out. Raw red patches on legs, shoulders, belly were swabbed and already encrusting with crystalline protection.

The crowd in the bay exhaled a sigh as she appeared, a sound so dense it gained a visible presence among them. Everyone was talking, but Bradley fixed upon Mara and Tsubata and watched their painfully slow progress toward him. An aisle formed among the crew, keeping his vision unblocked. Mara's mouth hung slightly open as she breathed deeply and her face had a white pallor. Her eyes retained their fierce glint and they fixed on Bradley.

"They told me about Corey," she said as Tsubata brought them to a halt. "You can write off another experiment."

"Another man lost," Bradley said mildly. "Among many."

"One more technological fix for the human condition. And like all the others, it didn't work out." Mara said this without her usual undertone of bitterness. Despite the deep lines of fatigue in her face her eyes danced. Her lips described a wry, downward smile.

"Perhaps."

"Why do you always tinker with the mind, Bradley?" Mara said with sudden new energy. "Why not design people who can digest newspaper, or learn to use photosynthesis directly? Why jiggle DNA to increase intelligence? How can it possibly work? Hell, the humans who are doing it are defective–that's the reason for the project in the first place."

"I know."

"Yes, yes." Tsubata hugged her gently and Mara

seemed to relax into his grasp. People milled around the nucleus formed by the three, *ooh*ing and *ah*ing, inventing stories for each other. They were all a part of the entire matrix, Bradley thought, a wholeness. Out here, far from where they had started, there was an emptiness that could be filled only by the interlacing between people. A community.

"Come here, Bradley," Mara said. "I want to whisper something to you."

Bradley leaned forward primly, hands reaching out to steady her.

Impulsively she slid into Bradley's arms. She lifted her head to the side and placed her mouth on his, almost as though to stop him from talking any further. Her eyes crinkled with delight. It began as a simple kiss and then she slipped her tongue between the wrinkled lips and deep into his mouth. The warmth touched him; he blinked in surprise. Then, without thinking, he relaxed into the instant and took a veiled pleasure in it. And felt a curious familiar stirring in his loins.

She pulled back at last and smiled knowingly at him. "Indeed," she said.

She tugged at Tsubata and hobbled onward. The people parted before her. Bradley nodded to himself and in her swift movement he saw not a new dimension but a continuing, infinite parade that would–that must–leave him behind.

FIVE

2061

TITAN

An aged man is but a paltry thing,
A tattered coat upon a stick, unless
Soul clap its hands and sing, and louder sing . . .
                                        —*W. B. Yeats*

Outside, Titan tilted.

Bradley Reynolds watched impassively, letting the pitch of the Walker roll him in little oscillations on his bunk bed. He had wedged his neck into the pillow so that he faced squarely out the port. With the room lights darkened the Titan landscape gained detail and colour. He could make out jutting shelves of rock that broke through the reddish ice. Dingy snow clung in crevices, pocked with gravel. All was bathed in the penetrating red glow–the rolling cloud ceiling above, the glimmering pinnacles of ammonia ice, the weathered boulders.

The scene tilted again. The Walker settled with a pneumatic wheeze. Bradley recognized the heavy thump as the forward legs thrust jerkily out; they found a purchase and the Walker lurched forward. He felt the momentum damped by the shock absorbers, and then the rear legs swing ponderously forward, bringing the floor back to level.

A hell of a clumsy way to get around. How much easier in the fractional gravity and dense atmosphere to use the helicopters—jet-assisted, triple-sensor navigation, fast. The 'copters had opened Titan to full exploration, and Bradley had assumed he would visit a few of the crystal-lattice sites in them. But he had not reckoned with Najima, the nominal chief of Kuiper Base.

Bradley raised his eyebrows wryly; his instincts must be getting rusty. He had specifically announced that he was retiring to the compartment for a nap, knowing that Najima was bursting with frustration and would inevitably squawk too much to the others—and then, soothed by the gently rocking cradle of the Walker, he had actually dozed off himself. Good strategy, lousy tactics.

He lowered his legs over the side of the bunk bed. He had long ago developed a sense of possible danger all elderly people possess, a perception of unbalanced forces and moments acting through a fragile, brittle axis. Ankles, knees, the base of his spine—flaws in the armour. He spread his feet wide against the turgid sway of the deck and made three steps to the hatchway. The hatch swung back easily. He dogged it on the wall and peered through the gap.

The three of them sat in bucket chairs. Before them opened the transparent hemisphere of the Walker. The landscape seemed to curve and compress around them, refracted by the thick, transparent organiform port. As she studied the shifting terrain, Mara seemed pensive. Tsubata and Najima were talking. Najima alone manipulated the Walker's controls.

"—do not have a precise fix on the blowout point yet," Najima was saying in his clipped, breezy way. "If the sliding continues—"

"Enough to justify turning back?" Tsubata said.

"No. The subsidence is forty-three kilometres—" Najima pointed, "—that way."

"Not close enough for a fracture line to reach us?" Mara spoke dispassionately, with interest.

"We've never measured a fracture locus that large." Najima swivelled his chair toward Mara, and Bradley ducked hastily out of sight. "I wish we had. Then I could quite easily take this old man back to Kuiper and be done with him."

"You mean," said Tsubata, "you'd have a pretext then."

"A solid reason," Najima said stiffly. "I do not deal in pretexts."

"This whole Walker idea is a pretext," Mara said.

Najima bristled. "How?"

"You want to show off the part of Titan you've studied most," Mara said lightly, as though the answer were obvious. "So you pretend this clanking Walker is safer than a 'copter."

"If I must explain again—"

"Don't. I didn't buy that guff the first time and this trip proves me right."

"A Walker cannot tip over."

"No, but it can't *levitate*, can it? When a fissure opens under it?"

"Unlikely. Most improbable. And I object to your word, pretext. Where—"

"Look, Najima, I don't give a holy damn how—"

"—whereas I *know* 'copters can be dangerous now, when the storms are building."

"They have good pilots."

"We've lost four men and a woman. The winds—"

Mara snorted. "How many in Walkers?"

"Ah, a few."

"Or several?" Mara laughed and Tsubata, usually imperturbable, made a growling sound of mirth.

"Very well," said Najima. "In all, four. A rock ledge sheared away and crushed them."

"The prosecution," said Mara, "rests."

Najima ploughed on with an explanation, but Bradley turned and moved carefully back to his bunk, out of sight. It was amusing to hear Mara at work on Najima, but he had already guessed nearly all of what they'd inadvertently revealed. He lowered himself tenderly into the welcoming embrace of the bunk. He was looking out the port again, at a weathered brown pinnacle, when the voices suddenly swelled in volume.

"All *right*," Najima was saying sharply. "I *am* trying to keep close tabs on him. For his own good."

"To be sure he doesn't collapse on you," Tsubata said gruffly.

"Of course. His death here would reflect badly—"

"How bothersome," Mara said sarcastically.

"—on all of us," Najima finished pointedly.

"What you don't follow, Najima, is that Bradley is here for personal reasons, not as an official inspection," Mara said.

"But he *said*—"

"A pretext. You didn't invent deceit, you know."

"For what?" Najima sounded genuinely puzzled.

"He doesn't give a damn about the efficiency of Kuiper Base," Tsubata said.

"Or your executive talents," Mara added. "He wants to see the lattice. That's all."

"We send holographic—"

"No pictures. Bradley wants the experience. He has an odd way about these things. He . . ." Her voice teetered uncertainly.

"Reynolds can *frange* his tourist impulses," Najima said savagely.

"He's your boss, legally," Tsubata said with a gravelly assurance.

"We're halfway across the solar system from the Orb. Why should anybody around Jupiter tell me what to do on Titan?"

"It's all the same research project," Mara said.

"Completely different," Najima said, blandly certain.

"Spherical whales in Jupiter, superconducting crystals on Titan–it's still *life*," Mara said.

"We don't *know* they're superconducting," Najima said. "Not everywhere in the matrix."

"You have a genius for sliding away from the point," Mara said.

"What *is* the point of this?" Najima said angrily. "Coming here, wasting my time? I thought I had to make a good impression on this old man if I wanted to get a bigger budget. Hell, twenty-eight men operating out of Kuiper Base cannot—"

"Before you fuse off," Mara said, "remember that we didn't want him to come out here either."

"You are right," Tsubata said. "He is too old for this."

"You should have stopped him," Najima said.

Mara shrugged. "He wanted it. All the way out under high boost, with his joints aching and unable to move around in a half gee, he talked about Titan. Even when he received a message from Earthside—"

Mara's abrupt halt brought a silence filled by the heaving thump of the Walker's ponderous progress.

"Go on," Najima said. "What did the message—"

"How long has that hatch been open?" Mara said, her voice rising.

Bradley heard the thump of boots crossing the deck and immediately shut his eyes. He sensed a presence at the hatchway. "It's all right," Mara said in a stage whisper.

He rolled over and said in a blurred voice as though from sleep. "Come in."

Mara grinned, the expression filling her face with compressed energy. She stepped in and dogged the hatch.

"A very neat dodge," Bradley said.

"What . . .?"

"Deflecting his attention after you gave away the fact that we got that squirt from Earthside."

"It was that obvious?"

"To me, yes. But you're not exactly transparent. You never told me you'd read that transmission. It was clearly labelled for my eyes only."

"Well . . ."

"Never mind. So you know they've ordered me back."

"Yes. But they had no right when you were halfway to Saturn to pull the rug—"

"They have every right. I didn't tell them I'd left the Orb until we were out of Jupiter orbit."

"But to recall you for this *one* infraction—"

He smiled and waved a brownish spotted hand in the air. "Merely an excuse. The Anti-Senility Acts prevented them firing me outright, even with Rawlins's reports in hand. But to leave the Orb? Take an unauthorized passenger flight on the regular supply shuttle to Titan?" He made a clucking noise with his tongue and shook his head sorrowfully. "They have me, Mara. I'm a plucked goose." He boosted himself up in the bunk, grunting, and the sallow slack folds of his face formed a wry smile. "This is as far as I'm going to get. Not bad, really–the outer limit to humanity. The farthest spot from Earth. I've always had a certain curiosity about Pluto, but that can wait. There may be other lifetimes, you know."

"They *can't*—"

"They can. Most easily."

"What will you do?"

"Go back. It was a fluke that I got to the Orb at all. I required this job as a condition of my support and testimony for the project."

She leaned against the seamed blue bulkhead, arms at first folded tightly under her breasts, then hands moving to her hips and then securely wedged behind her, snug in the twin spaces between the wall and the small of her back. "You can't be sure. Maybe they'll ask you to step down and take a lesser role."

"Mara, life is the art of drawing sufficient conclusions from insufficient data. I know how this is going to come out."

"But you were the one who brought us together in just the right way. So we could crack the Alpha Libra puzzle."

"So? Now they have what they wanted."

"There's so much more. We've got some math out of the Alpha Libra stuff, sure, but—"

"The most important point is to know we could decode it at all. That tells us there are basic similarities between intelligences."

"They can't simply impose a new director on us from outside."

"They won't. They're too smart."

"Who then?"

"Maybe you, Mara."

She gave a sharp barking laugh and began pacing the pie-shaped room. In the enamelled light she seemed to Bradley to exude a penned energy. The deck surged underfoot from the Walker's slow, thumping stride. "Not me. Rawlins, yes. That I could see."

"I've pretty well finished him off," Bradley said. A flush of self-pride surprised him. Until this moment he hadn't realized how past abrasions had been stored, collecting bile, for the moment when he could see Rawlins as a distant, defeated enemy. To regard a score as settled was a sure sign that, somewhere deep inside, the game was over. *I grow old, I grow old, I will wear my trousers rolled,* he thought. It had been decades since he'd read Eliot–an adolescent enthusiasm–but the lines sprang too easily to mind.

He felt a settling quiver in the Walker. Something odd in the cadence made Mara halt her pacing. Abruptly someone was banging on the hatch, making a muffled, indecipherable shout. Mara swung the hatch free and Najima stood framed in it. "Dr. Reynolds, I . . . come look."

Bradley rolled off the bunk again. He took it swiftly and landed with a too-casual grace. The deck had stilled and luckily he made it; he strode with erect certainty to his swivel chair. "What's on?"

"There," Najima said simply. His finger was unneeded; a ruddy blister towered on the horizon. White clouds roiled upward from its nippled peak. As they watched, fresh gouts belched from the mottled skin. Dark clusters like grapeshot spewed out with the escaping gas, arcing high into blunted parabolas and then showering downward through the thinning clouds. *Black seeds against the moist flesh of a sliced apple,* Bradley thought. "An ice volcano," he said.

"Precisely," Najima said. "We knew there was unrelieved stress in this area, of course. But these things cannot be predicted. You do understand?"

"I do."

"We must turn back at once—"

"No."

"My concern is with your—"

"I said *no*."

Najima swivelled his chair and assumed a patient, relaxed air. He laced his fingers and studied Bradley with eyes that glimmered like small black beads. Bradley tried to think of his best move.

"You're not worried about the lava, surely?" Bradley said. Often it was better to give an opponent a simple question to answer, to gain time for thought.

Najima accepted the bait and launched into a thorough explanation of the eruption mechanism. Titan was a massive snowball, the crust frozen, a kernel of rock at its centre. Between these solid boundaries was a great slush of dust, ice, and liquid. Compression and the sputtering decay of radioactive dirt gradually warmed some regions in the snowball. Hot liquid percolated upward, pressing, and gushed forth in a lava of running methane, ammonia, and water.

"Scarcely dangerous," Bradley said. "Hot by Titan's standards, granted, but still at least fifty degrees colder than we are."

Najima shook his square, close-cropped head. "The boulders flung out—"

"We don't seem to be in their vicinity," Bradley said, with his there's-a-good-fellow voice. "I can see them rolling down the flanks."

Najima's smooth dun face took on a veiled, knowing

look. "Then you can see the cracking."

Bradley squinted through the thick organiform at the volcano's snout. Beyond the nearby hills, alabaster clouds writhed upward into the unchanging deck of pink. Around the curiously bloated peak, thin filaments worked down the slopes. As he watched, a few of the lines thickened. Gas puffed from one. The volcano seemed to be straining to be free of its encrusted skin, bulging and bloated. "Faults in the ice," Bradley said.

"If we fall into one . . ." Tsubata began.

"We can navigate around them," Najima said with clipped certainty, his face a sudden mask.

"Not if they open under us," Bradley said. He smiled to himself. He was certain that Najima had intended to use the fissures as an excuse to turn back toward Kuiper Base. But the argument cut both ways, as Tsubata had anticipated and subtly indicated: any movement, toward or away from the volcano was dangerous.

Najima tilted his square head at an awkward angle, as though thinking. "Well, there is always—"

"I would suggest—realizing, sir, that this craft is of course still under your command and I am but a passenger— that we hold fast until this disturbance has subsided." Bradley spread his hands warmly.

"We can't," Najima said.

"We have supplies . . ." Mara began helpfully.

"Yes, but in a hostile environment it is foolish to run low. As we would, if we stayed here very long." Najima sat forward earnestly, his calculating mask forgotten in the desire to focus on the problem. Bradley reminded himself that Najima was, after all, an engineer first and an administrator a very poor second. "This site is not safe," Najima went on. "We rest upon an ice sheet laced through by rock. It could split."

"Not soon?" Bradley said.

"I cannot possibly predict such a thing."

"I propose we strike out for firm rock, then," Bradley said.

"I could call a 'copter—"

"To land on ice? That might be dangerous in itself."

"I doubt that point."

Bradley allowed his face to pinch into a cool, distant look. "How often have you tried it?"

"Why, never. We avoid such situations. As we have been instructed."

"Then you have no experience."

Reluctantly: "No."

"I am still your commander, Mr. Najima."

Najima looked from Mara to Tsubata to Bradley. Technically Najima remained in charge here. But there is a psychological force often stronger than legalisms, and the oppressive silence of the three made Najima's eyes slide away from direct contact with Bradley's. He cleared his throat with a deep grumble and said, "I believe I take your point, sir."

"Way Station Four is not too far from here," Bradley said neutrally.

"We can put in there?" Mara said.

"*All* our stations are secure," Najima said. He was studying Bradley, as though not quite able to keep up with the drift of things. "You seem to know a great deal about our operations, sir."

"I always do my homework," Bradley said. He kept his voice even and remote. Above all, he could not let Najima know how much hung in the balance here. If the man became suspicious he might very well beam a query Earthward. If that happened, the precious few days Bradley had left would shorten still more, and events would enclose them all.

The Walker made good time as it angled away from the seething volcanic dome. Bradley pretended to need a rest again and returned to the pie-shaped section that was their bunk room. The Walker was a dome atop hydraulics and rocker arms, with the control cabin taking half the dome space. The rest was sliced into three storage and personnel rooms. It was an interesting commentary on humankind, Bradley thought, that the designers opted for separate rooms even though each had to be so small. Offhand, the claustrophobia of living constantly inside, sealed away from the grit and feel of Titan, would seem to call for large rooms, a feeling of airy space and expansiveness. But people wanted privacy even here. The abrasions of continual contact proved too exhausting.

Small, small gestures in the face of the alien, he thought.

Bradley peered out the waxen transparency of the port and tried, against the waddle of the Walker, to find what he had come so far to see, the great ambiguous crystal lattices that spanned Titan. They were common near here, he knew. The Titan orbiter had missed them entirely. Beneath the crimson-brown blanket of clouds, the white filaments spun a seemingly random web. Early speculation had focused on Titan as a chill, primordial soup rich in methane and ammonia. The lattice did seem to incorporate some oily chain molecules, but there the analogy with Earth ended. The crystal was a simple monoclinic array in some spots, shading into complex interlocking matrices as the white strands wove through ravines and ice fields. The first manned expedition had sprinkled yellow dye near the lattice. Weeks later patches and dabs of lemon oozed forth kilometres away. There was digestion of sorts–subtle degradings of the oils the men injected–but no sign of how the energy was used. Conceivably it provided electrical power for the occasional bursts of jittery currents that laced across Titan, but even that single, simple point was still uncertain.

Bradley lay back, tired of squinting. Najima and the others at Kuiper Base expressed continual surprise in their reports at the failure of their experiments. Devising clear, accurate checks required a working hypothesis. But even more crucially, experiments demanded that the scientific method apply in the first place.

After Jonathon's frenzied dance, after Corey's mad

fall, Bradley was no longer so sure. Each discovery had come from the raw edge of human experience, not the warm comfortable spot near the orange glow of humanity's campfire.

Was there a moral here? Revelations and how he had hungered for them, without recognizing the appetite– came from the unexpected vector. The consensus reality was barren.

The Alpha Libra Puzzle was not proving logical to the last comma. And Jonathon's preposterous love of circles, the perfect curves–reasonable, given one premise as absurd as rheumy old Plato's tinkertoy rules, but without it . . . No, there had to be a middle ground, he sensed.

Then . . . perhaps his meditations in North Africa, however calming, were a deflection from what he really sought. To find that thing defined by a dimly sensed void, should he try to catch the unexpected? Should he try to glance, crafty and quick, out of the corners of his eye?

Mara opened the hatch a fraction and peeked in expectantly. Her arched eyebrows seemed to lift her face into an expression freshly minted; he had never seen it before. A concern, unknowingly condescending, for this addled old wreck bound on his overearnest mission?

"Come in," he boomed. "There's a limit to how much I can sleep."

"Sleep, was it?" She dogged the hatch shut. "I don't believe that."

"Oh?"

"You're figuring how to sidestep Najima. How to deal with him if he decides to turn back."

Bradley grinned. She had guessed one reason, but not the more desperate one. He said, "I don't think he will turn back."

"Check. He's daunted by you and doesn't want you to break a leg while you're under his wing. He'll hole up in Way Station Four until the volcano dies. Or until Earth denies you permission to be on Titan at all."

"Najima doesn't suspect that I'm in trouble Earthside?"

"He may."

"Did he say anything to you?"

"Only that he didn't like your showing up suddenly. He thought Titan was just getting supplies from the Orb."

"That's what I wanted him to believe."

"So that he wouldn't have time to complain Earthside?"

"That, and figure out a way to keep me confined to Kuiper Base."

Mara sat on the end of his bunk. Her brow wrinkled, as though she sought to see in the prism of his last sentence some converging inner part of him, his true essential spectrum. "You're getting pretty Byzantine, Bradley."

"By not telling Earthside I was coming to Titan?"

"Yes. That was dangerous."

"A gamble."

"What's so damned important about this iceball? The Zeta message is the crucial—"

"Mara, Mara. How did we decode the Puzzle, after all? The conventional wisdom is that you learn about the universe by looking through a telescope."

"Sure, A radio telescope."

"What we finally saw we got by looking in a mirror."

"Well . . ."

"See what's happening to the Zeta message? A new branch of science is pushing out of the womb. Did you see that breakdown we got last month?"

"The first nonmathematical element?"

"Yes."

"I'm not sure what it means."

"*Nobody* is. One school of thought renders those squiggles as–how does it go?"

"The phrase is, 'Ability to confer survival benefits in

an enlarging manner upon another being.' That's a crude translation."

Bradley smiled. In the viewing port he caught his pale reflection and was reminded of often-folded butcher paper, a web of worn crinkles. "Why not translate it less crudely as *love*?"

"Um. Possibly."

"Eventually the message will raise questions like that. There'll be specialists fighting over the poetic reading versus the practical one. Whole university departments, conferences, doctoral theses—"

"I don't see how Titan can help."

"Why by giving us a new *context*," Bradley said, surprised that his point had been missed. "We can't measure ourselves by some illusion of uniqueness. It's people like Rawlins who believe in rigid definitions–his fear of you lies in simple ignorance. And it's our job to expand definitions until even Rawlins himself can no longer use them for camouflage." He folded his dry, speckled hands across his belly and felt a cozy drowsiness begin to seep into him. *And to find even in the alien,* he thought, *a forgiving soul.*

Hours later, Way Station Four ignited its exterior lights on command, a welcoming flare in the ruddy Titan day.

A rust world, Bradley thought. A thin fraction of the visible spectrum filtered through the shroud above, giving the humped land a glow of rot. Framed by the flare, the Walker cast a shadow like a marching spider on a nearby slate-grey valley wall. Its clanking feet stirred puffs of dust as it backed into the station's air lock.

Najima powered down and secured the control panel. He glanced over at Bradley. "I thought I would save you the trouble of suiting up. Our rear lock connects directly into the station."

"Thank you, but all the same, I—" Bradley stopped, realizing that the less Najima thought about the fact that

Bradley carried a Titan-rated suit, the better. The illusion of helplessness would be helpful. "Are those white lines the lattice?" he said conversationally.

"Yes, I believe so. They are thick around here."

From the rear of the Walker there came the wheeze of the lock cycling and a sudden gust of bitterly cold air. Bradley shivered. The blue collar of his jumper waved limply in this fresh breath of Titan. The Walker's insulation was good, concealing the fact that the tumbled and frosted landscape outside was a hundred degrees below the freezing point of water. Dabs of pink ice speckled the hill; on Earth they would have blossomed into a burning gush of ammonia vapour.

Tsubata's dry voice called out that the station was secured. Najima swung out of his chair, but Bradley held up a palm. "We're on a sort of rock island, aren't we?"

"A ridge jutting up through the ice, yes." Najima's blocky head waggled in agreement. "You needn't worry –these sites are the most stable on Titan. Kuiper Base is simply the largest of them."

"They *could* sink."

"Unlikely, sir. These valleys have a long life."

"Like dirt in an iceberg."

"I suppose. But it is a spherical iceberg and the ocean is *inside*. This makes the crust relatively stable."

Bradley nodded. Given a chance, Najima's mitigating mildness broke through the varnished base-commander manner. Bradley's show of caution brought out a softer side in Najima, and during the days of confinement in this station he could work on that facet. Unless they all relaxed and dulled their edges, trouble lay ahead.

"I suppose the lattice knows this?" Bradley asked mildly.

"You *assume* it knows. That it is sentient."

"As an hypothesis."

"Unproven. We have no evidence of neutral—"

"Why are they clustered in the safe areas?"

Najima's olive face furrowed. "Why, they are mostly

silicates and metallic elements. It seems natural that geological forms arise—"

"—where their building blocks are abundant," Bradley finished for him.

"Of course."

"Couldn't the crystal evolve to seek out the safe areas?"

"The idea that electrochemical processes in the lattice represent life—"

"—is unfashionable," Bradley said. "So were trousers once. But what could be more reasonable, if the crystal matrix can sense the tiny shifts in Titan crust?"

"How do we know it can?"

"We don't. If long ago there was a slight survival benefit in knowing where the land would slip and splinter, that's an evolutionary mechanism."

Najima's hooded eyes brightened. "How did you know the crystal moves?"

"I didn't. There's nothing in your reports—"

"We are not sure. We do not like to make claims before the measurements are complete."

Bradley chuckled. "Okay. Now, what's the preliminary result?"

"Some of the long chain molecules appear to trigger a slippage in the crystal planes. This propagates through the entire structure, like a ripple, and moves it a few millimetres within a year."

"So the crystal strands *can* migrate. The better it perceives its surroundings and understands them, the safer it becomes."

"But the crystal is *one* thing," Mara said, Bradley looked up. She had clearly been standing behind him and enjoying the argument. She stood hipshot and challenging, her black hair gleaming in the Walker's enamelled light, her red lips like a dark emphasis.

"So?"

"*One* creature can't evolve," she said. "It doesn't pass on genetic material to any children. No reproduction, no selection."

Najima appeared relieved at this sudden help from an unanticipated quarter. "That is most reasonable," he said.

"Conventional wisdom again." Bradley felt suddenly weary. "Suppose each filament of the lattice is a child?"

Mara frowned. "There's no evidence . . ."

"These are *groundless* speculations," Najima said, with earnest seriousness, and Bradley now understood why he made a good, solid leader out here. "What we need, sir, is more data. For that—"

"—you require more resources," Bradley said. "A syllogism I may have stumbled across before, just possibly." He sighed. "Shall we ponder the matter over dinner?"

The cookers fired, a meal emerged: a braised pancake of stuff, chewy; cranberry cakes; a lemon froth with a curious aftertaste of chalk. There was talk over the central table, and then the familiar clatter and swishing sounds of the washup. The homely air of this ritual made human the double-domed spaces of the station, drew the four together. The station approximated a sphere, to give the greatest volume for the least surface area exposed to the lashing winds of Titan. There were two levels, the upper (and warmer) for quarters. Here, too, the need for privacy ruled; each person occupied a narrow cell of his own.

After the meal, conversation lagged. Tsubata selected a film to read; Mara went for a long steaming bath; Najima wandered the station, idly checking the equipment. The ceramic walls were hung with wrenches, low-temperature grapplers and calipers, taped hammers, snub-nosed pliers, intricately sprocketed and socketed devices whose function Najima clearly knew but Bradley could only guess. The work areas were cluttered, as every place is which has no one man responsible for it. Loops of brass, milled and threaded chunks of metal, chips and curls of gleaming copper, odd tangles of wiring, slabs of microcircuitry–all were strewn through the working shops. Najima arranged, sorted, filed, stored. The tide of clutter receded.

Then, boots clanging on the steps, Najima went below, to the supply and communications level. Bradley chewed his lower lip. There was nothing he could do but wait.

Lifting himself free of his chair, he glanced at the large, shimmering view-screen. The even twilight of Titan stirred with wind. Cloaks of dust blotted the horizon.

Turning, he went into the cramped quarters of his room and closed the door. The Walker was docked at the ground floor, where Najima was prowling now. Bradley reviewed the layout of the station, but nothing suggested itself. He thought of sleep, of searching out Mara for talk, of eating some of the station's reserve food for energy. But he lay down and began studying a map of the station's vicinity instead.

Hearing Najima's knock, Bradley tucked the map away before answering. He wanted the psychological equality of being on his feet.

Najima's face clouded as he stepped inside. "We should speak alone," he said tensely.

"You called Kuiper." It wasn't a question.

"They have received a directive from Earth," Najima said formally. Bradley sensed that the man was unnerved, and this stiff manner served to keep Bradley at a comfortable distance.

Bradley said nothing.

"You lied to me."

"I did not."

"You said you were on an inspection visit. An official—"

"I *implied* it was official."

"You let the implication stand without correcting it."

"So I did."

Najima put his hands on his hips and glared at Bradley. "Earth did not know you were coming until you

were near Titan. When they ordered you to return to the
Orb and then Earthside, you sent a signal saying you
would."

"And I will," Bradley said mildly.

"Earth did *not* authorize a Titan landing. You were to
remain in orbit."

"True."

"Then for three days I have been running unnecessary
risks. If you had died on the surface, under my responsibility—"

"I know. I apologize."

"You are too old for this, Dr. Reynolds. Go
Earthside. You are a–a madman."

"I know. A madman." Bradley felt the words loft
free, emptying him of this last charade. "A stark, raving
madman."

Lying in bed that night–artificial night, of course, for
Titan's ruddy glow never varied–when the bleached lights
finally dimmed, Bradley listened for the sounds of settling in from the other three.

Tsubata first, Mara only a moment after. He ought to
talk to her, he wanted to, but the session with Najima
had sickened him of words. All his life he had sought the
rough, true feel of things, instead of the halos of words
that surrounded reality. The essence, the core, the thing
behind the symbols: that was what he wanted. Not more
words, reports, arguments.

He was sure he would not find anything solid
Earthside. Najima would turn back tomorrow, if the
volcano wasn't actively spewing its icy wrath. Back to
Kuiper, then on the waiting shuttle. A shallow ellipse to
the Orb. A longer one for Earthside after that, and the
madman would be tucked into a snug pigeonhole.

He would retire into the embalming opulence of Luna
or the satellite cities. Below, a Spartan Earth would undoubtedly carry on with the Alpha Libra Puzzle and
with Titan. The madman might watch, no more: peer

downward at a bulging blue-white planet. Disconnected, dessicated, dead. An old man hooked to a humming life-support module, watery eyes tracking the fabricated action on a 3-D, slumped into a cushioned world, stroking a collie dog in his lap. Contentment. Reward. An ending.

No. *No*.

Najima still stirred on the upper floor of the station. Bradley closed his eyes to rest a moment. He'd slept as much as possible in the Walker, knowing he might need it, and now he did.

Sounds receded. He dozed and sleep took him unaware.

He woke slowly, sensing himself free of his body. Bradley drifted for one teetering moment, something in him questioning whether he should slide back into the battered, wrinkled carcass prone between the sheets, or elect to loft outward, toward some new and cloudy destiny. Framing the question so, the gaudy hums and splashes of life swelled up in him: the grainy texture of the firmly resisting material world; the delights of companionship, of a simple talk over a brimming sludge of coffee; of work, and of rest after work. All spread out before him as at an immense feast, a fest, as something to be seized and won each day. He woke to the competent whir of the air circulators, his waking an act of will, as though he had relaxed his grip on an anchor and now drifted lazily up, finally bobbing to the surface.

It was time. (Yes, no denying that) Time was it. Time. Time. Time.

He got up and cracked the door and let it hang open a centimetre. No sound. The station lights burned low. He invaded the shadowed corridor.

At the next door he paused and listened. He had a sudden vision of Mara and Tsubata entwined just inside this doorway, smooth limbs among the knotted bedclothes, a union he had to some degree arranged. Had he seen in Tsubata the fresh, the practical, and

nudged Mara in that direction? It was not accidental
that these new men were often from Asia, at least cul-
turally, and came with a sure grace into a world once
made gaudy by the West. They were part of the pend-
ulum swing of human history: East, West, East, West.
Perhaps Titan would ultimately yield to such men. But
at another level Bradley was not so sure. The East
lacked one quality the West possessed–was it brashness
or simple stupidity?–and he feared that element might be
the key to what lay hidden here.

He shook himself free of the mood and shuffled down
the corridor. He moved cautiously. The stairs descending to ground level rang faintly beneath his hushed feet.
He crossed the circular lower bay, weaving through
stacked equipment. In a sunken rectangle an engine
hung, an immense metal baby ready for washing and
diapers.

Bradley reached the spot where station and Walker
were mated, and paused. Was that faint, occasional
chugging coming from above, from a restless Najima?
He strained to resolve the sound. The medica insisted
their arts kept his hearing as good as a man of thirty, but
he knew he now missed the low, ponderous notes in music, and probably other sounds: thin whispers, distant
conversations.

Unconsciously he put out a hand and was startled at
a sudden stab of cold. The wall of the bay retained its
customary chill; the station had not yet fully warmed for
its guests. The station spent long months at Titan tem-
peratures, a piece of this world, its very air a liquid soup
stored in tanks.

The sound had not returned. Bradley knew he could
not hear well enough to detect pursuit, not once he entered the Walker. Very well; there was no going back
from here. He went through the Walker lock and directly to the suiting area.

The Walker was built for flexibility, including the
chance that an injured or weakened crew member might

have to go out into Titan alone. Four suits were racked on smooth-swivelling braces. Bradley swung his in an arc until it clipped onto the self-suiting platform. The suit was bulky with insulation and moved ponderously.

Bradley backed into its enfolding grip. The S-suit liner sealed snug. He jackknifed over to worm his arms backward into their tubes. Tensing, straining, he worked his head into the neck ring. Even though the rack supported the suit and automatically slipped it about him, its embrace had the quality of shaking hands with a corpse. He stood, pushed a button, and the rack zipped him up the spine. His helmet lowered gently into the neck ring. A last quick shove; locks snapped and clicked home.

Bradley methodically checked his interior systems and rested for a moment. On suit radio there came the mindless peeping of the station homing signal, but no other traffic. No point in waiting, he told himself; he freed the suit from its rack; its weight settled on his shoulders like a blanket. He took a step, then another. An ankle protested. Still, he could manage. His burdened carcass shambled forward.

Safer, far safer, to exit through the Walker's smaller lock. He went to the cylinder head that thrust up from the Walker floor and punched in instructions. A slow cycle rate; that kept down the pump noise. Inside this suit he could hear nothing, but the Walker probably absorbed most of the lock's sounds before they escaped into the station. Or so he hoped. The crucial point was getting away from the station unobserved, so they would not know which way to follow.

The lock light winked over to green. Bradley popped the lid, which tilted smoothly back, and climbed awkwardly into the mouth of the lock. He triggered the cycle and waited as the nurturing human air leaked away. With a gush he felt through his boots another presence came into the lock: Titan's thin chill breeze, slightly cloudy. Then the lower door opened and he stepped out onto the face of the alien.

He felt a leap of joy at getting free of the station's stale space. Even more, he had been right: this world was a new place, fresh and oddly sparkling, viewed this way. The thick port of the Walker had warped and refracted this frozen gallery of a world, like an aquarium that distorts fish into bulging, artless creatures. Now he was free of it.

He stepped out from under the sheltering circle of the Walker, shedding its roof. The mottled sky pressed down. A brittle ground crunched underfoot. Rumpled hills beckoned. Something stirred at his feet and Bradley was surprised to see a little whirlwind turning a few metres ahead of him. In it whirled bits of dirt, flakes, a swirl of ice. A circular presence outlined itself by its cargo. It sprang high, sucking at the ground, moving away from Bradley. He walked forward and through it, half expecting to feel the brush of its wind. When he looked back the circular dance was gone.

He looked at the dim ports of the station and the Walker. No movement. No face peering out, shocked, white eyes widening. Only the exhaust grilles, slashed in the station's walls, turned upward in a frozen expression of startled dismay.

A wind churned through the clearing around the station, fleeing a dark edge at one horizon. A storm might be kindling. If it grew strong enough Najima would not be able to call in helicopters to search for him. A good sign, but first Bradley had to get clear of the station.

He marched away, deliberately pacing his steps with his shallow breathing to set up a pattern. He headed uphill. He had memorized the map of this area and guessed that the Walker could not negotiate the ridge line four kilometres away, upgrade. If they pursued him in it they would have to take the long way around, paralleling the ridge until a break came six kilometres to the north. By that time he should have reached the thickest part of the lattice lines, just over the peak of the ridge.

Eddies of frost swooped through the air. To Bradley

the land glowed with its own light far brighter than it had appeared from inside the Walker. The cloud banks above diffused their dim radiance evenly, ladling out the energy that filtered from the unseen sun. Titan had a night side, slightly chillier, but light warped through the dense air to banish any true night. It was impossible to see even Saturn, looming banded and bright, through the cloud deck.

Bradley glanced back; the station was hidden behind a pitted hummock. The ground here was dark and metallic, like an iron loam. His boots scuffed up fine powder. He could hear only his own sighing breath and the occasional rock and wheeze as his suit adjusted. He could see this world, but not smell or hear or feel or taste it. The alien under glass.

He splashed through a puddle. It seemed like water, but a droplet that spattered on his faceplate steamed away immediately in a curl of smoke. Ammonia? He clicked on his flashlight and its lemon beam bobbed and leaped on the violated face of the pond. He switched off the light, lest the station have some way of seeing this far, and the land around him dimmed for a moment by contrast.

Bradley marched on, heart thumping. The uphill going was harder than he'd thought it would be, even in Titan's light grip. It struck him as improbable that such a moon, with only slightly more gravitational acceleration than Luna, should have inherited a thick atmosphere. The terrible chill was the secret: the sluggish methane and hydrogen seeped out of the gravitational bottle slowly. Inside his thick insulation Bradley felt only the reassuring rub and stretch of the S-suit. He paused for a moment to urinate into his suit pouch, panting slightly. He had a fantasy in which he popped the suit open and peed on Titan directly. Where it struck, the yellow stream would freeze instantly and the cold would spread, racing up the stream, a thin pale column turning crystalline in a flicker, the ammonia in solution perhaps sputtering free as the cold reached the tip of his penis and rushed up through his guts, clasping each organ in turn as the spreading wave turned him to stone.

Grotesque, yes, and funny, yes. Bradley stamped his feet to ease a tingling and began walking again.

"Bradley. Bradley!"

Mara's voice. He stopped, stunned for an instant and then marched on.

No point in replying. They could lock on his carrier wave and get a directional fix.

"Bradley, come *back*."

He negotiated his way through a field of humped and scarred rock. Pink snow stirred at his feet. He had to be careful. A fall could snap a bone and stop him for good.

"He isn't listening," Mara said faintly.

"He must be." Najima's voice was edgy but firm. The radio hiss swallowed his next words, then: "We must start a search pattern now."

Mara: "How?"

"Air support . . . No, that will prove too slow."

Bradley pushed on. His breath came now in harsh gasps.

"Which way would he go?" Tsubata asked, his voice resonant.

Mara: "I don't . . . wait. Toward the crystals. Of course."

Tsubata: "That is what he wants."

Mara: "Yes." A pause. "Yes."

Najima: "I could launch air-ground survey fliers. They could detect movement."

Mara: "He could see the launch."

Najima: "So? To remain unseen he would have to stand still. They will slow his progress, at least."

Mara: "Good. Good. Hey, the *radio*. He can—"

The air went dead.

Bradley walked faster, swinging his arms. The ridge-line stood jagged against the pink sky a few hundred metres away. He sucked a chewy kernel of dried fruit and worked at it earnestly. Then a long drink of metal-flavoured orange juice, and finally a gust of pure oxygen, heady and cool.

A stone turned beneath his boot and he staggered. Careful, careful. The rocks here were pocked and worn. Erosion? Streams of ammonia and methane carving this high land? Or the repeated freezing and thawing of ammonia in the rocks, fracturing them, pulverizing the seams of iron? The cliffs and boulders betrayed no lines, no mark of evolution. Everything here was pure. The debris of the primordial solar system had washed up here, cluttering the skin of an ice ball. No shale, no sandstone, no granite; nothing that spoke of process, of being baked at the interior or laid down by patient seas. A fresh world with scum for a surface, laced by—

Laced by—

The ridgeline loomed above. He scrambled up an incline and abruptly over the peak. A narrow valley lay before him. Gullies like fingers crawled up the slope toward him.

Laced by strands of white . . .

Downslope a few hundred metres he saw a thread of ivory. But a shallow crack blocked the way; he would have to edge along the ridgeline until he could find safe footing downward.

The sky flickered. A searing white glare burst above him, shadowing the land.

A survey flier. Bradley stood still, hoping his blue suit would not stand out.

He grimaced. Of *course* it would be obvious; that's why the colours were chosen. So now they knew where he was. Perhaps, if he spoke to Mara . . .

No, pointless. Talk wouldn't slow Najima's pace.

Bradley began walking quickly parallel to the ridgeline. His boots slipped on caked ice; he felt a twinge of pain. And marched on.

He stepped through drifted dust, past slabs of pink-

rown ice. The worn machine of his body began to ache,
and though he concentrated on his path, images began
to flit through his mind, pictures of Vonda and Mara
and Corey, memories of times he had strained on Mars,
sweating in his globed helmet. His body was a tablet on
which these people and places had written, his skin a
carved and wrinkled text. In his body he could discover
any record he wished: a burn of food rotting in his belly,
from the night's meal; the sweet needle of a protesting
ankle, recently banged when he lost his balance in the
Walker; pain of a sour and blurred shape, from his exer-
tion; a silvery pinch at his calf from an infinitesimal
hitch in the suit; a throb in his nose that somehow recalled Jonathon's dance; the dull pressure in his thighs
that echoed of the years of meditation in North Africa;
a puffing ache as he marched on, on.

Time blotted into an endless series of steps, boots
crunching on gravel, breath whooshing out of collapsing
lungs. A numbing cold seeped up his legs. His vision
tunneled, the helmet air thickened and tasted foul.

How much time? Najima could run swiftly. But if Najima could not find him . . .

Bradley turned and headed downslope. He coughed.
There were large boulders here, taller than he was. He
wove a path among them and then looked back. Unless
Najima were to stand on the ridge directly above Bradley, chances were he could not pick out the blue suit
among the shadows.

Bradley searched the sky. No winking lights of a
copter, no dot of a flying survey craft. On the rolling
horizon the volcano's funnel belched steaming brownish
clouds. Black specks danced in the plume . . .

Specks . . .

Bradley blinked, and saw that purple dots buzzed
dizzily at the edges of his vision. He could barely make
out the cracked pink snow at his feet.

Abruptly he began walking, a frantic energy boiling
up in him. His breath rasped thin. It was a good suit, but

it could not give him energy and reserves he did no
have. A warm suit, a heavy suit. All the comforts o
home. Product of the West. What was that remark o
Najima's? That when Gandhi had come to England, i
the twentieth century, and a reporter asked him what h
thought of Western civilization, Gandhi said, *"I think
sounds like a good idea."*

Yes, and it had been. Many ideas, really. And one i
particular: to look, to try, to rummage through the uni
verse.

To sit as student to the stars.

To stamp and march and breathe—

The sandpaper land slid away from his boot. H
clutched at a boulder and regained his balance. A smal
landslide pooled away the dust beneath his boots.

His nose dribbled, his eyes stung. He drank, and the
liquid oozed like oil down his throat.

Bradley angled away. He had lost his bearings, and
now his only hope was to work downhill. Eventually he
would intersect the strands of crystals. He had to. Smal
stones gritted against his boots, robbing him of balance
and speed.

He lurched forward, and the stone parted before him

He saw it first as a dab of light.

He took a step and could see the high square crystal
ivory, at least two metres tall. It wove away among the
boulders. Bradley instantly thought of an undulating
country fence thrown up from casual stone, but this
thing rose as one from the ground and rock face, seam-
less. As though it had grown there.

The crystal. The matrix, Bradley felt as though he
were falling. He could see golden flecks swimming deep
in the milky crystal. Glinting. Turning.

He blinked. His eyes were failing. But no . . . the thing
did seem to move.

Bradley shook his head to clear it. The purple dots
were gone. He breathed deeply, and the added flush of
oxygen tasted sweet. He looked away, beyond the
crystal, where the hill ran steeply down to a jumbled

lley. Then he looked back at the contours of the lat-
tework. They did not move, but formed a frame for a
risting of lines and perspectives.

A cold, prickly tremor ran through him. He saw—
—running antelope, wounded, flank spotted with
ried blood, tongue lolling—
—the enveloping cloak. A broad plane of a billowy
orld, an expanse of ruby cloth tumbling, now golden,
ow amber—
—power and mass, a bleached Earth groaning under
e weight of seven blazing circles . . . that laughed—
—a precisely defined space, miniatured facets of light
ad grace and form, soft curve of shiny apples; moisture
eading on plump Concord grapes—
Bradley shivered. His scalp tingled.
—thick, rich foam that lapped at stars—
—the rotting pinks of Titan, rusting world, stench,
aste, hollowness, echoes—
He snatched his eyes away and focused on the jutting
rey boulders. Slowly he let his gaze slide back toward
e glowing crystal. A rectangular splotch: here a side,
ere a joining; two lines, if extended, met *there* . . .
—a woodcut, burnished oak, of a swarthy man who
eckoned into the gale, wind snarling his hair—
Bradley stepped toward it. He blinked back rivulets of
weat. The images fluttered. Men, worlds, warped
eings, twisted leafy things, and jagged slashes of light.
He drew nearer.
He saw crevices in the lattice, like cuts in custard. The
aw face of it swarmed with a mesh of lines and colours,
ll rendered stonework. Each small incision was a pyra-
aid, a cube, a ragged thing of points and angles; but
aey summed to more.
He saw a mountain with insect machines at work on
, gnawing its lower slopes. Abruptly the mountain was
hole into the night sky that lazily began to fill with
aimmering water. Then a cone, an anthill. A comic face
ith hooked nose.
(Vonda?)

(Mara?)

All these in the flash of a second, with no thoug
possible between the jumps.

His head spun in a high and hollow place, airless.

He looked, and saw deeper. Etched in the milky fa
were rhomboids, many-sided sculptures, acute interse
tions in warped perspectives, polyhedrons that joined

Closer: the plain cube was a field for finer carving
smaller than a fingernail but perfectly rendered. Pointe
stars, whirlpools, threads that spun a gossamer ball
lines in a vibrating space.

They meshed and blended into something; somethin
that clutched at Bradley and made him look away. Eac
layer of complexity . . .

—man crying soundlessly, shaking—

. . . brought forth a rushing tangle of emotions in him
How far inward did the order go? Microscop
sculptures chiselled finer than the eye?

He teetered back and gazed upward. The cloud
thinned away, as fog does when you approach it, and h
saw the parent Saturn holding Titan in its grip. Beyor
the banded giant, ten billion stars made a galaxy and te
billion galaxies made a universe. The Milky Way wa
fog, a spinning discus a hundred thousand light-yea
wide. The discus spun, swarmed like embers, and Brad
ley could not see who threw it.

—loam rich and fine, with deep earthen smell
opened at his feet—

—a needle-fine point of fear parted the flesh, its swe
forgiving sting—

—frozen pillar of urine leaped from the silken ruste
land—

He cried with a sudden bursting release. Cried. He fe
to his knees, student to the stars. Wept. Saw it an
sensed it and enfolded it all.

The sky shattered.

Something broke inside him.

EPILOGUE

I

Mara found him.

He lay stretched on the gravel of Titan a few metres from the crystal's growths. His suit environment was intact but his body was cold. The medcap index on his back registered no signs of life.

They made ready to return him to the Walker. Perhaps his body would go to Earth, or perhaps they would be ordered to bury him here. She did not know.

She studied the crystal for a long moment. There were striations deep within it that seemed to form some kind of pattern. It was fixed, immobile. An interesting problem for the solid-state physicists, she thought, and turned away.

Without looking back, they carried him away from that place.

II

Seventeen days later Bradley Reynolds's body was encased in a vacuum, sealed in a sack and lofting out from Titan at 12.3 kilometres per second. Mara, already drugged against the numbing boredom of the long arc Joveward, thought again and again of the dry hunk that they carried. Yet her mind turned to the future, to the Orb and work beckoning, and she knew that events would press on with their own momentum, gathering

211

her up in them and slowly blotting away the traces of Bradley Reynolds in her mind and in the world.

On Titan the methane monsoon had begun. During the long, mild winter ponds had formed of methane, no more than a few metres deep. As the land slowly warmed near the poles, the methane suddenly could no longer exist in the liquid state. It percolated, boiled, flashed into vapour. Gusting winds stirred the sluggish pink clouds. Heat was carried on these storms to other ponds and lakes. They, too, boiled in a moment and fed the process. The towering cloud banks swept across the ragged face of Titan, raking the land and sending the men of Kuiper Base scurrying into its lowest depths.

Thus it was that few were on duty when the gigantic burst of electromagnetic radiation washed over the base. The wave was composed of very high frequencies and lasted seventy-three seconds. A later spectral analysis showed complex components, but no overall scheme. The intensity of the signal was too immense to classify; many receivers at the high frequency end of the base's sensors overloaded and died.

When the monsoon abated and damage was patched up, several scientists searched for traces of what might have caused the phenomenon. The obvious solution was the monsoon itself. This became accepted conventional wisdom, until years later, when the next coming of spring to Titan brought another monsoon.

The methane winds howled, but there was no electromagnetic burst. Only after this did a less popular theory, earlier brushed aside, come to the fore. The crystal lattice of Titan had showed curious depletion of energy resources after the earlier monsoon, but suffered none during the more recent one. Had the lattice somehow been responsible for the burst?

This began a new direction of study, experiment, and hypothesis. By this time the death of a weathered old man had been forgotten, and no one thought to connect the events at this late date.

III

Understanding the new and strange is not so much a matter of work and effort, but of intuition and time to let ideas come to fruition. The first hints of the true nature of the Titan lattice came fifty-two years after the death of Bradley Reynolds, and a full understanding—with all that it implied—required two decades more.

The lattice was a transmitter. The lattice was a sensing matrix. The lattice was a slumbering, fitfully brilliant intelligence. Yet the lattice was more than the linear sum of these terms. It merged with the world around it and yet remained apart, analysing.

It made an intricate three-dimensional antenna wrapped around Titan. The focus of this mesh was a region of space described by less than two seconds width of arc. The strands of the lattice delicately shifted and changed, constantly focusing on this spot.

Yet the lattice did not always transmit. Only when it was intensely coupled to its environment did it flex and sum and spurt out a tightly coded narrow-hand electromagnetic beam. For the scientists who studied it, achieving this intense connection took twenty-seven years of steady work, and even then a genetically designed telepath was required. And when the lattice spat out its encoded beam, more decades were consumed in understanding it.

Meanwhile, Titan was a booming source of cheap hydrogen for the entire solar system. Men lived and prospered there. The riddle of the earlier lattice transmission, now buried in an antique past, puzzled only a few scholars.

IV

A hundred and twenty-three years later a ramscoop vessel, decelerating from high boost, sighted the Beta Omega system. It comprised seven planets, none

Earthlike, and lay at the exact centre of the Titan lattice focus. The unmanned ramscoop streaked through the system and noted that one planet seemed encrusted with something glinting and complex.

The next probe, manned, arrived in fifty-six years.

The men who returned from Beta Omega were not the men who went. Things learned there could not be unlearned, and humanity was forever changed because of them. But one small note will signify enough:

In the third year of their explorations, after several had died and one had seeped into the cloudlike things above the crusted lands, they found the vault to which they had been led. After a journey they came to the place where the Earthlike worlds were recorded. There was a humming, close feel to the spaces there.

They found him in amber.

He was layered, a mica red intersection enclosed in a jewelled, oiled place. Nearby were others: the library of intense experiences from other worlds, other times.

The builders of the Titan lattice were stasis life, trying to fix what they knew as an impermanent form, *fluxlife*. To collect the diverse and fragile things of the flux-worlds was a task begun at the first glimpse of the galaxy, and now coming slowly to fruition. These beings knew that the hotworlds would spew out life, much of it memorable, and they sought to clasp it to them. But one cannot save technology, or even art. Only the essence can be preserved. Whenever a contact came, in however brief an instant of intense connection, the lattices trapped this moment, this being, and claimed it for the galaxy.

So nearby the race of Jonathon dwelled, their endless migrations now ended. The spheres of Alpha Libra swam forever in their hyperbolic seas. And rodents of a far star chattered; ocean minds murmured in the vast chasm; animals dead for longer than men could measure sang with eternal life.

The amber Bradley Reynolds spoke to the thing who

was like Jonathon. He was of the lattice and yet not of it, and the men who found him could see in the glinting, turning sheets of crystal an echo of man, of what they all were. Bradley Reynolds, thinking at that moment of the day to come when a star being would come here to reside, sent them a silent goodbye, and turned back to the game he played with the fluxfigures he knew, and lived again the agony on Titan, and then
Smiled.
Everlastingly.
Smiled.